The Owners Volume II:

Storm Clouds

– CARMEN CAPUANO –

An environmentally friendly book printed and bound in England by
www.printondemand-worldwide.com

Mixed Sources
Product group from well-managed
forests, and other controlled sources
www.fsc.org Cert no. TT-COC-002641
© 1996 Forest Stewardship Council
FSC

PEFC
PEFC/16-33-415

PEFC Certified

This product is
from sustainably
managed forests
and controlled
sources

www.pefc.org

This book is made entirely of chain-of-custody materials

www.fast-print.net/store.php

The Owners Volume II: Storm Clouds
Copyright © Carmen Capuano 2012

ISBN 978-178035-474-3

First published 2012 by
FASTPRINT PUBLISHING
Peterborough, England.
Printed by Printondemand-Worldwide

Chapter 1

I t was raining.
Of course it was.

Thick tears of rain streaked the window and were mirrored on his face.

The daylight had a *strange* quality to it, which made the image of the window reflect subtly onto the boy's features, so that the real tears and the reflected raindrops, seemed to be competing with one another, vying to be the biggest and most glistening. Ghost like, the phantom tears ran parallel to the real ones, down across his cheeks, only to be lost in the pattern of the thick checked shirt that he wore.

The boy brushed the tears away roughly with the back of his hand, smearing them across his face, till they were nothing but droplets of evaporating moisture.

"I know honey. It's hard for me and your dad to send you away too."

There was something not quite right about his mother's voice. Like the time she had fallen down the stairs and badly sprained her ankle, he got the sense that she was hiding something from him. Back then it had been her pain and fear that she had broken some bones, which had put that false quality in her voice, the lightly said, "no I'm ok," when she clearly was anything but. And now? Now?

"I don't want to go!"

He was surprised at how quiet his voice was, almost as if all the fight had gone out of him.

"Dan you have to!" She stepped towards him and grasped his shoulders in her hand, turning him away from the window and towards her and the muted TV which blazed its images out unheeded.

Shoulder length blonde hair cut into a neat bob, which curled cutely under her chin, Stacey Ryan stood eye to eye with her twelve year old son. He was so like his father, standing there, that it made her breath catch in the back of her throat.

A thought came unbidden to her mind and she voiced it without concern. "You know Dan Ryan, another year and you will be taller than me…"

She had said it many times in this past six months and always finished with the semi-jest, "and then I'll be calling on you to fetch me things down from the top cupboards."

But now these words would not come. She could not let them. They would be her undoing. So she bit them back and forced a wan and unsteady smile instead.

The words hung in the air unspoken between them. Almost tangible but not quite. Because they both knew they didn't *have* another year. Not *together* anyway. Instead, she inclined her head towards the TV, her eyes seeming to lock onto the images which lingered there.

An elderly woman was being air lifted to safety, taken from the roof of what had presumably once been her home, but was now a floating island in a sea of floodwater.

And even as the woman was safely pulled into the helicopter, something else could clearly be seen swishing around in the current - a baby's bassinet. Dan's stomach gave a sickening lurch as the news camera struggled to focus on it and its contents. There was a baby inside. Unable to help anyone or anything, Dan averted his eyes. In his mind it was a form of respect for the dead and drowning.

"Come with me mom. If *you* come, dad will come too, I *know* he will." It was a desperate plea but his mother would not relent.

"You wont be gone forever honey. Just till this is over. Then we will send for you." She smiled but her mouth forgot to tell her eyes how to lie and it was unconvincing. Dan kept his eyes locked to hers. He tried to burrow into that part of her mind which controls decision making, as if by the very exertion of his will, he could make her change her mind.

"No you won't. Because you won't be *able* to! If it really gets as bad here as it is there," he was forced to nod towards the hateful TV, which now showed the multitude of waterlogged bodies floating to their watery graves, "it will be chaos. And..." He trailed off, unable to complete the thought that maybe, just maybe, she wouldn't survive it.

Under his direct gaze, her smile faltered. And in the split second that her face took to change to an expression of deep sadness, he saw something else there. He saw the truth.

He saw her fear and her love for him but he also saw that she completely understood the finality of what she was doing. What was about to be done, could *never be undone* and they would all just have to live with that. If living was even possible. She had made her choice and there would be no going back on it.

"Your dad has his clients and he can't just up and leave them." Her voice was firm and had a mechanical note to it. It had become a mantra, often repeated to smooth over Dan's protests at his dad's absence from anything he might have been expected to attend.

School sports days, birthday parties, Little League tryouts, family vacations…all these things and more, his dad had missed. All in the name of his work.

"Gee, look at my dad waving like a crazy guy!" his best friend Tommy would snigger, as *his* dad cheered him on from the sidelines. And Dan would nod and smile at Tommy, as inside him something with sharp claws, curled itself into a ball, in the very pit of his stomach. And it grew, bigger and stronger and more desperate for release.

He didn't envy Tommy, he didn't want to take away his friend's happiness and make it his very own. He just wanted the same for himself. That feeling of being so important in someone's life, that they will give anything for you. He could only try to imagine how wonderful that must feel. How wonderful it would *make you feel*.

Dan was tempted to ask his mother what was so vital in his dad's law firm, that he would risk his life for it. *Give* his life for it. But that was the whole point really wasn't it, he reflected sourly. The firm *was* his dad's life. And his dad - and making him happy - was his mother's life.

"And I can't leave your dad, honey." This time her smile was completely genuine and full of sadness. "What would he do without me to look after him?"

Stacey Ryan had made her choice.

For a moment then it didn't matter that he was twelve, that he was almost he same height as her, that he ate more food in one meal, than she did in the whole day.

For a moment, none of that mattered and he wanted to hide himself in the folds of her skirt as he had done when he was very little, burrowing and folding his little body into her larger and protecting one, place his hands over his eyes and make the world go away.

Or failing that, to flee to the sanctuary of his room, with its posters of helicopters and planes still on the walls and its collection of stuffed toys, that had found its way to the bottom of the wardrobe. He had a sudden urge to just run there and pull all of the furry bears out and cry into them, letting their fur soak up his tears. But he could not do that either.

So he swallowed the lump that came to his throat.

"I've put some pictures of us all together in your bag…" Her voice broke now and for the first time he saw how hard this must be for her. "Just so you will still recognise us when we come to fetch you." He wasn't sure if this was an attempt at a joke or not, so he stayed silent.

"And your Uncle Jack will look after you, you know that." There was a breathless silence which followed, as if there were many things which needed to be said between them, but which neither knew fully how to voice.

"Dan…I," whatever would have followed, was lost in the foghorn blare of the truck which came to a halt, directly opposite their front door.

"The trucks are here!" she stated rather unnecessarily, already reaching for the large suitcase which stood on the floor between them, seemingly separating their two worlds. Arms outstretched, she tried to pass him the bag but he would not take it. To have taken it, would have been to admit that he was going, leaving his mum and his dad behind to die.

His mother sighed but she did not place the bag back on the floor. Instead she lugged it with one arm and wrenched open the heavy front door with the other. Then she was out, onto the sidewalk with the torrential rain pounding down on her, soaking her fine clothes and turning them to rags which clung to her slim frame, making her look as miserable and diminished as an old bag lady.

"Dan! Dan! Hurry!" she cried urgently. It seemed to take all of her strength to swing the bag up to the waiting soldier in the back of the truck. The soldier caught the bag and stowed it neatly under the bench on which he sat. The bench where there was a Dan sized space, waiting just for him.

And then he saw something amazing. He saw his mother reach out, wet and bedraggled and grasp the ankle of the young soldier, capturing his attention and making him call out to the driver, "wait just a minute longer."

To wait just one minute more. His mother, who avoided all physical contact with strangers at any cost, had grabbed this man's ankle. His mother who would *cross the road*, to avoid talking to someone she might be expected to greet with a warm kiss on the cheek. And he caught the look of desperation that she cast towards the young man wearing the army uniform.

The soldier, face pale as a winter moon, regarded her sombrely. The legend 'Private Curtis Wood' was embroidered on the top right hand side of his uniform and Stacey used it with authority now.

"Please Curtis, wait for my boy, please wait a moment."

The use of his first name rather than the conventional 'Private Wood' seemed to be effective. Something in the soldier's face softened and revealed the boy he had so recently been.

"Call him, lady, call him! These guys won't wait for ever." He hooked his thumb backwards to indicate the unseen driver and any soldier companions he may have.

Immensely grateful for even this small mercy, Stacey used her free arm to beckon to Dan. "Hurry Dan, come on!" He could see her lips moving to form the words but the words themselves, were lost in the surrounding noise.

Many tannoyed voices shrieked from loudspeakers positioned on top of the dozen or so trucks, which now drove slowly, from one end of the street to the other. All relayed the same message: "Bring out the children to be evacuated. One bag per child. Bring out the children to be evacuated. One bag…"

Amplified and repeated, at least ten fold, it was a cacophony of noise. And still the rain fell.

They were waiting for him. But they wouldn't wait for ever. Couldn't wait for ever. His mother turned towards him, body brutalised by the heavy downpour but still clinging to the leg of the soldier.

Her eyes were beseeching, begging him to come forwards. And he couldn't tell if it was rain on her face, or tears which suffused her features so. Either way it didn't matter. She loved him to the best of her ability. However much or little that was, it was as much as she could give.

The soldier waved his arm. 'Come on!' he indicated. Dan stepped out into the rain and away from the home he had known all his life. Not once did he give it a backward glance. To have done so, would have implied a knowledge that he would never see it again and he would not do that.

Rainwater swished and swirled around his ankles and even in the few moments that it took to reach the truck, he could feel it rising, creeping higher and higher, straining to reach his shins. It was rising fast, much faster than he would have thought possible. A new horror blossomed in his mind. He had assumed that his mother would have a chance to get away, to one of the safe places the Government had organised. But would she?

The sudden realisation that that was perhaps unlikely, made him stop just as he reached the truck. He stared stupidly at the soldier, eyes unfocused and not even really seeing him. Because what he *was* seeing was an internal picture show…an image of his mother, sat on her bed with her photos all around her …as the water rose and rose, uncontrollably and unstoppable.

Then strong hands grabbed at him, hoisting him upwards and inwards. Some involuntary reflex action of his body strived to push itself up, using his foot to lever and lift, and for a moment he was airborne, before finally taking up his place on the bench next to the soldier.

"Go, go, go!" He felt the force of the breath which was expelled in the shout, smelled the pepperminty essence of it and heard the young masculine tone of it.

But he did not see it happen. His eyes were glued to his mother.

He took in every detail of her face. Every little line and blemish. The angle of her cheekbones, the curve of her hairline...everything was stored in his memory...imprinted there with the indelible ink of his love.

The truck lurched once, strangely bringing into his mind a memory of a camel he had once seen at the zoo, which had to lunge forwards, before it could get up from kneeling on the ground. One forward lurch, then the truck began to move. He felt his mother's hand brush past him, as it was wrenched off and away from the soldier. And there was no time for more goodbyes.

Only dimly aware of other children, friends and neighbours climbing into other trucks that stretched the length of the road, he watched his mother fade from view, becoming smaller and smaller, till she could no longer be distinguished from all the other grieving parents who stood alone in the road.

His mother was gone. Or he was. It didn't really matter which way round you looked at it, the end result was the same. And his dad hadn't even stayed home long enough to say goodbye. He hoped that she wasn't alone at the end, that she found some comfort in the arms of the other parents on their street. But he couldn't bear to think any more than that, it was too awful to contemplate.

A shuffling around him, caught and forced his attention to his present situation. The truck was full to capacity. Eight benches lined the inside of the vehicle and children were squeezed in like sardines in a can, as close as possible on every bench.

"Full back here!" the soldier cried, presumably to someone in the front. Immediately there was a change in speed, as the truck revved up, no longer cruising for passengers, but now eager to reach its final destination.

The soldier offered a smile to the assembled children, then turned his attention to tying down the canvas flap which served as a back door for the vehicle.

A low muffled sob reached Dan's ears and he sought out its source. At least eighty pairs of eyes, regarded him sullenly. There were children of all shapes, sizes, dimensions and ages here. Some he knew well, others vaguely and some not at all.

But in one way, they were all the same, all identical. Silent and terrified, they sat huddled together, their clothes wet from the dash to the truck. There was a strange smell too. More than likely it was only the scent of so many damply clothed bodies drying off. But Dan thought of it as the smell of desperation.

Without exception every face displayed the same expression of shock and disbelief, as if the enormity of what was happening was just too huge to be comprehended. And perhaps it was.

Chapter 2

Hard unpadded bench beneath him and a solid backrest behind, separated him from the rest of the passengers but only minimally. A boy roughly Dan's own age sat on his left and the young soldier to his right.

At every pothole and bump in the road, the occupants were jostled into one another and almost catapulted from their seats on more than one occasion. Elbows were shoved accidentally into ribs and knees knocked jarringly against one another. Yet still the silence was unbroken. All except for the plaintive sobbing, which still issued from an unseen source at the furthest end of the truck from where Dan sat - and of course the rain, which continued to beat a deafening tattoo on the metal roof of the truck.

Dan looked around. Even the faces that he knew, were rendered almost unrecognisable in the strangeness of the situation. Then movement other than what was expected due to the lurching of the truck, caught his eye. Someone was trying to stand up. It was Jimmy Tulley.

Placed in different classes in the same school year, Dan and Jimmy had naturally let their friendship drift, till it was little more than a passing "hi" as their paths met in the school corridors. Yet here he was now, bound for the airport just as Dan himself was, leaving their cosy Seattle homes behind them.

"Oops, sorry, oh…sorry…thanks…could I just get in there?" Half clambering, half falling over others, Dan watched Jimmy make his way down one row of benches and up another, till finally he arrived at Dan's side. He cast a glance at the soldier but Curtis seemed in no mind to tell him off, other than a rasped, "sit down before you fall down."

Dan shuffled closer to the soldier to make room for Jimmy but it wasn't much space at all. Then suddenly there was more room as the person on the far end moved to the opposite bench and *that bench* shuffled to make space. In a sort of domino effect, Dan watched at the final person in that row, then moved to the fist place in the next and it started like a ripple all over again, until finally the space that Jimmy had originally left was refilled.

"Dan, my man," the nickname Jimmy had always used for him seemed inappropriate here and now. "Didn't know you'd be headed for Arizona." Jimmy's large bushy eyebrows were raised, giving him the look of an inquisitive squirrel, which was only exaggerated by his shock of thick auburn hair.

"I'm not!" panic filled his voice. "I'm supposed to be going to New York, to my Uncle…he's expecting me…" And what if he never got there? What if they were all bound for Arizona? How would his mum ever be able to find him again? Fear, even greater than any he had felt before, clutched at his heart and he felt pinpricks of anxiety tramp across his scalp.

"I'm supposed to be going to New York!" he turned to the soldier, seeking confirmation.

"We're headed to the airport, is all I know. Flights out of here are heading to anywhere that's safe." He paused for a moment before adding, "well at least safer than staying here I guess."

He turned to look directly at Dan. "Can't help you there fella. But I figure there's a good chance there will be planes heading New York way. Last I heard, things were ok out there."

"Don't stress, Dan," Jimmy's words were meant to allay his friend's fears but his eyes were filled with anxiety and his voice had an unsteady quiver to it. Dan felt the pupils in his own eyes actually dilating and contracting in fear. A cold film of sweat broke out along his upper lip and made his hair cling uncomfortably to his forehead.

"I'm supposed to be going to New York!" he told Jimmy once more, seemingly unable to do more than repeat this one phrase.

"Yeah and you will." This time Jimmy was more convincing. "I'm going to mom's cousin Marjory!" Jimmy rolled his eyes in exasperation and a little of the 'old Dan' was resurrected for just one brief moment.

"You mean 'Margarine' from England?" enquired Dan, slipping back unconsciously into the nickname they had used for her when she had come to visit. A rather generously proportioned lady, Dan and Jimmy had invented the nickname due to her insistence that only low fat spread be used in the preparation of her every meal. Sandwiches, creamed potatoes, waffles, everything she ate, was subjected to the low calorie spread. Which would have been fine, if she had then not gone on to consume huge quantities of the food, exceeding her body's needs at every opportunity.

"Yeah Margarine, you got it, my man!" sniggered Jimmy, obviously caught up in some memory of his own. "Mom and dad are gonna go to the shelter and then when this is all over, they'll come get me." Jimmy gave Dan a playful dig in the ribs. "Let's just hope that by then, I'm not so huge that they can't fit me through the doorway." Jimmy puffed out his cheeks and shoving both hands up the front of his shirt, he pulled it out in front of him so that he looked very fat.

Dan wanted to laugh. He really wanted that emotional release but it would not come. "You really think they'll get out? Be safe?" he asked. Jimmy's answer was immediate, no hesitation at all. "Sure man! The army sent trucks for us, like they said, didn't they? So they will send more trucks for our parents and take them to the shelters, just like they said they would!"

If that was true, and Dan had to admit, the first part certainly was, then maybe everything *would* be fine. "You honestly think so? Honestly?" And even as he said it, even as he asked his friend for honesty, a little voice whispered in his head. Right from the deepest, darkest corner of his brain, came the thought, 'just say yes. Just say you believe it. Say it *like* you believe it. Even if you don't. Just say yes!'

"For sure, Dan the Man, for sure." There was just the faintest note of uncertainty, a vague whiff of desperation but Dan chose to ignore it and focus on the words and the intention behind them. Jimmy leant across Dan and tapped Private Woods on the arm.

"Hey soldier man, did you see any of those trucks picking up adults and taking them to the evacuation places? Are they far behind this truck?"

"Sorry kid, I don't know nuthin 'bout that." The soldier's tone was direct and abrupt. Dan flinched at the words, as if the soldier had physically slapped him across the face. If this soldier didn't know [and especially because he was part of the unit who were on pick up duty] then there was a chance there *were* no other trucks…that there *was no* rescue planned for the civilian adults… But this was America, surely that could be true.

But then Private Wood spoke again. "Hey look, kid, what do I know? I ain't no Genral Patton," he gave the term 'General' a slur, as if it were a comedown from Private in his eyes. His mouth turned up at the corners – a weak attempt at a wry smile. "They don't tell me nothin' y'know! It's 'need to know' kid, purely 'need to know' basis they work on."

His attempt at reassurance failing dismally, the soldier made one more attempt, aware that every pair of eyes on the truck were now fixed solidly on him. He cleared his throat nervously. "They got hundreds o'trucks though. Hundreds rolling out day and night. So just 'cos I ain't done nothin but pick up kids, don't mean one hell of a bean in a peastorm, if you get my drift."

The expression was new to Dan, as was the soldier's dialect, which he couldn't completely place but none of that mattered. He got the essence of what he was trying to convey.

There were lots of trucks, lots of soldiers. And they were picking up from everywhere and around the clock. Everything would be ok. His family would be saved.

Suddenly, the truck gave a final lurch and screeched to a stop. Hands from outside grappled with the heavy flap which covered the back of the truck and roughly cast it aside.

Bright lights streamed into the truck, courtesy of the overhead strip lights and Dan blinked his eyes rapidly to acclimatise them. They appeared to be parked in a large hangar, which was currently half empty of planes.

A woman stood outside the truck, clipboard held protectively like a shield across her breast. "This is delivery SE 19/27 238764947 bound UK/ France/ Philippines and Southwest USA, right?" She read the numbers rapidly from a list full of red ticks and crossed out lines, from the clipboard which she now held in front of her. Pen poised on the brink of ticking them off, she awaited Curtis's response.

"This is SE 19/27," the soldier confirmed, "as for the rest, you are gonna have to hang on a moment there!" He fished an official looking piece of paper from one of his pockets. Folded and refolded till it was as small as possible, he had to take the time to unfold it and then smooth it out across his leg, before he could read out the series of numbers she was waiting for. The woman sighed impatiently, moving her weight from one foot to another, as if eager to be off and on to the next consignment of evacuees.

"Now, let's see," drawled Curtis, "yep, that's right! This is SE 19/27 38764947 but I don't know where they are bound." He didn't attempt a smile.

"Good, thank you *Private* Wood." Something in her tone, suggested she had fully intended it as the sneer that it sounded. "These evacuees are bound for the UK, France, the Philippines and Southwest USA, as I stated!"

The significance of what she had said suddenly hit Dan. The SE probably referred to Seattle, where they were now and he had no idea what all the numbers represented, or even if they were significant or not but one thing *was* clear – they were not taking him to New York.

Before he could get any words of protest out, Curtis spoke on his behalf. "This boy here is headed for New York," he stated matter factly.

"Well that's as may be, but that flight is leaving as we speak. So now he's going to England, or one of the other destinations instead, I'm afraid!" She didn't sound at all concerned.

Dan didn't think she was put out at all by this information, regardless of the words she used. "But...I..." he began, fearing that any words he said would fall on deaf ears anyway, but he couldn't just not try, could he? Eyes wide like saucers, he turned first to Jimmy for help, then finally Curtis.

Jimmy's face now had an unhealthy grey pallor to it, as if all the colour had been leeched away by shock and Dan had a moment to wonder if this is how he himself looked to everyone. Then he felt the soldier beside him stiffen and hold himself more erect as he addressed Ms Clipboard.

"Where it is? Where is the plane for New York?" Even as he talked he was already on the move, grasping Dan's arm and hauling him behind him.

"I...it...it's gone, I told you!" Querulous voice raised in defence to the man mountain who now towered over her petite 157cm frame, the woman tried to take a step backwards and away from Curtis. But Curtis followed, towing Dan behind him.

The woman came to a forced stop, banging her hip in the process against the side of another truck. Involuntarily, her eyes closed in the sudden flash of pain and her right hand fluttered to her side to rub the afflicted area.

Not prepared to waste any more words or time with her, Curtis merely plucked the clipboard from her hands and scanned it for details. "She's right, it should be leaving right now…" He turned to Dan, waiting for his cue.

"I *need* to go to New York," half wail half sob, Dan could only just make his own words out.

Curtis fixed the woman with the full force of his stare. "Runway two. How do we get there?"

The woman was scared but not completely cowed. "Look Private Wood, I already told you that flight has closed!" her former officiousness and anger, now seemed to be replacing any fear that she had initially felt. Dan longed for the soldier to really intimidate her. Not that that was the kind of thing he enjoyed seeing but because he thought it was the only way to save time and make her give the information quickly.

He got his wish. Bellowed as loud as any firecracker on the fourth of July, Curtis's voice reverberated round his head. "RUNWAY TWO! HOW DO WE GET THERE? RUNWAY TWO! ANSWER ME, GODDAMN YOU WOMAN!"

And then there was this little voice. Throat tight with fear, she issued the directions in a kind of semi-squeak and they were off, running across the concourse as fast as their legs would carry them, heading as directly as possible for runway two and the plane for New York.

Chapter 3

B reath labouring in and out of his chest, Dan felt as if his lungs were alternating between bursting at the seams with air and lying flat and crumpled in his chest cavity, like a deflated and burst balloon. Limbs on fire with his continued full-out run, he burned with pain from head to toe. And at the back of his mind he worried.

He worried that they wouldn't catch the flight to New York. He worried that they would get to Runway two and it would be already gone.

He worried that because of that, they wouldn't take him then on any other internal flights. He worried what would happen to Curtis because of him. But most of all, he worried about his bag...the bag that as far as he knew, was still stored under the bench he had been sitting on in the truck.

It wasn't the bag itself that he was worried about, of course. Nor even the clothes in it. It was the photos that it contained that he fretted over. Pictures of him and his mom and dad. Not only had he lost his parents because of this evacuation but now he had lost the only mementoes of them that he had.

Still running, being urged even faster by Curtis who was still in the lead, his mind tried to disassociate itself from each jarring step, to mull over the alternatives. But there weren't any. To have got on the wrong flight would have meant he could have kept his luggage, but at what cost? To have ended up somewhere completely different to where his parents expected him to be? So that if by some miracle, they all survived and tried to recall him home, they wouldn't even be able to locate him in all the confusion that there was likely to be.

So there hadn't been a choice really had there? His heart felt heavy with grief. It was so intense and so specific a pain, that he could pinpoint exactly where it radiated from. Cold pouring rain lashed him constantly whilst hot greasy sweat ran down his back and pooled on his forehead, running little rivulets of oily moisture down into his eyebrows. He was soaked, but not cold, the exercise was making sure of that.

They seemed to have been running forever. Across asphalt then grass, then clambering over barriers and charging over asphalt and grass again.

"C'mon kid!" panted Curtis heavily, holding out a hand to Dan, who took the proffered hand immediately. "Thanks," Dan only just managed to gasp out, as he was propelled onwards and forwards by the soldier. Running now, joined to Curtis by his hand hold, Dan was reminded of times when he had run like this with his mother. Not with this urgency of course and not for a few many years. But when he was much younger and they had been playing on the beach or in the park or just messing around in the backyard.

He would never run like this with her again. It was a loss that he hadn't even been aware of until now. Time had stolen from him that childishness that sought the comfort of another's hand in its own. And he hadn't even been aware of its passing, its loss - until now, when his losses seemed to be mounting up, towering over him in their enormity and threatening to crush him, when they toppled over from the sheer weight of them.

He had been so busy with his internal thoughts that it was only when he bumped into Curtis who seemed to have stopped for a moment, that he became aware of his surroundings again.

They had run out of runway. Behind him lay the way they had come. Ahead was a dead end. Asphalt simply petered out and there was nothing beyond, other than dead brush and waterlogged grass.

"This way, c'mon kid, we're nearly there!" urged the soldier.

"But it's a dead end!" he protested, unable to take his eyes from the waste land which somehow seemed to be a bad omen.

"No, up here. Hurry!"

Up where? Dan turned to ask the question and found that he didn't need to. A huge set of steps led from where Curtis now stood, to somewhere else, destination unknown. Hadn't that been a song title once? Dan's mind took itself off on another tack as his conscious mind refused to consider what was actually going on here. Left alone with no guidance from its counterpart, his sub-conscious kept his body moving automatically, placing one foot on the first tread and the other on the next, faster and faster, climbing higher and higher.

"We've …been in…the newest… part 'o…the airport…the part only built…a cuppla years 'go," Curtis relayed the information in bursts of used up breath, managing to scale two steps at a time with his long legs.

"This'll take us…to the old bit…runway two." He gave an extra huge heave as he said this last bit, hauling Dan up and over the last couple of steps so that they were on the flat again. Dan banged his shin against one of the stair risers but didn't even call out in pain. Instead he absorbed the sharp smart and filed it away as of no consequence in the grand scheme of things.

The corridor stretched ahead. Meant for the use of only airport staff, it had none of the luxurious feel that is normally associated with airports. No marbled walkway with eye catching murals here. Instead there was the bare grey of weathered concrete and hastily painted wood and metal, as if here the airport was stripped of its fancy trimmings, laid bare. Here, it was not the fantasy land of far-away dreams and fancyings, here it was about cold hard cash and big business and how many planes could be flown in and out of one place, in the space of twenty-four hours.

And maybe that was a good thing. Maybe it was good that he was seeing what lay beyond that shiny façade that lined the everyday world. The world where the school bus always arrived on time and there was always pizza for lunch on a Friday. Because that world was gone. Who knew if there would be pizza again on a Friday…ever? Who knew if there would even ever be a *Friday* again!

"Gotta stop, gotta…" legs like jelly, he felt himself crumple to the ground, chest striving to take in more air, more oxygen, which seemed suddenly to be in short supply.

"No kid, don't give up!"

Strong arms lifted him. Lifted him right up in the air, as though he wasn't nearly the same height as his mother and filling out every day! He was lifted and cradled against the soldier's chest and they were running again. Legs swinging slackly over Curtis's arms, Dan thought for a moment about the rain which now seemed both warm and soft, as it fell on him. Except that the corridor had a roof and was not open to the elements. And then he thought to look up.

Tears fell from the soldier's face and plopped onto Dan.

"I've got a kid brother, name of Walt. I just hope that what I'm doing for you, someone does for Walt, if he ever needs it!"

And then Dan understood. As much as the soldier had put himself out for Dan, he was really doing it for himself and for his own family, in the hope that all the old sayings had some truth.

"What goes around, comes around. One good turn deserves another. You scratch my back and I'll scratch yours." Dan found himself mumbling them all like a litany.

Maybe some of the sayings were true, maybe not. There were certainly *many* sayings about human behaviour both good and bad. But that was the thing about sayings…they were easier said than done.

"That's another one!" Dan laughed to himself, "easier said than done."

"Gotta put you down now. We're at the steps going down. If I carry you we may fall." Curtis didn't need to carry on the comment to its logical conclusion. One or either of them having broken limbs and or concussion at this time could prove fatal, even if the initial fall wasn't. The airport was in the process of evacuating everyone and was chaotic, to say the least. How long would it be till they would get help and medical attention? Would they get it at all in fact? It was not an option.

"Can you move again now?" Curtis enquired with worried eyes.

"Yes, thanks!" His legs were still slightly wobbly but he was able to take the steps going down better than those going up. "Will we be too late?"

"Don't honestly know but we've been running for about four minutes now. Depends how far we still have to go!" They reached the bottom of the stairs. Sheltered for a moment from the driving rain, they stood transfixed at the sight which met their eyes.

A huge sign bearing the title 'Runway 2' stood just ahead of them. And on its asphalt, stood the biggest, shiniest jumbo jet Dan had ever seen. And as they watched, it slowly and inexorably, began to move.

"Noooo!"

"Noooo!"

Simultaneously they voiced their dismay and horror. To have come so far and tried so hard, only to be defeated at the last split-second was just too hard to bear, too crushing a defeat.

Once more, Curtis surprised him. Thrusting Dan away from him, in the direction of the back of the plane, Curtis ran for its nose, running long and wide in an arc that would take him to the tarmac, immediately in front of the taxiing plane. The pilots in the cockpit would be startled but could not fail to miss the tall soaked soldier, standing right in their path.

Without looking back Curtis called to him, "run! Get ready to get on to that plane, when I get it to stop."

Get it to stop? Dan was bewildered and terrified all at once. But he was not petrified into inaction. He was not stuck rooted to the spot in fear. Instead he picked up his heels and ran as if it was for pleasure – nothing more than a race with a friend in the park. Because a little part of his brain told him, that if he thought about what they were doing, what they were really attempting, he would be more likely to just throw himself under the wheels of the plane and be done with it.

A myriad of eyes regarded him from the plane. Divorced from the rest of the faces, he saw only the eyes, watching him with surprise, horror or anxiety. The faces they were set in, seemed to be colourless blurs. Only the eyes held his attention and he focused on them more and more as he drew closer and closer.

The plane seemed to be picking up speed. He tore his eyes away, searching for Curtis, only to see him at the last second catapult himself in a huge bound, right onto the runway directly ahead of the plane. Dan's heart beat double time. By his reckoning, if the plane didn't stop in the next sixty seconds, it would roll right over this brave and noble man. Not just brave *soldier*, for it was kind of expected that all soldiers were brave, Curtis had been elevated in Dan's opinion to that revered position of a 'Man', going above and beyond the call of duty.

Curtis would not have time to avoid his fate, if the plane did not stop. Too wide, too heavy and too fast, it would crush him to death, as surely as a grasshopper was crushed under the wheels of an oncoming car.

Breath now coming in huge whoops of air, Dan struggled to keep pace with the plane. He waited for it to hit Curtis, before continuing on its way, uncaring of the devastation it left in its wake, the body left torn and brutalised. Some cold clinical part of him wondered what noise it would make as it rolled over his friend. Would there be a bang? An exploding noise? Or a quieter squishing noise as it crushed and burst every organ and cell in his body? Inwardly shuddering, Dan forced his aching legs onwards, arms cycling at his sides, in an unconscious attempt to go faster.

Was it his imagination or was he speeding up? Catching up?

No, the plane was stopping. An ear piercing screech of brakes and the warm and not unpleasant smell of burned rubber permeated the air. Freed from having to run so fast, Dan slowed to a stop and folded over at the waist, hands on his hips and clawing at the air for breath.

The plane had stopped. But had it been too late to save the soldier? Was he even now pinned, alive and squirming, under one of the wheels, his body mortally wounded and shutting down forever?

From the position he stood in, Dan was aware that if he just bent slightly lower, just bent down a fraction more, he would be able to see the undercarriage of the plane. He would see its wheels and what lay beneath them. But he couldn't do it.

Luckily he didn't have to!

"Don't just stand there kid!"

The voice had a recent familiarity and Dan could just have laughed and laughed with sheer joy, at the sound of it. Before a couple of hours ago, this man had been unknown to him, merely another inhabitant in a huge big world. Now he had played a pivotal role in Dan's life. How was that even possible? How could someone previously unknown have come into his life and so radically altered it from the course it had been designated by fate to take? Or had fate sent this man, directly, to make this change? Who knew? And really, who cared. 'Grass is green, whatever way you look at it,' Dan thought. It didn't matter if Curtis had altered his fate, or whether fate had meant him to intervene. All that mattered was that the plane had stopped.

The plane for New York.

Chapter 4

Heavyweight doors swung open to admit him, and a ladder was rolled down for him to climb up. Hesitating only a moment on the lower rungs, he held on tight with one arm and used the other to grasp Curtis's arm.

"Thank you."

It was such a simple sentiment and yet it conveyed everything. The soldier's eyes were cloudy and Dan instinctively knew what he was thinking.

"I'm sure your brother will be fine." The lump in his throat prevented Dan from carrying on. He wanted to say Curtis's brother just *had* to be fine… because there was really no other choice. There was no choice for any of them now.

"I know kid, I know."

There was nothing more to say. Dan flicked his lips up, in an attempt at a smile and turned away from the man who had surely altered his destiny.

A large hand placed firmly in the small of his back, served to usher him higher up the ladder. One foot in front of the other he climbed, until he reached the very top. Urged on by a pale faced stewardess, he was finally hauled into the interior of the plane.

"There are no seats left honey, you're gonna have to squat down in the aisle," she smiled an apology for something that was not her fault. "You have a good friend there, you know."

"Yes, I know."

"He risked being crushed…" her attention was caught by something or someone further up the plane and she hastened off in that direction. "Just stay seated till the seatbelt lights go off and you'll be fine, ok?" she called back to him.

Dan didn't know much about planes. It was a fact that hadn't really bothered him before but he figured he was no more, nor no less safe in the aisle, than he would be in the seats anyway. After all, if there was a mid-air collision, he didn't figure many of them would stand a good chance of survival, seatbelt or not.

Suddenly the vastness of the space that he was in, was just too ridiculous. He had never thought about how big planes where before, how wide and long and heavy they were. Yet they were strangely able to glide high in the sky, in between the clouds, as if they had fooled the laws of physics into believing they were no heavier than a feather.

The door he had entered was closed with a heavy thud, severing his daydream in mid flow and bringing him back to reality in a flash. This was the last time he would ever see Private Curtis Wood. There was also the small unbidden and hastily denied thought, that it was perhaps the last time he would see his home area, the place where he had spent his whole life...till now.

He had to find a window to look out of. There were small ones set above each row of seats. But to see through any of them, he would have to climb and clamber over all the occupants of the seats. It was not something he even had to think about. It was just something that had to be done.

Throwing himself across the knees and legs of the other children who sat slack-jawed, acting as accidental barrier between him and the window, Dan scrabbled into a semi-upright position. Elbows and knees digging sharply into the flesh of the seated passengers, Dan didn't even spare them a glance as he scrabbled on top of them.

Finally reaching the window, he banged forcefully on the glass, whilst sending a desperate thought message to Curtis to look up at the plane, look up to where Dan was frantically waving to him. And the soldier did. Just in the nick of time, as the wheels of the plane started to move along the runway once more, Curtis raised his head and saluted, rainwater running off his arm at the elbow and splashing onto the tarmac.

And that was all it took. The fear of the unknown and what lay ahead was too great to be denied. Dan had lost everything and everyone. That final salute, a last gesture of kindness and humility in a world which was becoming increasingly terrifying and unknowable took its effect. As he raised his own arm in a mirror image of the soldier's salute, Dan's face crumpled, and was once more awash with hot salty tears.

"Good luck," he whispered, although in truth he wasn't really sure if he was saying it to the soldier or to himself. The plane gained momentum and glided into the thick storm. The heavy rain must have drummed and lashed against it but the noise was lost to the occupants of the plane. In a strange way it reminded Dan of watching the TV with the sound turned onto "mute".

For a moment, it was almost like he was caught between two worlds - one which was safe and warm and the other, which was wet and wild - and he didn't know which one was the real one anymore.

Suddenly he was suffused with guilt and shame. In his desperation to see Curtis and say a final thank you, he had been guilty of the very thing he feared people doing to him – treating him and his life as of no consequence.

Shamefacedly aware that he was no doubt crushing the children he almost sat on top of, he uttered a half apology and wriggled off of their laps.

The three children mutely regarded him as if it were almost an everyday occurrence. Two boys and a girl, they sat with arms linked together. There was no mistaking their facial similarities and resemblances and their beaten attitude. The eldest of the boys, who looked just a little younger than Dan, sat nearest the window, with his sister, the youngest of the three, at his side and other brother at the far side, next to the aisle.

"Dad says I have got to be in charge now. I've got to be the man of the family and look after Katie and Jim-Bob," the oldest boy told Dan. There was a determined set to his face but there was some shaky note in his voice which betrayed to Dan, the fear that he was not up to the job.

"I'm Dan. I don't have any brothers or sisters. Wish I did, though, 'cos then it wouldn't just be me." Unfortunately that came out as rather an obvious statement but it worked as he had intended and served to draw the other boy out.

"I'm Ben. Pleased to meet you Dan!" Ben extended his hand across the lap of his brother and sister to clasp and shake Dan's hand. Dan thought it was a strangely adult and formal gesture and didn't fit with the age of the boy at all. And then he realised that the boy was copying what he knew his father would have done in the same situation. Ben was being "the man of the family," in his dad's absence.

Katie and Jim-Bob looked on and suffered the hands to be shaken across them without saying a word. "Pleased to meet you too Katie and Jim-Bob!" Dan smiled as wide as he could. He wasn't sure if it looked genuine; it certainly didn't feel it but perhaps if he did it for long enough, it would start to feel even just a little bit right.

Jim-Bob smiled back but Katie remained quiet and unchanged. Now he looked closely, Dan thought that she didn't really seem to be looking at anything in particular. It was almost as if her gaze was fixed at some point in the far distance. Or at some image inside her head. This last thought seemed to radiate from somewhere on the inside of Dan's brain, as if he too were controlled by his sub-conscious mind. As if reading Dan's thoughts, Ben said, "Katie hasn't spoken since mom and dad dropped us at the airport." His voice was quiet and worried.

A tannoyed voice interrupted them. "Ladies and..." the official sounding voice stopped mid-flow before recommencing in a softer tone, "my apologies for that mistake. Let's start again. Boys and girls, I am Captain McKinley and I am flying this plane with co-pilot..."

Dan missed the co-pilot's name when Katie chose that moment to speak. "I couldn't bring Binx. Dad said they wouldn't let him on the plane!" Her voice was thick and tears spilled down her face. Dan's eyes were drawn downwards to where Katie shrugged free of her brothers' arms and began to kneed the fabric of her skirt, mashing it and ripping at it.

"And he was right. Mom will look after Binx, Katie, you know she will." Ben tried to console his sister but even to Dan, his words sounded flat and unconvincing.

"...on our way to New York..." the Captain droned on.

"And I had to leave Fin and Fat behind!" wailed Jim-Bob in response.

"But they are FISH, stupid!" his sister snarled back at him, her face contorted with supressed anger.

Dan felt Jim-Bob sink back into his seat, frightened by the ferocity of his younger sister's features.

"...and so I want you to stay in your seat and just raise your hand if you need anything..." the Captain was sounding increasingly self-assured as if he was coming to the end of his speech and relieved to be doing so. Dan wondered if the Captain had flown his own children somewhere safe, or whether they had ended up on the wrong plane like he almost had. He was willing to bet that the Captain wouldn't sound so self-assured if Dan ever got a chance tell him about his near-miss.

"They aren't exactly going to drown in all this are they?" Katie buried her face in her hands and sobbed loudly and wetly. Dan only just made out the snivelled, "but Binx will. He's an old cat...And mom and dad will drown too!"

"But they are *tropical fish*, they need warm water!" Jim-Bob's voice took on the whine of a much younger child and he too burst into tears. Ben's eyes met Dan's, across the two crying younger children. Dan could tell that Ben was fighting his own impulse to cry, fighting to be the man of his little family just as his dad had instructed. Dan nodded slowly and quietly.

"It's going to be tough. But we will all get through this, I promise you." He said. Listening to his own voice, he tried to be objective but his mind cast images of his own mother saying the very same thing and how, even then, he hadn't been able to bring himself to believe her.

"Cats can swim, you know," he tried another tack, striving to keep his voice light and matter of fact.

"Really?" Keeping her hands where they were, in front of her face, she instead looked sideways at him, her little face still looking worried but with the slowly blossoming flower of hope beginning to take root.

"Sure they can. They don't like it much but they *can* swim!" Gaining ground, he felt it was safe to let his tone be more assertive now.

"You are really sure they can swim?" She had dropped her hands to her lap now and her face was smoothing out, the worry being replaced by a shining light of faith in what he was telling her.

"Haven't you ever seen a cat catching a fish in a small stream…" It was only a second after the words were out of his mouth, and a fresh bout of sobbing began, this time from Jim-Bob, that Dan realised his mistake.

"…but cats only eat river fish of course…" he tried to amend quickly. Thankfully that seemed to do the trick and all sobbing stopped. Dan managed somewhere between a smile and a grimace and was rewarded when Ben laughed.

But the brief reprieve was shattered when Katie turned to Dan and asked, "mom and dad will be ok too, won't they?" It was half question and half statement and one that he didn't feel disinclined to agree with. But what was he to say to her?

He had been semi squatting on the floor of the aisle and he used the excuse of settling himself more comfortably before he answered her. The floor still felt rather slanted upwards as if the aircraft was still gaining momentum and height and he wondered when or even if, it would level out. Or perhaps it would just keep climbing in the sky. Climbing until there was no fuel left and then plummet back to earth.

He realised that he was procrastinating. Wasting time so that he had space to think up the answer to the question, or if his luck was in, time for something else to happen, which would distract the girl from her original question.

But she was not to be deterred. "They will, won't they?" she asked, voice small but demanding of an answer.

"Yes, they will." He was surprised when the answer came out of his mouth. It wasn't that he had decided to say something different or that he had decided anything at all. The answer just came out. No-one asked him how or why he knew that, they just accepted it and for that he was thankful.

Perhaps the best idea all round was to talk about the future, not the past. "Who is collecting you when we land?" he asked, hoping that it was someone the children knew and liked.

"Georgia," supplied Katie, her immature voice giving the name a slight slur, so that it sounded more like 'Joorja'. "She's a kid doctor." Katie seemed proud of having some information to impart.

Dan's brow furrowed as he thought about this statement. "Do you mean she's a doctor but she's still a kid? Wow, she must be really smart!" A moment of stunned silence followed, where Ben, Jim-Bob and Katie all stared at Dan, before simultaneously cracking into laughter at Dan's stupidity.

"Georgia's not a kid, she's *old*. She's a doctor *for* kids, dummy!" exclaimed Katie as if she thought he had the learning capacity of the average five year old. "And she's from *Engaland*." She managed to make it sound very exotic.

"England," Ben corrected before adding a comment of his own. "She's a paediatrician," he sounded the word out as if he had practised it long and hard, giving it an elongated sound, so that it seemed like 'peed-e-a-trish-on' to Dan's ears.

"She peed on what?" enquired Jim-Bob, his ears pricking up at the merest hint of toilet humour. The others decided to ignore him and Jim-Bob turned his attention to studying the clouds which passed by the window.

"And mum told you to call her Auntie Georgia, Katie!" Ben reprimanded. Katie shrugged her shoulders in response. "She's not our auntie though! She's mum's friend from when they were at school together."

"College actually," Ben corrected, "and you were *told*, Katie!"

"Blah, blah, blah," Katie responded, no longer interested in the conversation.

"What about you? Are you being picked up?" Ben turned back to Dan, angling his whole body so that he was directly facing Dan and sideways to Katie, who was clearly enjoying annoying him, a little smile now playing on her face.

Before Dan could answer, there was some commotion behind him, at the back of the plane. The aisle was quite narrow but he could see two flight attendants moving slowly towards him, row by row. They were leaning into the children in each row they passed and doing something to them. Something which made them cry.

Like a wave coming closer and closer to the shore, the noise built upon itself, becoming more ferocious and undulating as it did so. It was the sheer scale of the increasing voices, as one by one, new children joined the wailing choir, which made it so deafening.

"What's happening?" asked Ben anxiously, as at the very same moment, the seatbelt lights came back on, and the Captain switched on the tannoy again.

"...please place your seatbelt buckle firmly around you and..."

Dan wriggled in the aisle trying to see around the bodies of the flight attendants, who were now only four rows away, without actually standing up and bringing attention to himself.

They had something in their hands.

"They are doing something to all the children, but I don't know what!"

Three rows away now. Dan saw what it was each woman held in her hand. It was a gun! All at once he felt the blood drain from his face. How could that be? It didn't make any sense at all.

Two rows away.

The Captain's voice droned on overhead, his words passing their ears unheeded, until just one word lodged in Dan's brain.

"...vaccine..."

Dan froze in place and listened.

"The attendants are going to give you all a shot of vaccine kids. Don't worry, it won't hurt and it will keep you safe. The attendants..." It was a recording, looped over and over, whilst the attendants carried out their work.

One row away.

And then they were by Dan, squeezing past him and into the rows either side of him. He mashed himself closer to Jim-Bob. The attendant vaccinating this side was the same one who had helped him on board and he thought she looked a little more gentle that the other one, her face a little less stern.

"Do you have any allergies, that you know of, children?" she addressed them all and included Dan in her gaze.

"Mom says I'm allergic to being clean," Katie said, her eyes wide with innocence. The woman smiled, "that's fine then honey. This will only hurt a little second, alright?" And in one swift movement she had fired the drug into Katie's right arm.

"Oww, you LIED! That hurt A LOT!" Katie shrieked, full of indignant fury, before pulling her knees up into her body, she lulled herself with her own tears.

Dan wondered why the woman had chosen Katie to be first in the row. Surely it would have made more sense to have started with either himself or Ben, and worked from one side to the other. The woman's next statement, provided the explanation.

"Ok, the youngest of you has been done. Who is going to be the next bravest then?" She looked from one to the other, waiting patiently.

"Is that the 'Doomsday' vaccine?" Ben asked, his eyes darting nervously between the flight attendant, Dan, Jim-Bob and the still crying Katie.

"Yes, it is honey. And you need to have it. We all do!" asserted the woman, a slight tone of impatience, starting to leak into her voice.

"But mama said she spoke to Aunt Georgia about it. And Aunt Georgia said it hadn't been tested enough. Mama said it was too big a risk to take it!"

Dan heard the unconsciously spoken 'mama' and understood that Ben was lost in a moral maze. Unable to stop something happening to his sister that their mother would not have approved of, he had slipped back to the comforting language of his younger days. Dan's heart lurched in sorrow and pity for his new friend.

The 'Univacc', or 'Domesday Vaccine' as the popular press had nicknamed it, had many supporters but there had been a small but growing band of people who opposed it both loudly and publicly. Cobbled quickly together, it was a mish-mash of existing vaccines for a variety of contagious diseases. Cholera, Diptheria, Dysentery, it covered all of these and more.

"Well this little girl has already had it…and you need to have it too." Without further ado, she leant across and zapped Ben in the arm, allowing no time for refusal or further discussion.

Dan remembered an overheard conversation between his parents about the vaccine. They had been watching a news broadcast about the worsening weather and the studio had cut to a shot of a government laboratory, where some mad scientist was talking about the new wonder vaccine they had created.

"The vaccine to end all vaccines!" his dad had laughed at the TV screen but there had been no mirth there. Instead, Dan had had the strangest feeling that his dad was afraid and that he was attempting to cover it with humour.

"That's as may be but if we get the chance, we should take it." His mother's voice had been quiet and calm but there had been a note of strength in it too, which was unusual for Stacey Ryan. In fact, Dan couldn't remember a single occasion when his mother had ever contradicted his dad. Apart from this one time!

The flight attendant quickly turned to Jim-Bob and gave him a shot of the vaccine. Jim-Bob's eyes were red with tears and he and Katie clutched at each other for comfort, all previous spates forgotten and forgiven.

"I still think we should have it, if we get the chance." Stacey Ryan had repeated and closed the conversation, holding her hand up as if to physically stave off her husband's objections. Dan replayed the conversation in his mind's eye. It was so clear, so precisely remembered he could even see the deep furrows between his dad's eyebrows as he had muttered, "if survival comes to that, we haven't got a hope in hell anyways, Stace!"

The flight attendant stooped down to him now, vaccine gun at the ready, pausing only to reload it with a fresh dose, all for him. What was he to do? Follow his mother's belief or his dad's? Lost in internal struggle, he was too late to stop the contents of the vial being injected into the fleshy part of his arm. In his imagination, he tracked the progression of the drug through the muscles and capillaries of his arm until it hit the bloodstream.

He imagined he could feel it burning through tissue, like acid, leaving a wrecked and ravaged trail of muscle and sinew in its path, seeking that final terminus – his heart. There, it would suffuse the chambers with poisoned blood and cause his heart to implode with one last shattering beat.

But of course nothing happened. Instead, the sharp sting of the shot faded away to leave just a faint throbbing a memory of what had been - and a warning for the future.

Chapter 5

It was a long flight and Dan was grateful for the company of the other children. After a while Ben swapped seats with Jim-Bob so that the younger boy could continue to gaze out of the small window and Ben and Dan could talk more easily. The sky had grown ever darker as they travelled and the rain continued unabated. Dan didn't know if the sky darkened because of the worsening storm or whether it was because it was just getting late.

It occurred to him that there was a possibility that New York was in a different time zone to Seattle and that therefore whatever time it was now back in Seattle was not necessarily the same time as all the different regions that he was flying over. The fact that he didn't know what time it was in Seattle only confused the issue further and he made a conscious effort to put it out of his mind. His stomach rumbled slightly and he realised it had been some time since he had last eaten.

"Do you think we will ever come home again?" Ben asked. His voice seemed very small and very-far away, even though he sat within arm's reach. There was a depth in Ben's eyes too, that Dan hadn't noticed before. Only searing honesty would fully answer the question and Dan wasn't sure either of them were really ready for that. But to lie, even a white lie, seemed somehow dishonourable to Dan, under the circumstances they found themselves in.

"I hope so, Ben, I really do!" Dan squirmed uncomfortably on the floor. He was getting sore sitting there, with no barrier between his body and the vibrations of the aircraft engines. But the squirming wasn't caused solely by physical discomfort, instead it was a manifestation of inner turmoil.

There was a moment of silence between them, thick and laden with unspoken fears.

"Here, swap with me for a while and have this seat," Ben offered, standing up and sidling out around Dan. There was a distraction here, offered and accepted by both boys, a moment when they could both put more pressing fears to the back of their minds, being merely boys being boys, for just the briefest of moments, and they giggled over the necessity of scrambling over one another in the process.

"Thanks. Wow this is comfort!" Dan sighed, settling himself into the still-warm seat that Ben had vacated. Both boys sat in their new positions for a few moments, neither wishing to broach the subject which still infused their every conscious thought.

Like a noose around his neck, Dan felt a constriction that he could not shake off. Perhaps talking about the very thing they feared would make it less frightening, chasing the bogeyman as it were.

On the other hand perhaps it would make it worse, giving a weight and depth to it, that would not allow it to be hidden any more. But once again, there was no real choice. The words burned in Dan, pushing themselves to the forefront of his mind, demanding to be spoken aloud, to be considered ...challenging him to deny them.

"I really do hope that we get home one day," he echoed, as a preliminary to what he was about to say, giving his brain time to put the emotions into some semblance of order. "Because if we *don't* get back then it will mean that *everything* we ever knew is gone." Even if his mom and dad survived and he somehow managed to be with them, it would not *really* be enough. Without his home and the familiar surroundings of his everyday life, things would never be the same again.

"Yeah, I know what you mean. We moved once, just after Katie was born and it was weird, leaving my bedroom and my school. But I knew it was still there. It still existed. It was just that I didn't go there anymore. But this..." Ben's shoulders slumped.

"It's kinda like your whole life up till now has been wiped out...like maybe you don't even exist anymore...cos nothing and nowhere that you know still exists, so why should you," Dan agreed.

"Yeah, that's it exactly! Like we won't exist anymore," Ben couldn't help his eyes being drawn to Katie and Jim-Bob who were sharing a book, reading by the dim overhead light, all fears of what lay ahead and behind them forgotten for the moment. Dan saw the look and understood how Ben felt. Wouldn't it be a relief to be just that little bit younger, as to be able to let all these cares be shrugged off for even just a short time.

Feeling the weight of his gaze perhaps, Katie's eyes were drawn up and towards Ben. With a shock Dan realised how wrong he was. Like a porcelain doll Dan had once seen in a store window, Katie's face was a rigid mask of false cheerfulness. Eyes pinched and tight at the corners, her skin appeared to have been stretched to cover too-wide cheekbones and a mouth that was too small for the rest of her face.

To have come so far from the mute staring child she had been when he had met her, to this...this caricature of a small girl, was too far a journey in such a short time and her feared for her sanity. Dan felt all of 112 years old, as if life itself had worn him down.

Suddenly weary, he closed his eyes. Like a machine shutting down, he had the strangest sensations of a switch being flicked to 'off'. As his muscles relaxed, his body cooled and his breathing slowed, until he descended into sleep. His body rested in slumber but his mind was not afforded that luxury.

Intensely sharp images invaded every dream, pulling at the edges of them, peeling the sweet, soft familiar things away and replacing them with new things... things unknown and coloured by fear and uncertainty.

He was at school, sitting where he always sat and listening to Mr George drone on about the Civil War and how issues then, were still relevant today. The light breeze blew the tree outside the window just enough to distract him from wondering how long it had taken Mr George to grow his weird moustache...and then, unaccountably really, because it certainly wasn't raining outside of the school, Mr George was being swept away to his death on a tidal wave that burst through the classroom door. Hands grasping at anything that could afford him some purchase, he fought his way to the surface just once, his once proud moustache now tangled with seaweed [strange how the mind works], before being pulled back into the centre of the wave, forming a spiral of current that seemed to suck him deeper and deeper down.

Bathed in a sticky hot sweat, Dan wrestled free from his nightmare only to find that it hadn't been a complete fantasy after all. Ok, so there was no tidal pool devouring humans here, but he *was* on a plane bound for a destination across the country, with his mother and father and his whole life left behind him. His waking mind tried to shroud the truth from itself, insisting that it was all the product of a fanciful imagination but in the split-second that Dan rose from sleep to wakefulness, the fraction of a second that his eyes remained closed whilst his hearing became 'switched-on', there was no denying what was reality and what fantasy.

Eyelids flickering open, he found his head was turned to the side and Ben was in his direct line of sight. Conscious that he was in the younger boy's seat, Dan felt guilty.

"Sorry. Was I out for long?" he asked, fighting the urge to stretch and yawn, not wanting to rub the other boy's nose in it.

"Yeah, a while. They gave us some food. I saved yours for you but to be honest if you are not that hungry, you might want to leave it." He offered up a sandwich that looked like it had seen better days and a Rock cake that actually looked like its name. Dan was willing to bet that it tasted like it too.

"Thanks for the advice, I think you are probably right. I'm not actually *that* hungry!"

"We are coming in to land now. The pilot just announced it. That's maybe why you woke. Hearing the loud announcement, I mean."

"Oh right. You better have this seat again then."

It was only on getting up, that Dan felt the stiff sore place on his arm and remembered the site of the vaccine. He felt an urge to rub the area but as soon as he put his hand on it, there was a searing pain and a burning sensation. As if the vaccinated arm was on fire, he withdrew his hand rapidly, before it even made contact. He was desperate to get a good look at the skin where he had been injected but it would have to wait.

"Does your arm ache? You know, the place where we had that shot?" he asked, not in the least surprised when the boy nodded his agreement.

But then Ben qualified the nod and Dan became uneasy again. "Yeah, but no more than when I got a shot for tetanus last year, when I cut my hand on a rusty knife." He offered up the once injured hand to show the faint scar which bisected the palm.

"Oh!" It was all Dan could say on the matter, his mind busy wondering what the injection site actually *looked* like, hidden as it currently was.

"You talked." It was said so quietly that Dan almost didn't hear it.

"I talked?" Dan had no idea what Ben was referring to.

"In your sleep I mean." Ben tried to explain himself better. "You talked in your sleep." He stopped, waiting for a reaction from Dan before continuing.

The plane made a slight shift in altitude, a slight drop in height that very few passengers would probably even notice. But Dan did. He noticed it because it mirrored how he felt inside.

There was no reason to feel the way he did. As far as he was aware he had never talked in his sleep before. He'd been to plenty of sleep-overs at friends' houses and not once, not *ever* had anyone told him he had been talking.

Full of curiosity and more than a little bit of dread, for a moment he still actually considered dismissing the comment as of no interest. But that wouldn't be true. Nor was it of no importance somehow. Looking at it logically it clearly was of importance to him. Perhaps not the *waking, conscious him*, but certainly *the him* that he became when he was asleep. It was good logic…if his mind hadn't been caught on something, he certainly wouldn't have been dreaming about it, much less talking about it in his sleep.

"What did I say then?" he enquired, hoping that his voice sounded light and unconcerned.

"Well you mumbled a bit at first and I couldn't quite make out what you were saying. Then you shouted "SNOW!" really loudly, then some stuff about your mom and …leaving her in the storm," Ben's voice caught and wobbled and Dan knew he was thinking about his own mom and dad, left all the way behind them in Seattle.

It didn't take a brain doctor to figure out what had been on Dan's mind but his face burned with the knowledge that he had so publicly announced his upset. To think that he had shouted aloud to the other passengers was almost unbearable and he vowed to avoid contact with them if at all possible.

"Snow huh? As if we don't have enough trouble with the rain!" His attempt to make light of it was gratefully accepted by the other boy, who looked less like he wanted the seat to swallow him up.

"Yeah…" anything else Ben was about to say was swallowed up in the screaming which issued forth from most of the children, as the plane took a sudden lurch upwards into the sky, from where it had only recently descended.

Dan was pushed back as forcefully as if someone had punched him in the chest and he banged the back of his head on the floor of the aisle. Eyes level with the row behind Ben now, he could see that all the children were forced right into the back of their seats by the speed and angle of the plane's ascent.

Then, just as quickly as it had changed altitude, the plane levelled off.

"Sorry about that, children." There was a hesitation in the pilot's voice and a slight shift in tone when he continued, "The airport was not quite ready for us there. We will be circling around and land in five minutes. Please stay in your seats and keep your lap belts on."

Something about that shift in tone signalled a lie to Dan.

He had certainly heard enough lies in the last few months to be able to identify one.

"Meteorologists confirm the storm in the Midwest is not worsening." That had been one of the first, and quite a good one apparently, as most of the folk he knew in Seattle had believed it. Even his parents had. Neighbours had stopped each other in the streets and confirmed its truth to each other as if they more people who said it, the more who believed it, the more real it would be. Confirmed it and by their sheer numbers, willed it to be true.

"Hey Joe, didya hear that meteorologists confirm the storm in the Midwest is not worsening," a man would call to another across from him, as they both collected their morning papers from the dry front lawn, using the *exact same words* that he had heard on TV.

"Yeah Pete, I heard that too. It's a real relief isn't it? So you up for a beer tonight?"

Dan shook his head at the memory. How could they have got it so wrong? And when they realised they were wrong – what did they do about it? Tell the truth? As if! They merely trundled out the next lie.

"Meteorologists confirm that although the Midwest storm *is* now worsening, there is no indication that conditions will escalate further or that the storm will spread to other regions. Lie.

Then it was,"meteorologists accept that whilst the storm does seem to be holding strong in the Midwest, it has also widened its area but this is still contained and it is believed the storm will soon peter out." Lies, lies, lies, LIES.

And here, right now, had been another one. He didn't know the reason for the sudden increase in altitude but he knew for certain, that it wasn't because the airport wasn't ready for them. The only reason he could think of was that they had been about to collide with another plane, when the pilot realised this and took action.

Dan didn't know whether to be worried about their imagined near miss or just be grateful it hadn't happened.

He settled for being grateful as once more the plane began its descent.

Chapter 6

The airport was huge but had the feel of a small place because it was so busy. Dan had never flown before but he had seen pictures of airports on the TV and he knew they didn't normally operate like this. Herded from the plane like a bunch of sheep, the passengers were hurried through empty corridors which terminated in little rooms with counters in them.

Apart from his fellow passengers, and the two flight attendants who led the way, the corridors and rooms were deserted. No-one asked his name or checked his passport or anything, which was really lucky 'cos he didn't have one anyway.

"Follow this next corridor to the end and you will be in the main area of the airport. The person who is collecting you will be there and your luggage will arrive on big conveyor belts. We have to leave you now. Good luck children." The attendant's eyes were watery and betrayed her fear and anxiety.

Dan knew exactly how she felt. He had tried to stay beside Ben, Jim-Bob and Katie but as he was actually in the aisle when the plane landed, he had had to get off before others behind him could get past and in the rush, he had been pushed to the front of the crowd. Now with no flight attendants to hurry him along, he hung back, letting the other children surge past and beyond him, seeking out his friends.

Right at the very back of the crowd, they were a while in catching up with him. Katie looked exhausted, her face small and drained and somehow too tiny for the rest of her seven year old body. Jim-Bob looked little better, with the hair on the back of his head sticking up where it had rubbed on the back of the plane seat. Dan drew a hand over his own hair, wondering what he looked like to them.

"You're being met by your Aunt, right?" he checked as they walked and he and Ben half-dragged Katie up the fast emptying corridor. There was no real need to rush, the corridor did not have any intersections where they could possibly take the wrong turn, it just went on and on with a light curve or bend every so often.

"Yes, the doctor who pees on things!" Jim-Bob tried the joke again but it fell flat this time. He grinned anyway, his smattering of freckles mixed with the unkempt hair making him look impish and mischievous. Dan thought Jim-Bob would be ok. His sense of humour would serve to carry him through the difficult times ahead. Even Katie would probably be fine once she was well rested. She was younger and therefore probably even more mentally resilient.

It was Ben that Dan feared for. Ben who held a responsibility that would daunt an adult. Ben who had been charged with looking after his younger brother and sister.

Ben's eyes were hard and sharp.

"Yes Aunt Georgia. We have to find her as quickly as possible so that she can let mum know we are ok."

It was the same thought that had already occurred to Dan about his own situation.

"I have to find my Uncle Jack but we can all look together."

Ben smiled in response and Dan understood that they were both grateful for each other's support and friendship.

Footsteps from behind, alerted them to the fact that they were no longer alone. Dan glanced behind. There was a crowd of children of varying ages approaching at a fairly fast pace. Jammed together by the relatively narrow confines of the corridor, the crowd would surely sweep them up and along at its own pace. Katie would not withstand it. And they would not be able to stay tight together.

In his mind's eye, Dan saw her flagging, all energy gone, all the fight and resilience worn out of her. He saw the force of the crowd tear the four of them apart. And he saw Katie fall to the ground without the support of the two older boys keeping her upright. And he saw the crowd surge over her, careless feet trampling on her little hands, the weight of the crowd pressing the breath from her lungs, the life from her body.

"Press yourselves again the wall, and hold on tight to each other!" he commanded, dragging them all over to the side of the corridor. He flattened himself against the wall and tightened his grip on Katie, using his other arm to try to shield Jim-Bob.

Out of step with each other, the crowd looked less like an army than a militant mob. Children or not, it was a scary sight to behold. Perhaps the very fact that the crowd was entirely composed of children was what actually served to make it scary. Dan wasn't sure and in truth didn't have the luxury of time to ponder too much on it.

Bodies ripping past him in extremely close proximity, his arm was battered by the sheer force of the crowd. Tensing his muscles against the onslaught, he pressed further back against the wall, forcing Katie and Jim-Bob at his side to do likewise. Once or twice he thought he was going to lose his grip on the children, especially when a particularly large teenager crashed into him, winding him severely, so that all his breath left his body in one huge 'whumph' of air. And suddenly there were too many bodies around him, too many faces blurring the air right in front of him so that he couldn't even draw a breath back in, didn't have enough space in front of his own body to even expand his lungs and chest back to their normal size.

Then it was over. Like a tsunami, the crowd washed over them and moved onwards, uncaring for what it had left behind. Coughing at the desperate rush of oxygen back into his deprived body, Dan doubled over in pain, dropping his arms to clutch at his burning chest. Katie and Jim-Bob still stood where they were, eyes still fear-widened, bodies still pressed as flat as possible against the cold wall of the corridor. The pallor of their faces exactly matched the shade of paint on the wall and Dan had the oddest feeling that if it weren't for the contrasting shade of their dark blonde hair, that they might just be absorbed by the wall. It was of course a stupid and impossible thought but eerie enough, that he couldn't immediately shake it away.

"Come on then, let's get moving again." Ben pulled at his sister's hand to encourage her. Dan smiled and worked hard to keep the expression on his face. It served a dual purpose and that was just fine by him. It encouraged the others but more importantly it provided an excuse to say nothing...and that was important because right now he was feeling more freaked than he had been before, even on the plane. Something about the single-mindedness of the children who had passed them had been *more* than terrifying.

Not like anything he had ever seen before, even in the packed corridors of school, when a bell sounded to signify the end of one lesson and the start of another, causing the whole school to empty into the corridors in search of the next timetabled classroom, it had scared him at a primal level.

In school, there was so much *noise,* footsteps of course, but other noise too. Noise that was banter, snatched conversations and thrown jokes, humour and derision, eagerness and reluctance, depending on the twist of the timetable.

But not this. Not this crowd which had just passed them. Silent apart from the echo their feet made as they pounded along the corridor, the crowd had an intent feel to it, as if their purpose was too important for them to be distracted by chatter. Yet it was not unique he realised.

"They weren't talking at all!" His voice sounded slightly different to normal he noticed and wondered if that was the after effect of near suffocation, when he hadn't been able to draw a breath.

"No." Ben didn't seem surprised at the remark and Dan wondered if the other boy had noticed it before his comment.

"But neither was anyone in the crowd we were with." Ben's voice echoed around the now empty corridor and in Dan's head.

"Yeah, I know." There didn't seem to be anything else to say. Neither boy seemed able or willing to supply a theory as to why that was and Dan thought maybe it was best left that way.

They walked in silence a few minutes before a turn in the corridor brought them face to face with a set of closed double doors. Clasping the door on the left side with his left hand, Dan waited till Ben grasped the handle of the right door with his right hand before he began to pull the heavy door open. They would need both doors open simultaneously to get Katie through with them supporting her on either side.

Glancing over at the little girl, his eyes fixed on the exhausted droop of her features, he didn't immediately see the scene which had been hidden behind the closed doors. Only the soft gasp which emerged from Ben's mouth alerted him to the fact that herein lay something unexpected.

Reluctant to have to face any more unfamiliar situations, he felt his brain scrambling for a reason. An excuse to just turn around and go back the way they had come. But there wasn't one. Going back was not only pointless, it was impossible. There was nowhere to return to, only the long stretch of corridor which now lay behind them.

Eyes slowly drawn upwards, he saw the scene from the ground up. A strange perspective perhaps, but one

which afforded him the fullest sense of the sheer volume
of people who crowded the airport terminal. Like
livestock on their way to market, the people were pressed
up so close to one another, it was difficult to see where
one ended and another began. And it was not a still
picture, but rather one which flowed and melded as the
people who made it up, struggled to move past one
another, within it.

Now that he looked more closely in fact, he could
make out individuals, those who seemed to be fighting
their way to the outer edges of the crowd, whilst others
fought to enter into the thick of it. And everywhere,
hands. Hands held up in the air, holding names written
on thick cardboard, hands moving other people along,
hands reaching out and seeking something…someone
else.

And a cacacophony of noise. Adults and children
alike, shouting their own names or those of the people
they were expecting to meet. Crying and wailing mixed
with the odd scream or screech. And above all that, a
tannoy which informed the unlistening crown that
passenger arrival schedules were available at the kiosk on
the right side of the terminal, under the big wall clock.

Unheeded, the tannoy continued to play the
recording, whilst the whole of humanity [or so it seemed
to Dan] continued to push and shove around each other.

"Aunt Georgia's *in there?*" the unbelieving tone of
Jim-Bob's words turning the statement into an
unintended question.

"I guess so!"

Dan wasn't sure if Ben's response was intended as an
answer to what he thought was a question or whether it
just reflected the boy's own sense of amazement.

A sudden tiredness in his wrist made him realise that they still stood on the far side of the door, holding it open without going through.

"And your Uncle Jack."

Of course, it was true. Somewhere in that crowd, Jack Ryan was searching for him. Indeed he may have been searching for some time already. In fact, wasn't there the horrible possibility that Uncle Jack had already gone away, had already reported to Dan's mom that he wasn't on the flight? With a burgeoning sense of fear, Dan realised that no one had taken his name when he had boarded the plane late.

"Did you give your name?" he asked urgently as he motioned to Ben to step beyond the doorway. The heavy doors closed slowly behind them but if they just stood exactly where they were, stood with their backs to the doors, they would not get sucked into the melee, he thought.

"Give my name?" Ben sounded dazed now and Dan became even more panicked.

"Give your name? On the plane?" Desperate for an answer, but also fearful of what he already knew, he could not bear to wait for a response.

"Did you give your name to anyone on the plane? Did anyone write it down or cross it off or anything?"

Ben's slack face changed as he realised what Dan meant and strove to think back. "Yes, I told them who we were and who we were meeting. It was the other flight attendant, not the one who injected us. She wrote it down in some kind of book."

"He won't know I'm here…" Dan wasn't even sure if he merely thought it or said it aloud.

"How are we going to find her?" Jim-Bob's voice had more than a slight wobble in it. "We will lose each other if we even try to get in there!" Dan recognised the truth of what Jim-Bob had said. If the crowd of children had been a threat to their unity, this was an even bigger one.

"Give me your belt, and yours too," he demanded of the two boys, the smallest grain of a plan forming in his head. Taking his own belt off, he fastened the buckle of his belt to the last hole in Ben's belt, and the buckle in Ben's with the last hole in Jim-Bob's and made one very long and strange belt from the three.

"Ben you need to go at the front so that you can look for your aunt, then Katie, then Jim-Bob then me. I am the tallest anyway so I will see over your heads." It sounded good, even if there wasn't that much difference between his height and Ben's but he knew it was important that he sounded confident.

Standing directly behind Jim-Bob, Dan rethreaded the now giant belt through two of the loops in his jeans, before passing it through a loop on the left side of Jim-Bob's trousers then past Katie who had no loops on either her skirt or her top. Then he threaded it through two loops of Ben's, around Katie's right side, through the loop on Jim-Bob's right side and back to himself, where he buckled it tight. Pulling them all as close as possible together.

The modified belt bit into him a little and the holes in the final strip of belt were slightly too small for the pin of the buckle on the first belt but it would have to do.

"Ok then, let's go."

It was difficult to walk all trapped together and made him think of himself as part of a huge centipede thing. For a moment he considered telling this to the others but he knew what Jim-Bob would do with the end syllables of the word and he didn't think he could take any more toilet humour without bursting into tears in despair of their situation, so he kept the thought to himself.

Partly to distract himself and partly because it could only help their search, he asked Ben what his aunt looked like.

"She's got longish dark hair but she normally wears it tied up...and she's pretty."

"Dad says she's not as pretty as mom, though." Katie's voice was small and quiet but hearing it offered so freely again, made Dan's heart glad.

"Duh Katie! Dad just says that. Aunt Georgia is way prettier than mom!" Jim-Bob seemed more than prepared to sacrifice family loyalty for the truth.

"That's not true. Ben, that's not true is it? Tell him off!" Katie almost shrieked, the intensity of her hurt at odds with the importance of her brother's statement.

Recognising that there were deeper currents here, Dan worked at diffusing the situation, allowing Ben to distance himself from it. "Guys, I don't think that's really what's important right now." The belt dug further into the soft area underneath his ribcage, as Ben lurched forwards into a space which had opened up in front of him, dragging the rest of them along in his wake.

Bodies pressed around them in every direction, pushing, pulling, shoving and being shoved. It was every person for themselves here, survival of the fittest. As sorry as Dan would ever be to have to admit it, he was aware that he himself would do anything he had to, to keep his little band of people ok. He just hoped it wouldn't come to more than this. For all their sakes.

Chapter 7

There was no knowing how long they struggled in the crowd. Time seemed to have lost all meaning. And it was strange how many women there were with long dark hair.

"We're never going to find her." Katie's voice had become increasingly slurred, an indication of how exhausted she was.

"Of course we will!" Dan hoped his voice did not betray his own doubts. But what if they didn't find Georgia? Or Jack? What if they just wandered around and around till they could go no longer. What then? Would they just stop where they were? Could they find somewhere to sit or lie down? Impossible. They would be more than likely crushed to death by the hordes of people who would literally walk right over them.

Dan knew he wasn't a pessimist, he wasn't a cup half empty kind of kid, but he was a realist. And like it or not, if they stopped moving in this crowd, the crowd would not part and flow around them...oh no, the crowd would step right over them and grind them into the marble of the flooring. There would be no malice, no hurt intended, and in fact he had no doubt that as individual human beings, the people in the crowd would try to avoid stepping on them.

But the crowd as an entire entity would not be able to manoeuvre itself to avoid them and they would be crushed underfoot. Still mindlessly pushing one foot out in front of the other, he knew this to be true. They had to find Georgia and when they had done that, then he would have to find Jack.

Bumped hard from the side he was almost knocked off his feet and stumbled against Jim Bob's back. Wearily he looked towards his assailant, expecting his eyes to be met by the sight of no less than a full quarterback, complete with helmet and padding, the force of the knock had been so strong.

Instead he encountered a slim dark haired woman dressed from what he could see of her, in green hospital scrubs. The significance of the clothing for a split second escaped him.

"Aunt Georgia," he croaked, meaning it to be a call to the others ahead of him. But head turned to face the woman and away from the other children, his voice was consumed by the crowd. Only the woman herself heard him, her head snapping towards him and eyes widening, even as her brow furrowed in lack of recognition.

The belt bit deep into his flesh as Ben, unaware of what was happing behind him, forged deeper into the crowd ahead. Feeling as if the belt was literally going to cut him in half, Dan tried to stay is ground. Forcing his fingers under the belt where it cut most into him, he tried to draw the others back to where he still stood.

Excruciating pain ripped into him but he knew he could not give up, could not let them miss the woman they had spent all this time searching for.

Dan strained against the belt.

"Ben, wait, come back this way!"

Jim-Bob, his ears probably ringing from the loudness of Dan's shout so close to them, joined in the cry and passed it on to Katie who in turn managed to get Ben's attention.

Finally the belt slackened as Ben, in the lead, stepped back towards Dan. Using the slight slack, Dan struggled to turn around within the circle of the belt, so that he was facing the woman he had surprised.

Reaching out to him, she grasped him by the shoulders, her hands strong and firm and holding him in place as the crowd tried to buffet him first one way then the other.

"Who are you?" Even the surprise of her English accent didn't disguise the puzzle in her voice from him. Her eyes searched his face for any recollections of him, her blue eyes seeming to darken as they latched onto his.

"Aunt Georgia!" shrieked Katie at his side, her eyes impossibly huge and excited. Dan watched with a feeling of strange detachment as the force of the crowd, thwarted by their inability to move them forward, shunted them kind of sideways, so that they now stood side by side, the belt still around all of their waists but tighter now.

"Katie! And Ben and Jim-Bob!"

Relief replaced the worry which had been etched deep into Georgia Wade's face.

"Oh thank God I've found you at last!"

"Oh Aunt Georgia, he's not God, he's Dan!" Katie supplied, taking Georgia rather a little too literally.

"Well then, thank you Dan!" laughed the woman, her eyes twinkling at Katie. She smiled at all of them, Still holding tight with one hand on Dan's shoulder, she moved the other one to Katie's chin, cupping the child's face in her hand and lifting it upwards slightly. "You are so like your mother Katie."

At once Katie's expression changed. Her face fell and hot tears splashed down her cheeks, leaving a trail through streaks of dirt. Elbowing others out of the way, Georgia did what Dan considered to be virtual suicide and crouched down in front of the little girl. "Don't worry, Katie, everything will be ok."

Dan hoped she was right but he wasn't that sure. But he was pleased that Georgia hadn't offered empty promises that they would be back with their mom soon. Katie and her brothers were young, but they weren't stupid and he was willing to bet that strange as their short lives had already been up till now, they were about to get even stranger.

"Come on, let's get out of here. I have already got your bags in the car. Your mum labelled them well. I knew them as soon as I saw them 'cos she used the old cases from when we were roomies together and both liked old time swing. As soon as I saw Michael Bubble's face on the bags, I just knew they were yours." Georgia smiled wistfully, remembering better days.

Replacing the smile with a pale rendition of brightness, she let go of Dan's shoulder and instead reached both arms behind her and grasped Katie, pulling her behind her and tight in her wake. Caught by the belt, the three boys were pulled into some semblance of order, with Ben following Katie, then Jim-Bob with Dan bringing up the rear.

Pushing and shoving, straining against the flow of the crowd then conversely being swept up in it, it was a surprise to find themselves suddenly outside the building.

Georgia let Katie go and turned around to face them all. "Well wasn't that a good idea," she pointed towards the imprisoning belt and reached towards it, unfastening the buckle and rolling the belt up into one huge coil.

"What a clever idea to keep you all together." Head cocked to one side, she reminded Dan of some exotic British bird, he'd seen once in a book. "Come on kids, let's get you home and into a hot shower."

"I…I can't go…I can't leave here. I have to go back inside." Four faces regarded him in astonishment. It would seem that having spent so long in finding their aunt, the others had forgotten that he had his own person to find. His own life to lead.

"I don't understand." Georgia looked from one to the other of them, waiting for an explanation. Light drizzle landed on her hair and eyelashes, making them sparkle as if jewel encrusted and like a bolt of lightning, for the first time, Dan realised that it was raining here. Not hard and relentless like back home but fine and almost unseen. A shiver ran down his back and a feeling of inescapable dread roiled in the pit of his stomach. Rain. Always rain.

"Dan was on the plane with us. But he's not with us. He is supposed to meet his uncle here." Ben explained.

"Well not *here*. Inside," provided Dan just in case there was any further confusion. "So I have to go back. Inside I mean."

Georgia was clearly torn. Her desire to look after and protect her three charges did not extend to the idea of re-joining the melee inside the airport. On the other hand she was loath to leave Dan alone to the mercies of the crowd. "Ok look, I've got an idea. My car is over there. We can go over and put Katie and Jim-Bob inside and Ben can look after them, while I go back inside with you.

It was as good a plan as any and secretly Dan was relieved not to have to go back in alone. But the farewells at the car were hard on all of the children, especially Katie, who demanded that Dan kiss her on both cheeks and promise to come back to Georgia's house with them, if he couldn't find his uncle.

"Yeah of course I will." It wasn't a lie, just an easy promise to make under the circumstances.

"Ok then. See you later Dan." She settled herself in the back of the car, knees huddled under her chin and was snoring softly by the time he had said goodbye to Jim-Bob and Ben.

"Your Dad would have been proud," he murmured quietly so that only the older boy could hear.

"So would yours Dan. And your mom too. Thanks."

Dan felt a lump of emotion clutch at his chest and tears well up in the corner of his eyes. Unable to say anymore, the two boys hugged each other fiercely, before almost reluctantly, Ben got in the car with his brother and sister and Dan turned once more towards the airport terminal.

"Well, what proved to be a good idea once, is an even better idea, second time round," stated Georgia as she modified the huge belt, taking one of the larger belts off the roll, so that it fitted snuggly around her and Dan.

"Are you ready?"

Dan didn't trust himself to speak so she nodded his agreement.

"Here goes!"

Launching themselves into the crowd didn't seem so difficult this time. Perhaps because Georgia was in the lead, they managed to cut through groups of people, slicing through the throng with no real trouble.

Round and round they went, both of them searching faces for Jack Ryan as Dan remembered him – not quite as old as his brother Kevin, tall and with a thick crop of reddish/blonde hair. It wasn't much of a description for Georgia to go on, even Dan had to admit, but it was pretty much all he had. Unbidden, like a sour taste in his mouth, the memory of the photos he had forever lost haunted his memory. But what was done, was done.

And then there he was, far, far away in the distance and yet standing above the crowd, surveying it as it churned around him. And he was moving. Moving yet managing to stay in the same spot. Confusion clouded Dan's brain as he struggled to understand what he was seeing.

"He's over there! I can see him!"

Georgia followed his gaze. "He's standing on the carousel, jogging to stay in the one spot!" Something about her tone suggested she was impressed by this. Either the endurance required to do so or the actual idea of it, tickled her somehow and Dan felt the tiniest glow of pride.

"We have to get you over there. Do you think he has spotted you?" she asked, changing direction and heading more directly for Jack.

"No, I don't think so. Oh!"

A pile of discarded suitcases blocked their passage and even as they watched yet more luggage slid off the conveyor belt on the carousel, landing with a thump on the baggage already there. Bizarrely Dan focused on a single pink shoe which teetered on the very edge of the belt but did not tip over onto the pile. Instead it was secreted away, back through the gap in the wall, as it continued its journey.

Perhaps the rest of the luggage it had been travelling with had been eaten by a strange beast which lurked the bowels of the airport. Or perhaps it has just been badly packed, in a case which had finally burst its contents all over the carousel and all that remained was the one solitary shoe.

"You are going to have to climb up there and onto the belt and head towards him. If we both try, the pile will fall and we will lose too much time. This way, if you climb alone, I can hold the pile steady for you."

She was right of course. Their combined weight would topple the pile of luggage over and in the ensuing chaos they would lose too much time. Time in which Jack Ryan might just move elsewhere in his search. Time was of the essence. She untied the belts around them.

"Yes, you're right. Thanks for helping Georgia."

"Good luck Dan!" she smiled and he saw how fearful she was. Her mouth was wide and honest but her eyes tried to hide her fear from him and failed.

"We will be fine and so will you. Look after them." He was disturbed at once more having to say a forever farewell to a new found friend. How many times was the human heart expected to break and keep healing itself, he wondered. How many times could he do this?

"Come on! Go! GO, go,go!" she cried, thrusting herself against the pile of baggage, pinning it down and holding it in place as he scampered up and over it.

And then he was on the conveyor belt itself. Bags and holdalls and suitcases came towards him at speed, threatening to push him back to where he had been. The strip of metal which bordered either side of the moving belt was too narrow to walk on, so he had no choice but to leap and hurdle every obstacle in his path.

Sweat beaded his back and made his clothes cling to him once more but he was getting closer and closer to Jack and that was all that mattered. Vaulting a particularly large case, he was suddenly within earshot of his uncle.

"Uncle Jack!" he panted, aware that he was so out of breath he had to rest soon. "Uncle Jack!"

"Daniel!"

Jack's face was ecstatic and he caught Dan up in his arms, sweeping him up so that his feet momentarily dangled above the passing luggage.

"Come on let's get out of this madhouse!"

But in the instant before he leapt back into the crowd, with his uncle at his side, Dan used his high position to seek out Georgia's face amongst the crowd. She stood where he had left her, by the pile of luggage, off to the left.

For the last time she caught his gaze and smiled. For a short moment he smiled back and then he did something that neither of them expected. He lifted a hand to his mouth and blew a kiss in her direction.

He was too far away to see if the smile she sent him back reached all the way to her eyes, but he was gratified to see her reach for the kiss as if to catch it and hold it close to her heart. He sure hoped Georgia Wade and her nephews and niece, his *friends*, would all be ok.

For now, the promise of good luck was all they had to cling on to. With that thought weaving trails around his head, Dan held tight to Jack as for the second time that day, he fought his way out of the terminal.

Chapter 8

The drizzle outside seemed somehow colder and wetter than it had been only a short time ago. It clung to them, blurring their vision and forcing them to squint against it. Disorientated for a moment, it took longer than he would have liked, before Dan began to recognise his surroundings. They were not that far from where Georgia's car had been parked.

Hope fluttered in his chest for a brief moment before he realised that the car which now occupied the very same spot, was not hers after all. Her car had not been silver, he was sure of that. If nothing else, at least it meant that she was on her way home with Ben, Jim-Bob and little Katie. But he was still sorry that they had gone before he had introduced them all to his uncle.

Jack's car was not so much a car as a truck. It was not at all what Dan was expecting him to have. His surprise must have immediately shown on his face as Jack wrenched open the passenger door and waited for him to get in.

"What, you don't think this suits my style?" Jack's smile, so like his brother's, Dan's dad, caught at Dan's heart with a little tug.

"I guess I never really thought about it," Dan considered, "except that dad always says you have this great reporter job in New York, so I guess I kinda thought…"

"You *kinda thought* I'd drive a little sporty car like your dad huh?" It was teasing but of the nicest variety. Jack shut the car door firmly and raced around the tailgate at the back of the truck to climb into the driver's seat.

"No sporty little car for me. I like the freedom this gives me. Besides, it reminds me of my roots. Speaking of which," he reached into a pocket in his jacket and withdrew a slim cell phone.

"Don't you go forgetting your granddaddy was an Irish farmer before he came to this country, and proud of it too, he was." Delivered in what was probably the best imitation Irish accent Dan had ever heard, Jack's smile was radiant. "Guess you'll be needing this!" With a magicians flourish, Jack presented Dan with the phone, his mom's number already showing on the screen.

All restraint and manners gone in his haste, Dan couldn't prevent himself from grabbing at the phone. He muttered a brief, "sorry. Thanks," under his breath and knew that he hadn't offended Jack really.

Like the peal of church bells, the phone rang out on loudspeaker, each ring seeming to ricochet off his eardrums and around the cab of the truck. Four rings, five and finally six, Dan began to wonder if it would ever be answered. And then she was there, voice filled with hope and fear, concern and relief.

"Jack! Jack have you got him? Is he there? Can you put him on?" Her words all rolled together in her anxiety to get them out.

"Mom, it's me. I'm fine and I'm with Uncle Jack."

"Oh baby, that's so good." Her voice sounded strange, far away and hurt like she was about to cry. "Kevin, it's Dan, he's with Jack," he heard her call to his father.

"Dan, we love you." It was his father's voice but words that he had never heard from him before.

"I love you both too you know," that lump which kept appearing in his throat was there again but this time he couldn't swallow it down.

"We know son, we know," Kevin Ryan's voice was full of heartache and Dan could hear his mother crying softly in the background.

"Dan pass the phone to Jack now, we might not have long to talk." Handing that phone over was one of the hardest things Dan had ever had to do. But in the moment of passing it over, Jack gave him a twisted smile of reassurance. As hard as this was for Dan, it was also hard for Jack.

"Jack? You there?"

Something about his brother's tone made Jack's eyes flicker nervously. "Yes, I'm here Kev. You are on speakerphone." His eyes shot towards Dan and away again before Dan had a chance to read anything from them. Had there been a warning implied within the information that Dan could hear everything said?

"Uh ok, take me off the speaker!" There was no doubt at all in Dan's mind that whatever it was that his dad was about to say, was not meant for his ears. That unfortunately only served to make him more desperate to hear it. He squirmed in his seat, trying to get as close to Jack and the phone as he could, arguing internally with himself about whether it was best to keep his head near to Jack's in an effort to listen, or pull away slightly so that he could focus on his uncle's face and gauge what was being said by that. In the end, he was forced to settle for a mixture of both, catching the odd word and accompanying expression.

"…out…don't know…can…"

"I understand."

"…tell him…miss…"

"I will, I will. Bye Kev …and take care." Jack was troubled. He replaced the phone in his pocket and reached for the car ignition. Dan stopped him with a hand on his arm.

"What was that about?" he demanded, eyes drilling into Jack as if to force an answer from them.

"The army is starting to evacuate the adults. It's still raining but your dad says it's ok. The ground floor is flooded but it's only up to his knees he says." He tried to smile but failed miserably, "your dad wanted me to tell you they miss you. He said they will phone us later when they know more about what's happening. The signal is poor but your dad thinks it will be easier to make the call than to receive it."

Dan nodded, lost initially for words. Instead he turned his head and looked out of the side window. On another day, in a different situation, there would have been much that would have caught his interest. This was New York after all, one of the most vibrant and exciting places in the world. But under the circumstances it might as well have been the dark side of the moon, so scared, confused and unenthusiastic was he.

He closed his eyes against the blurred rushing of garish colours as the traffic zoomed past on the wide highway and let the motion of the car lull him into a doze.

"We are home." Even just coming out of a heavy nap, he heard the wince in his uncle's voice. "Well, I mean it's your home for now…" Jack Ryan hastily tried to amend.

"S'ok. I know what you meant Uncle Jack."

"Ok, then. That's good." Jack suddenly slapped the flat of his palm against his forehead. "Your luggage! We never collected your luggage! Damn it!"

"There was no luggage. I mean there was at first, when I first left home, but it got lost before I got on the plane. Cos I nearly missed the flight and there was this soldier…it's a long story, perhaps we ought to go inside first?"

Jack smiled. "Sounds like you have a tale to tell young Dan. How's about you tell it whilst I fix us both something to eat?"

Dan thought that was nothing short of an excellent idea and he nodded enthusiastically. A white hot flash of guilt suddenly raced through his mind. How could he even think of food whilst his mom and dad were still not safe?

"Come on then." Jack sprang out of his side of the truck and waited for Dan to do the same. But something in Dan's expression must have wordlessly conveyed that very idea to his uncle. "You can't help them kiddo. You can only stay strong for them. Ok?"

Dan nodded but didn't even attempt a smile. It would only have pained his face and lay like a stone in his heart anyway and he was grateful that Jack made no effort to jolly him along.

For the first time Dan looked up at the building which lay ahead of them. A huge brownstone, it was so far architecturally removed from Dan's own clapboard and white picket fence home, that it was like comparing a horse to a chihuahua dog.

"Wow, you live here?" Dan couldn't keep the impressed tone out of his voice and felt a stab of conscience that he could so easily put his parents' peril from his mind.

"Yeah. But only in one apartment, not the whole building, you know," he laughed, "but it suits me just fine."

He held the heavy wooden door open as Dan entered the building, no longer disinterested in his surroundings, attempting to take everything in at once, his eyes scanning the painted walls and the smooth tiled floor. He stopped at the foot of the stairs, black banister spiralling down from the many floors beyond, like a thick black snake finally uncoiling itself to relax.

"I've never been anywhere like this. Though I have seen them on TV. I thought you'd have a house like us. Dad never said."

"Yeah well this is ok, but there are better buildings, better neighbourhoods," Jack began to ascend the stairs. "You ok climbing the stairs? We could take the lift but it's only two flights up and since you have no luggage..?"

"No, the stairs are great and anyway I could do with stretching my legs a little bit." He ran his hand along the smooth wood of the banister as he climbed, liking the cool solid feel of it.

"My apartment is smaller than you are used too but we can have a bedroom and a shower room each and I won't mind if you put your feet up on the sofa either." It was a gentle jibe at Dan's mom, who was known to physically move people if she thought they were making the room look untidy.

Dan was grateful for the chance of levity and immediately pounced upon it. "Do you know she once made me change my socks before I sat on the sofa. She said they looked dirty, but I reckon she just thought they didn't match the colour scheme." This last bit was snorted out as Dan laughed through his own words at the memory.

"Yes, that sounds like your mom alright!" Pulling his apartment key out of the lock he pushed the door open and ushered Dan inside.

Chapter 9

Swinging his legs, sitting at the bar with a fast disappearing hot pepperoni pizza and fries in front of him, Dan recounted the tale of his airport ordeal and rescue by Private Curtis Wood.

Jack pulled a bar stool around to the other side and listened intently, not even taking his eyes off Dan as he took a long swig of some Mexican beer Dan had never heard of before. But although he never once commented, Dan saw how Jack's grip tightened around the bottle when he heard how Dan would have possibly been lost forever, if not for the intervention of the young soldier.

Fingers taut around the bottle neck, Jack's knuckles were drained white and the muscles in his forearm were rigid with tension. He worked hard to keep the anger and relief from his face.

"Looks like there are some good guys left in the world. That's good to know." He tossed the empty bottle into the trash and stood up.

"Look Dan, I have to go to work. I've got to cover a big baseball match. But you will be fine here. The bed in the spare room," he stopped himself and rectified, "the bed in *your room* is made up and there are towels for you laid out in your shower room. Make yourself at home and have anything you want from the fridge. Except the beer of course!" he smiled. Get to bed, no later than midnight and I'll see you in the morning. Ok kid?"

"Sure Uncle Jack. I'm kinda tired already so I think I'll watch a little TV then hit the sack anyway."

"Ok, I'll see you later then kiddo." Jack hesitated a moment, unsure how to say goodbye. Finally he settled for ruffling Dan's hair. He grabbed his car keys, his still wet jacket and he was gone, leaving Dan alone for the first time since he had said goodbye to his mother. How long ago had that been? He wasn't sure of the time then or now but either way it had been no more than twelve hours ago. Twelve hours and a lifetime ago.

Jack had told him to borrow one of his tee shirts and jogging bottoms and where they were located. It seemed silly to just get changed without showering, so he decided to do that first before settling down.

Skin almost bruised by the force of the power shower he was still surprised when the tears came. Somehow he had thought he had already cried himself dry. Swallowed by the hot soapy water, his tears made no impact on it at all, just as he himself had failed to make an impact upon his parents' decisions to stay in Seattle. And now? Now whilst he luxuriated in the fancy shower, they were being flooded out of their home, lives endangered and in terrible trouble. His cheeks began to burn as the imagined discredit he was doing them, enjoying a hot shower whilst they drowned.

He let the tears fall until he was truly empty this time, before turning off the faucet and roughly drying himself. His arm was still sore and was quite red but didn't look *too bad* to him.

Jack's tee shirt was both too long and too wide for him and made him look like one of those poor orphans from the film version of Oliver Twist. That thought and the dire possibility that that was exactly his fate, made him cringe at his own self-pity. The tee shirt did the job and that was all there was to think about really, he decided. The jogging pants were also ok, once he had rolled the legs up a couple of times. The waist was loose but luckily there was a drawstring there which enabled him to draw it tight around him.

The TV was huge and took up one whole wall of the living area and it took him a moment to figure out how to turn it on. But when it did flare into life, he wished it hadn't. Colossal images of the disaster that was continuing to unfold took his breath away. He staggered to the sofa, walking backwards and unable to take his eyes off the screen. Because these pictures were not of the storm in the Midwest anymore. They were far more familiar to him than that. They were of Portland, Spokane ... and finally... chillingly... of Seattle. Parks, roads, shops and even *schools* that he recognised were flooded, debris floating on the churning water.

Heart hammering loudly, he had to turn the volume up to hear what the reporter was saying.

"...army has stepped up its efforts to evacuate all adults from this area."

His area. Where his mom and dad still were.

"Whilst the geographical and population centre of the United States has always been in the Midwest, where

80

these storms have originated, there is no denying that the volume of population here in the Greater Washington area is tremendously large. There can be no doubt that the ability of the army to evacuate this volume of people will be sorely tested…"

Evacute! The word resonated in his head. They would be evacuated. Safe. *Saved*. His eyelids felt like someone had superglued them open. All notions of sleep were gone. Instead he sat body erect and still on the sofa and watched the TV with a morbid fascination, as each image was replaced by another even more horrifying.

Chapter 10

"Try and get some sleep. As soon as I can, I will get us out of here." Georgia tucked the blanket firmly around Katie's little body and pulled her long hair to one side on the pillow.

"Is this where you live Auntie Georgia?" Her voice was sleepy and she struggled to keep her eyes open.

"No, honey this is the hospital where I work and this is the ON CALL room where the doctors who are on call, come to sleep."

"So if you are on call, why are you not sleeping with us?" Jim-Bob's question was valid under the circumstances but Georgia didn't have the time to explain fully.

"The hospital needs my help right now. I'll be back soon. Get some sleep. Night night."

"Night night mommy." The words expelled on her last wakeful breath, Katie's eyes were already firmly closed. Her mind had lapsed into the familiar bedtime routine, where her mother's voice was always the last she heard before sleep claimed her.

A cold clammy hand of dread clutched at Georgia's spine and twisted, so that her words caught in her throat. Prevented from correcting the girl, she bit back the words that could have come, the words that would have brought the children's current situation back into focus and ruined any rest they might otherwise have got.

Now Katie was fast asleep and Jim-Bob too. Only Ben remained awake, lying flat on the little camp bed, blanket raised to his chin but eyes wide open. The look which passed between them said it all. Georgia shook her head at him to show she had taken no offence from Katie's sleepy salutation and quietly slipped out of the room.

"Dr Wade, over here!"

Georgia turned and was astounded at the sight which met her eyes. There were people everywhere. Nurses hurried back and forth, their arms full of supplies, faces strained and white, the heels of their shoes making unheard clicking sounds that were absorbed in the general bedlam of the scene.

"Dr Wade," an intern with a large clipboard appeared as if by magic at her side, although logic told her that he had merely walked unnoticed towards her. "Dr Wade, thank you so much for coming in at short notice..." he puffed at her, his voice having a rather asthmatic nasal quality to it. She wondered if he was even aware of that. Shaking her head to clear any surreal thoughts, she focused on the shiny name badge that sat jauntily on the pocket of his white coat.

"Look Dr Harris, I have three young children to look after who have just arrived from Seattle, so make it quick!" Her voice was sharper than normal and the inexperienced doctor blanched under its directness.

"The ER is full but patients are still being brought in …"

She cut him off, aware that she was being unfair and using her higher rank against him. "But I am a paediatrician! Not an ER doctor!"

"Yes, we are aware of that, and a damn fine one you are too!" bellowed a voice from somewhere behind her. The loud blustery voice, so in keeping with Dr Bill Bently's physique, contained only a gentle reprimand.

Georgia blushed under the force of the compliment from her mentor. "Off you go, Dr Harris, I will handle this difficult but brilliant young doctor from here." Bill's tone was light and airy but Georgia knew it disguised a mind that was sharper than a pin and a will that would bend steel.

"Thank you Dr Bently." The young intern's relief was apparent and with a brief nod to Georgia, he turned away, presumably to harass some other unfortunate.

"What's going on Bill?" Georgia asked, as the older man took her by the elbow and led her down the corridor.

"ER can't cope. God knows the whole hospital can't cope. Every hour we are having more and more patients brought in. It's all hands to the deck Georgie-girl," the familiar nickname was delivered without the familiar smile to accompany it.

"But where are they being brought from? The closest flooded areas to here are too far away, for us to be receiving their casualties."

"Need to know basis only Georgia, I'm afraid." Bill Bently rubbed his not inconsiderable beard, his eyes guarded against her. Sweeping the hand upwards and over his eyes however, seemed to produce an incredible effect. At once, the guardedness was gone, replaced by an urgency and seriousness that she had only ever seen, when consulting on the very worst of cases.

"Listen well, and don't ask any questions." He glanced around furtively as if he were about to tell her the biggest secret in the universe. Unconsciously she leaned further towards him, sensing that what she was about to hear would land him in trouble if it got out.

"You were my dear Betsie's friend, God rest her weary soul. And she wouldn't have gone through with the cancer treatment if it weren't for you..." his voice was cracked with suppressed emotion and his hand was once more on her elbow. "And even though she didn't make it...you gave her that hope back. And for that, my dear girl, I will be eternally grateful."

Georgia placed her own hand on top of his. She had heard this sentiment before and knew it cost him dearly to express it. His heart grieved anew every day for the loss of his beloved wife, just as she herself did, for the loss of a true friend. Knowing it was best to let him carry on in his own time, she merely waited till his composure was regained.

"It's everywhere Georgia. Wherever it's not yet been, seems to be where it's headed."

Her heart reeled in fear. Surely he was mistaken? "But the news reports said that after the Midwest and now the West Coast area, the storm would have no substance. They said that..." she was unable to keep the fear from her voice.

He interrupted her, nodding and using his hand in a shushing motion, for fear that others would notice their communication. "They said that it would all be over soon. They said that it would never get out of where it started. Then when it did, they said it could never travel further, hell they even evacuated kids to here, but guess what they didn't say?"

Her face ashen, she could only wait for what he was about to say.

"What they didn't say, was that the storm was heading this way too."

She found a voice to use, although from the shrill reedy tone of it, she wasn't sure it was hers at all. "So why not evacuate the children somewhere else? Why evacuate them to here? And why have they not started to evacuate the hospital?" Her mind whirred with thoughts and emotions but she tried to focus on Bill. Focus on the answers she was sure he would supply that would explain everything.

His answer shook her to the very core. "Because *there is* nowhere else Georgia. This has come from on high, so I know it is true." Georgia remembered now that Bill's brother was somebody important in the Government. Presumably this information had come from him. Bill sighed deeply, as if what he was imparting was causing him much anguish.

"The information on the news, TV and radio has been censored. This storm is happening worldwide. There is nowhere that's safe."

Surely it would not be so easy to keep information like that from the general population, not with the efficiency and speed of the internet as a communication tool? "But the web? Surely it would be all over the internet?" Her voice sounded incredulous and she watched as he winced, surprised by her naivety.

"The internet is down Georgia. Whether it crashed on its own, or had a little help is not for me to say. But it sure makes it easier to keep people in the dark."

"But I have three kids to look after. What am I going to do? I promised their mum I'd keep them safe. And then there are all the kids on the ward...what will happen to them?" 'Stupid question', she rebuked herself, 'they will die, they will all die!' Georgia felt like she was falling into a bottomless pit where vipers snapped at her heels.

"Yeah, I heard about the kids. That's why I'm telling you this. Get out while you still can. Tell no-one, just get the kids and go."

"I can't just leave, people need me here! I took an oath to always help save lives... not run away from trouble!" She was aware that she was rambling, her words jumbled and slightly incoherent.

"Listen to me girl. The *right* thing for you to do is to get those kids the hell away from here. You soon won't be able to make much difference here anyways, so just concentrate on saving them."

"But my patients...those children..." her words were cracked out of a throat that felt as if it has been glued shut. Bill interrupted her firmly. "As for your patients, I have a little plan, that under the circumstances, has a strangely fitting biblical connection. You are going to have to trust me Georgie-girl." With a touch as light as any professional pickpocket, she felt him drop something into the pocket of her white coat.

"Those are the keys to my car and my house and my garage. My car will handle better than yours in *wet conditions*," there was the merest hint of a very dark humour in his intonation. "In my garage, out back of the house, is the trailer and the boat is already loaded on to it.

As you well know, it's old like me but just as well maintained." His attempt at a smile broke her heart.

"Take it and get yourself and those kids the hell out of here. Best guesses from the "guys who know these things" are that you should head for the very area the storms started. The place will be devastated, make no mistake but where the storm has already passed, it seems to show no inclination to return. So you should be safe there. Or at the very least, *safer* there than elsewhere. Now go! And God bless you Georgia Wade."

Bill's eyes welled up and spilled over, the tears trickling into his beard as if to hide themselves.

"Come with us Bill. Please!" She was crying herself now, because she knew the answer even as she demanded that he voice it.

"I can't. My Betsie is buried a few miles from here. I can't leave her on her own and I can't leave this hospital in its time of need." He saw the thought which burned at the back of her eyes, provoked by the words he had intended to soothe her with.

He knew from old, that the best thing to do with Georgia Wade was to tell her the truth, unshrouded by niceties and convention.

"I can't leave. But *you* can. And you must. Those children and their parents trust in you, and you must *not let them down*. And if that is done at the sake of any personal ideals you uphold about not letting patients down, then so be it." He held her gaze and she knew he spoke what he believed to be true.

"Trust in me to get your patients to safety. I promise you I will make sure the paediatric wards are evacuated. So you can safely let your patients down. Indeed, toss your doctor's conscience into the fiery pit of hell, if needs be so, but do not let that very same conscience, stop you from saving those three children." His voice was strong again, forceful and full of commitment.

"Because let me tell you something. If you fail those children...*if I let* you let that happen, for whatever misguided moral reasoning you can provide, then we are all doomed." His eyes burned into hers.

"Those children are the future and they need you." He suddenly took hold of her hand and thrust it deep into the pocket where he had dropped his keys. Her fingers closed around the bunch of keys, making a fist of them so tight she could feel the sharp edges cutting into her palm.

Releasing her hand, he simply turned and walked away. Head high, back straight he immersed himself in the throng of scurrying medics, disappearing rapidly from view and never once looking back.

Chapter 11

"No point in taking that off, 'cos you are heading straight back out there into it again!"

Jack scooped up his sodden coat from where he had just hung it on the back of his chair.

"The game isn't on for another two hours yet, so I thought I'd make a head start on some of this other stuff," replied Jack, indicating the pile of half written sports reviews which littered his desk.

"Hmm, that's as maybe. But fact is, the game's been cancelled Jack. The ground is too waterlogged."

"Oh." It hadn't really come as a surprise but Jack was annoyed that he had come in to work for no reason now, when he could have stayed home with Dan.

"Don't get too excited Jack, you're not heading home. I need you for another article."

Jack waited for instructions, forcing his arms back into the cold, wet sleeves of the coat, which snagged and fought against him as if alive.

"Ed wants you to go see some guy about an ark he's building." Bernie Lieberman raised his eyes as if to admit that he found the idea preposterous.

"Oh come on Bernie, gimme a break would ya? I got my nephew at home. He's been evacuated from Seattle and quite frankly I ought to be with him, not here!"

"Look Jack, orders is orders and it's come from on high. You don't like them orders, take it up with Ed!" And with that Bernie slouched off, shabby too-long jeans dragging at the backs of his trainers and making a flat scuffing sound on the tiles.

Jack fought his way back out of the still wet coat. The sleeves which had tried so hard to resist him inserting his arms into them, now insisted on clinging determinedly to him, so that when he did finally manage to get the thing off, it was twisted and warped, sleeves inside out and thoroughly bedraggled. With a grunt he threw the mangled coat onto the desk and went in search of Ed.

Knocking on the Executive Editor's door was always rather intimidating. Jack thought it was the big letters which proclaimed the man's authority rather than the thought of the man himself.

"Come in Jack!" boomed the voice from behind the wooden door in response to Jack's knock.

"How did you know it was me?"

It wasn't the first thing Jack had planned to say, but it did strike him as strange that Ed had known it was him.

Ed Malone smiled. It was a smile that did great things to his face, lighting it up from within. A small, thin man who sat behind the most enormous desk Jack had ever seen, Ed was the closest thing to a real life Wizard of Oz. Just like in the film, he was a man who hid behind his power and position, using them to convince the outside world of his importance when in fact he was both shy and unassuming.

"Could *only* be you Jack, with a knock as loud and firm as that," Ed explained.

"What's the idea about me covering a story about an ark?" Jack didn't wait for an invitation but instead settled himself in the chair facing Ed's enormous desk.

"Well see here's the thing. We had a tip off about this guy and I think it will make an interesting piece, don't you agree?"

"Interesting Ed? The guy's a nutcase surely. I mean of course there were floods in the Midwest and now on the West Coast…but an ark…jeeze…he's bound to be one of the 'end is nigh' weirdos!"

"Look around you Jack, aren't we all a little weird? And anyway I give you carte blanche as to how you write it up." Ed held his hands up, palms flat and towards Jack as if in submission.

"Come on Ed, you know I only do sports now," pleaded Jack.

"Yup. And I also know that before that, you were the best damn political reporter I ever had the grace to work with." Ed's eyes narrowed into thin slits, willing Jack to work at his meaning.

For all his seeming Wizard-of- Oz-ness, Jack knew that Ed's unassuming appearance held a mind so sharp and shrewd, it could cut through stone.

"You saying there's a political angle here?" Despite himself, his interest was well and truly caught and reeled in.

"Now I wouldn't want to be saying anything that wasn't in the best interests of our population. Anything that wasn't vetted by the White House team of lawyers.

Wouldn't want to be stirring up the masses, after all, in this good law abiding country..." Ed let his words hang in the air between them.

Jack was silent a moment too, letting the words sink in.

"Look around you Jack." But this time Ed was no longer smiling and his outstretched arm indicated the heavy rain which fell outside the large plate window behind his desk.

"Suddenly those White House lawyers are very quiet. Come to think of it maybe they've gone on vacation with our esteemed President."

Like a hot needle in the eye, Jack got the point of the cloak and dagger conversation.

"Carte blanche you said?"

"Carte blanche," Ed confirmed. "Oh and Jack," Ed called him back just as he was about to leave the office, "make it a good'un!"

Jack stepped through the doorway and closed it gently behind him. Snaring his coat from his desk, he picked up the slip of paper which gave the address of the biblical ark builder.

Still pondering Ed's words, he drove through a district that seemed suddenly unfamiliar to him, cloaked as it now was in a veil of lashing rain and malevolent storm cloud. Building facades, their stone somehow darker than usual, perhaps due to an extreme soaking, looked empty and abandoned, when in fact the very opposite was true. People huddled inside their homes, away from the worsening weather.

Roads, normally full of traffic, which although not now deserted, were definitely quieter than normal. But everywhere there was a desolate feel to the air. He tried a few radio stations, hoping for something to mask the sound of the rain on the hood of the car. Something that was easy on the ear would have been good. He could have let it wash over him whilst still contemplating things. But most of the stations were strangely absent, a white hiss of noise emanating from the speakers instead of the expected drone of what passed for music nowadays. It was as if they had gone off air and forgotten to carry on.

Jack pressed the search button on the dashboard. Numbers scrolling rapidly across the display, looking for a signal to latch on to, he watched with amazement as the digits grew bigger and bigger.

"…and Jesus said unto them…" Jack pressed search again.

"…it is man's punishment…" Another station bleating on about how mankind had incurred God's wrath for the last time.

"…throw down your heads and pray to the Lord…"

Jack hit the search button a little too forcefully and was rewarded with an earful of classical music. Frustrated, he switched the stereo off and resigned himself to the sound of the drumming rain, which seemed more insistent now.

And what of Ed's suggestion that the White House was strangely quiet? Was he suggesting that the President and his most valuable aides had been evacuated to safety? And what exactly did that mean if they had?

It took less time than he would have thought, before he pulled up at the address written on the slip of paper. Like something out of a movie set, the hulking old warehouse looked almost gothic with the rain lashing down at it in almost vertical swathes.

Parking as close as he possibly could, he ran to the front door with his coat collar up as high as it would go. The rain now fell with such force, that it seemed to bounce off him, rather than soak in, although the lack of absorption was more likely due to the fact that he was already soaked through. With his back to the rain he stood at the door and almost expected Frankenstein's monster to appear when he rang the doorbell.

Instead it was a man who looked to be in his late fifties, sporting a vividly patterned shirt and an unlit pipe.

"Sorry, never did smoke but I find chewing on the stem of the wood, helps me concentrate," explained the man, managing to get his words out and understood, despite the pipe waggling around in his mouth as he spoke.

"Erm yes," murmured Jack, unsure quite how to begin. "So tell me Mr…" embarrassingly the man's name completely escaped Jack's memory and he had to look down at his slip of paper to read it.

"White. Sam White. Pleased to meet you, Mr Ryan," he said, reading Jack's name from his press badge, which was permanently pinned onto the breast pocket of his coat.

Sam White's handshake was warm and firm and his welcome was equally warm. "Come in, come in! Goodness me you are soaked through. Ed should have given you an umbrella at least, before he sent you here, but that's Ed for you, he never likes to dawdle!"

Things in Jack's head were not adding up. This man did not appear to be nutcase but instead a very rational man. And if Sam White *knew* Ed personally then how had this call been to investigate a tip off?

Jack followed Sam through the doorway and into the vastness of the building. He was reluctant to say anything, preferring to wait and see what was unintentionally revealed, before he went for the proverbial jugular.

"Look I have kept the existence of this place secret. And let me tell you that hasn't been easy!"

Jack could see why. The entire interior of the warehouse had been stripped out and now it housed a gigantic…well…ark…was the only real definition of the thing that Jack now regarded.

"Wow!" In his amazement Jack found no other word would adequately suffice and he was unable to keep his silence.

Sam White laughed good naturedly, "wow indeed!"

"How long has it taken you to build this?" he began to walk around the perimeter of the vessel, Sam at his side. "When did you start? And why?" It was clear it hadn't been thrown together quickly, so they were perfectly valid questions, although Jack hadn't intended to pose them. He had hoped the information would come more naturally, but circumstances had overtaken that idea.

"Longer than I would have liked. It took so long to find the perfect place to build it for a start."

"I can see why." A thought occurred to Jack. "But the …ark…" he struggled to actually call it such a thing, "is bigger and taller than the industrial doors. How will you get it out of here."

"Ah, well that's the interesting science bit, young man. Come over here," and he led Jack over to a complicated looking series of switches and buttons. "It's fully automated. Once the flood water reaches a certain level for the ark to be able to float, these switches here will use a series of pulleys and winches to pull the vessel through the roof and set it down outside."

Jack looked doubtfully up at the large industrial roof. "Won't it just hit the roof and get smashed up?"

"No, the roof opens up, in two sections. Don't worry it will work alright. And the ark is a specific width so that it will pass easily between tall buildings without getting stuck."

This interview was not going at all the way Jack had anticipated. "Pass between buildings?" He had a mental image of Sam White, with his shock of white hair and perfectly trimmed goatee beard, dressed as a modern day pirate, sailing down Fifth Avenue. It was ridiculous. Wasn't it? As if on cue, a particularly large torrent of rainwater threw itself across the roof above them, deafening them momentarily with its roar.

"But the storm is set to blow itself out before it ever gets here." Even as the words came out of his mouth, he realised how ridiculous they sounded. What was that outside, if it wasn't the start of a mega-storm?

"Yup, sure is. Just like it was set to blow over within a day in the Midwest, just like it was set to blow over *before* it got to the West Coast. Just like it will blow over before it gets to *us*. Because of course, that out there couldn't possibly be the beginning of a storm, could it?"

Granted , he had a point there, though Jack.

"Look I know you don't know me from Adam, so let me tell you about me. For twenty years, before I had the heart attack that changed my way of thinking, I was the Senior Theoretical Scientific Advisor to a body with a long string of initials, but which was in effect part of the Government."

Jack listened intently.

"Now you would never have heard of the existence of such a department, but let me tell you that it exists. And this storm has been one of the most talked about scenarios for nigh on two decades!"

"You mean that two decades ago, it was known that this storm was coming?" Jack was incredulous.

"No, not *this* storm or *that* storm but rather the possibility of a *super* storm, one that spreads itself around so that it's everywhere. And now it's no longer a possibility. It's a reality."

Chapter 12

Fumbling the key into the lock, Georgia finally managed to get Bill's front door open. The house seemed cold and unwelcoming, bereft as it was of its owner's presence. She wondered if this is how it always felt now to Bill, coming home from a long shift at the hospital, with no Betsie here to welcome him.

It struck her that she had never been in the house alone before. Indeed she hadn't needed to be here now, except she wanted to do something before she left.

The children watched her from the inside of Bill's SUV. She had driven his car here and left the keys to *her* car on his desk at the hospital. A straight swap, except that she was well aware that she had had the better deal.

Unable to repay Bill, she had done the next best thing and given him back a cherished memory. It was one of the last good photos ever taken of Betsie and up till now it had had pride of place on her mantelpiece.

Dappled sunlight shone down on the two women in the photograph. Caught in that split-second before a gale of laughter overtook her, Betsie was radiant, her hair a shining halo around her face. Then as now, Georgia was overcome by how beautiful she had been, both in looks and in nature. By comparison, Georgia thought her own face looked plain and very ordinary in the photo. The smile on her lips and eyes could not compare to that of the other woman.

Each holding a glass of champagne up high, the women had toasted the lovely day, the picnic, life and love. Georgia could remember it so well, she could even still taste that slightly bitter effervescence on her lips, still hear the pop of the cork, still feel how at one she had felt with life and the universe, that summer's day.

Tears sprung to her eyes at the memory and she chose to let them fall. Somehow to have refused them, would have been churlish, as if it would have diminished the real friendship and love they had shared.

Betsie had died six months later, almost to the day, of that picnic. Bald and weakened from the cancer treatment she had undergone, she was a pale rendition of how she had been in the photo. She had become unrecognisable. It was the worst way possible to remember a loved one.

Georgia had had the photo copied for Bill but he had been unable to accept it. "I want to remember her that way," he had confided to Georgia over a large bottle of bourbon, "but it's just so hard."

He hadn't been ready then. Now he was.

Knowing exactly what she planned to do, Georgia had driven home to pack a few things for herself and the children and also to collect the photos, one for her and one for Bill. Now she placed the framed photo on the hall table, knowing he would see it as soon as he walked through the door.

"If you can, I know you will be looking down on Bill and also on me." Georgia was afraid of what she was about to say, about to do and despised herself for that weakness. "Please help me get these kids to safety. Help me to stay strong for them. You were the most courageous person I have ever known. And one of the kindest, most generous hearts I have ever met. And I miss you." Sobbed out, Georgia found there was a freedom in venting her grief alone and unencumbered by having to worry about anyone else's feelings.

Betsie merely continued to beam out from her image in the photo but something shifted in Georgia's heart. It was almost as if a little space had been made there, hurt and debris cleared away, to make a new pathway for a fresh start.

"Yes, you are right. It is time to move on, my friend," aware that no words had been spoken other than her own, she somehow felt that the idea had been adequately conveyed to her. "Look after Bill, Betsie. And if his fate is that he comes to you, I know you will do all you can, to ease his passage into the light."

Although not religious herself, she had an idea that what she was now experiencing, was not dissimilar to the lift that she had heard attending the confessionals gave practising catholics. Like an affirmation of belief.

There was no need to say anything further, so without ado, she closed the door gently behind her and placed the house keys in the little hidey hole Betsie had once laughingly shown her.

A little ceramic pig, it had a hidden drawer underneath its pot belly, which could easily store a set of keys. Betsie had bought it from a little curio shop several years ago because she said it reminded her of Bill, with its chubby cheeks and misunderstood ways. Bill had laughed and laughed and recounted the tale to every visitor to the house.

That had been the sort of couple they had been and that would be how she chose to remember them. She climbed back into the car and headed towards the back of the house and the garage.

The garage lock sprung open as soon as she inserted the key and from the residue left on the shaft of the key, she could see that it had been oiled recently. Bless him, Bill had needed to ensure that everything ran smoothly for her and had obviously planned well in advance of coming into the hospital.

She remembered the boat from before, past summers spent lazily sunning themselves before jumping off the edge and diving into the cool waters below. It wasn't a big boat. Not ostentatious in the least, Bill had wanted one that he could use whenever the mood took him and not have to fiddle about organising how to get it where he was going.

Already fixed onto its trailer, *The Betsie* looked every inch a cared for vessel. Gleaming white paintwork, overlaid with two blue stripes and a scrolled rendition of its name, she wondered if it was really up to the task ahead of it. If things were really going to be as bad as Bill thought, then could this boat save them?

Through the plastic weather shield and the cabin doors which stood slightly ajar, she could see bags and boxes, lined up and stored neatly inside. Had Bill been using the boat for storage? Unlikely, she thought.

Climbing up and peeling back an edge so she could clamber inside, she found the boxes were taped firmly shut and covered in plastic. They were also marked with a felt-tip pen. A note was attached to the biggest box which proclaimed "NON-PERISHABLE FOOD" in Bill's neat handwriting.

She ripped the note off the box and read it.

"Dearest Georgia, you were and are, the closest thing to a daughter Betsie and I were ever blessed with. You will remain in my thoughts and in my heart, forever. Take this boat and those children and go. And do not waste time in looking back. What will be, will be - and yours is the future to make happen. All our love ,

Bill and Betsie."

He had signed his late wife's name with the little heart shape she used to make, instead of the dot over the i. Georgia crumpled. She wished that she could rip up the letter, tear it into a thousand pieces and scatter it in the wind. But that would not turn back time, or change her reality. So instead she slipped the note into an inside pocket of her coat and checked the other boxes for their contents.

If the writing on the boxes was correct, which she had no reason to doubt, then there were two boxes of perishable food, four of non-perishable food supplies, three boxes of bottled drinking water, a supply of diesel and four individual sleeping bags all in their own little bags. Bill had thought of everything. If anything, she owed it to him to make this plan he had concocted work. Shifting the boxes slightly to one side, she went further inside the boat where she found a large map, with a route drawn in thick red pen across it.

The route took her from New York towards the Midwest but instead of ending at a final destination, it ended instead at a large circle. She figured that he didn't want to be responsible for her heading anywhere too specific. He wanted to allow her to know when and where to choose her moments when an opportunity arose, rather than be rigidly confined to a particular destination.

Aware of the passage of time and the fact that she had once more left the children alone in the car outside, she left everything as it was and went to fetch them.

"Wow, Auntie Georgia, are we really going to live on that?" Jim-Bob was beyond excited.

"Not really live on it, just travel on it when we have to, ok?" she smiled, glad that children always seemed to find pleasure in something, even at the most difficult of times.

"But how will mummy and daddy find us if we go away from here?" Katie's anxious voice cut right through Georgia's smile and she watched as the innocent smile on Jim-Bob's face was replaced by a look of shame. Guilt stabbed at her and she was aware that she had already failed the children by not thinking of their most basic needs. They needed to know their parents knew where they were going.

"We will phone them now ok?" Pulling her phone from her pocket she dialled her friend's number but there was no response. Hanging up, she tried the children's father's phone but again there was no response.

"They are not answering right now. We will try again later ok?" She worked hard at smiling and looking completely unfazed by her inability to get through to their mum or their dad.

"Let's get this trailer hitched up and we will be on the road again!" she exclaimed brightly. It did the trick, and the children were eager to help. Katie and Jim-Bob moved the boxes and sleeping bags into the inside of the boat, placing them under and on top of the seating area, balancing them securely against one another so that the weight was evenly distributed and less liable to make the boat overturn. Then they moved their own bags to the boat and put the map in the car. But Georgia left the picture of Bestie in the car, resting on top of the cup holder and facing towards the driver's seat. Superstitious or not, she wanted all the luck and help she could get.

Ben helped Georgia back the car up to the trailer so that the towing ball could be secured firmly and the electrics for the indicator lights fed through and connected up. Georgia had never done it herself before, she had just stood and watched as Bill did it, whilst Betsie insisted with a twinkle in her eye, that she loved her husband "to be manly." In retribution Bill had often responded that he liked his "woman to be womanly...so go and get the lunch on!" This had always been followed by much mock horror and booing on the part of the women, before all had climbed into the car to set off for the day. How she wished they were here now.

"Auntie Georgia, look!" Ben's voice brought her back to the present and she followed his gaze. The rain which had been falling heavily when they arrived, now appeared to be more violent in its downpour, bouncing off the ground and no longer seeping into the sodden earth. A nearby drain struggled to cope and even as they watched mesmerised, it abandoned any attempt to drain the surface water away. It seemed to just fill up and instead of draining, allowed the water to pool on its surface.

"Come on, come on, let's go!" she called to the children, ushering them all back into the car and driving out of the garage, with the boat on its trailer being towed behind.

Only the phone lodged in her pocket, its most recent calls unanswered, nagged at the back of her head, as she made the left turn that took them out of Bill's property and set them on the route he had mapped out for her, towards the devastated towns of the Midwest.

Chapter 13

"*A super storm?*" Jack couldn't quite keep the incredulity out of his voice. "And that's what you think this is?"

"Ok, granted, that's not the proper scientific name for it. But it's sure as damn it what it is. Look let me show you round while we talk." He walked around to where a ladder hung from the side of the boat and began to climb. Jack waited till he was safely at the top and then he followed. It was a surprisingly steep climb and Jack was surprised at how quickly Sam had reached the top.

Holding out his hand to him, the older man helped Jack haul himself onto the deck.

"I have lots of questions," Jack informed Sam's back, as the older man now pulled open a hatch and began to descend.

"Yes, I know you do. But time is short, so let's talk and walk."

Jack had no choice really. If he wanted to talk to Sam White, he would just have to follow him around like a puppy.

"Tell me what you know about this Super Storm and how long it has been theorised about and what has been done…" Jack tried to reel off all his questions at once, as he followed Sam through doors into the interior of the boat.

"Look, here are the toilets for this deck…and over there is the kitchen area…" Sam was either ignoring Jack or he was deaf…or he was just totally insane. He pointed the areas out to Jack, who merely glanced in their direction.

"Ok,ok. I get the picture. You won't pay attention till I tell you the full story." Sam sighed.

"Take a seat," he picked a seat at random from the many rows stationed in the middle of the boat and sat himself down, patting the seat next to him in invitation.

"One thing I ask is that you keep the questions to a minimum, or we will be at this all day and as I have already said, time is growing short. Agreed?"

"Agreed," Jack reluctantly stated. The seats were not unlike cinema seats he found, roomy and well sprung.

"Ok, let's see…where do I start?"

"How about the fact that this was supposed to be an anonymous tip-off but you actually know my editor Ed Malone?"

"Hmm yes, sorry about that Jack, but Ed figured it was the best way to get you involved. You see, I need your help."

Sam lifted a hand to stave off Jack's questions.

"I told you I used to be involved in high level research about the changing weather conditions. That was true. And I did have a heart attack, that was also true. But way before that, I had become disillusioned with the way things were going. We knew that one day there would be a storm the likes of which mankind had never seen before - except of course for the storm quoted in the bible and we all know how that went!"

"So you built an ark!" Jack couldn't help himself from interjecting.

"Actually, I built several arks." Sam watched Jack's eyes widen at this revelation and was impressed how Jack managed to still hold his tongue.

"Although this is the only one I have actually built myself, the others I just oversaw. The 'powers-that-be' knew we had to preserve humanity. But that's where the agreement ended. Some thought we should save the 'big thinkers', those people whose IQ sounds like a readout from a barcode, it's so huge," Sam chuckled to himself but it wasn't a happy sound. Instead it seemed derisive, as if he were both angry and disgusted at the suggestion.

"Others thought it should be the big wheels in the government and financiers and such like. But I ask you, do you think that a bunch of high fliers and big brains would have the common sense between them to change a lightbulb if it blew, 'cos I don't. And believe me, I know these sorts of people."

Jack couldn't contain himself any longer. "So where do I fit in? Or Ed Malone?"

"I'm getting to that bit. Then there were the others, the politically correct guys who said that 'The Salvation Project', sorry that's what it was called, should have told you that bit before, anyway these guys though that it should be a lottery and nothing more. Names drawn out of a computer and it didn't matter if you were doing life in the State Pen or an expectant mother - all would be weighted evenly."

Exasperated by the memory, Sam threw his hands up in the air.

"I mean I'm as much a believer in repentance and rehabilitation as the next guy but we were supposed to be saving the human race here, not helping wipe it out. Financiers, Government officials, prisoners...were those the people who would built a foundation for the survival of the human race?"

Jack put two and two together. "So you left and built your own ark, right?"

"Right and wrong. I had a heart attack, and with it came an epiphany. Feelings were bad by then between me and the others in the project, so yes I left and I built my own ark, smaller but just as good. And I set about making a list. This is where you come in."

"I'm listening." Jack found that he had unconsciously shuffled forward in his seat, so that he was now half turned towards the other man.

"I've known Ed Malone for years. He's always been a good friend. So when I went to him to explain my position, he was keen to help." Sam stopped momentarily, took the pipe out of his mouth, fiddled with the end of it for a few seconds but did not replace it between his teeth. Instead he held it by the long stem in his lap, while the fingers of his other hand closed themselves around the bowl of the pipe. If it had been lit, he would have been badly burned.

"I discussed it with my wife and we agreed what to do. The ark has a capacity for just over four hundred and fifty people." His voice was rough and Jack realised that whatever Sam and his wife had decided between them, it had not been an easy choice.

"Do you know how many people live in New York alone?" It was a rhetorical question and Sam didn't wait for an answer. "Too many. Too many to fit on this little boat. Too many to fit *on a hundred* of these boats!" He gestured around him at the space, that empty as it was seemed vast, but clearly not vast enough.

"Wise woman, my wife. She said to take the best. Not the richest and most powerful, or even the best academically, or in their field. But the best *human beings*. Because that's the only way for the human race to survive."

Sam's hands twisted harder around the pipe and Jack watched as his knuckles shone palely through the taut skin.

"It's playing God. That's exactly what it is. And I don't deny it, God help me. But if that's how it has to be, than that's how it has to be."

Jack was still waiting for the bit where he came into the story.

"Sally, that's my wife, had a friend who died recently. A lovely lady whose husband was the chief paediatrician at one of the big hospitals. Betsie made Sally promise on her deathbed, that we would take the children from the wards there. She said it didn't matter how ill they were, that they had never had a shot at life and they shouldn't be denied one now. But we couldn't save the children and not save their immediate family too, so we counted them all in. But only one hospital," Sam hung his head low, "there's just not enough space for more than that."

He lifted his head once more and looked Jack in the eye. "So then we were left with a few places for the right people. People who cared about others, people who would fight for the right thing in this brave new world that would be created in the aftermath of the storm."

"Go on." Jack's stomach was taught with apprehension. He suddenly knew where this was heading.

"People like the award winning journalist who gave up his political career to expose the corruption he had uncovered. An exposé that left him writing sports and nothing more…"

"I had no choice. I couldn't let them carry on doing what they were doing. Couldn't turn a blind eye to the injustice…"

"No. You couldn't. And you didn't. That's why you are top of my list. Along with forty-seven other names that between us, me, Ed and Sally compiled."

Sam attempted a weak smile and pulled a long scrolled piece of paper from his pocket which he proceeded to unfurl. A list of names, contact details and reasons for the selection.

"So perhaps you will excuse the cloak and dagger approach to get you here, the lie that there was an article to write. You see the very reason that you have been selected for this, is the same reason that Ed figured you would refuse it. You are just too moralistic and self-sacrificing."

Jack knew there was an element of truth there, that ordinarily he would never take a place that could have gone to someone else, someone more deserving…but was that still true now, now that he had Dan to look after?

"All the other preselected people will be collected over the course of the next 24 hours. Current predictions are that the storm will not completely overtake New York for at least two days, giving us a little window of opportunity. I would like you..."

He was interrupted by the ringing of Jack's cell phone.

Jack looked at the number displayed and hurriedly accepted the call.

"Kevin?" His voice was tight and he was aware of Sam listening but trying to look as if he wasn't.

"Jack. Thank God I got through to you. The army is moving us south. Or at least, those of us who are left! There are so many dead Jack...I've never seen anything like it...The Cusacks...the nice family across the road...they didn't make it Jack...didn't make it..." Kevin Ryan's usual composure was gone, replaced by a shocked and jitterey shell of the man that Jack knew.

"Hold it together Kev, hold on for Stacey. Where are they taking you and when?"

"We are moving out now. Heading to the Midwest. It's crazy man, that's where the storms started..."

Jack turned to Sam, his face strained and demanding. "Where are you heading in this?"

"The Midwest. Analysis suggests that the area will be devastated but safe from further storms. Then we can rebuild."

Jack looked from Sam to the phone and back again. Was everyone crazy? Rebuild in the Midwest? Rebuild the original area that had been flooded and storm battered? Then again, where else was there to go?

Jack needed Kevin to be more specific. "Where abouts in the Midwest, Kev?"

"I don't know. I have asked but either no-one knows or they are just not saying..."

"If you can, let me know where you are. But wherever the army take you and Stacey, STAY THERE AND I WILL FIND YOU!" He hadn't meant to shout the last bit but that's how it had come out.

The line went suddenly dead and he was left staring at the phone. He dialled Kev's number then Stacey's but neither even rang out, it was as if the phones were totally out of service.

"That was my brother. The army are moving the survivors," the word 'survivors' left a distinctly bad taste in his mouth, "to somewhere in the Midwest. I have to take my nephew there, so they can be together."

"Yes, of course. We will not leave your nephew behind. We can make a little space for him."

"Thank you, but I don't think Dan and I can wait till this thing is ready to go. I think we need to leave now."

"I don't advise that! Please reconsider. It is only a day or so till we can go and you would be so much safer than trying to do it on your own."

"Tell me one thing. Is it possible if I leave right now, that I could get far enough away from here before the storms reach here?"

"Well it's possible…but…"

"Then that's going to have to be enough. Good luck Sam. To you and this ark and all who will be on her. You are a good man and I hope to see you again." He smiled. "In better circumstances." The smile hurt his face a little with all the tension in his facial muscles.

"Maybe we will meet in the Midwest." Jack stood, bringing the conversation to a close. Sadly Sam led the way to the front door. "If you change your mind…" he began.

"Thanks, but I can't. I have to think of Dan," Jack acknowledged the offer. But as he walked through the door back into the deluge beyond, he could feel Sam's eyes burning into his back, wishing he would change his mind.

With a slight nod towards the other man, Jack climbed back into the truck and headed for home, his heart heavy with fear for the future.

Chapter 14

It was a miserable driving experience. Georgia felt as if she had her nose pressed flat against the windscreen and she blinked every time the wipers passed in front of her eyes. She was leaning so far forward in concentration, steering through the deluge and the wipers were moving so rapidly she felt she could be heading for either an epileptic fit or a stroke at any moment. She was grateful for the firm feel of the wheel beneath her palms and the sure way the tyres still gripped the road, even though the water continued to rise.

She had tried the children's parents on her phone before they had set off with the boat in tow but there had been no tone. No ringing, no beeping, nothing. She had turned the phone off and back on again but it had made no difference. She had tried the local deli she used just to check the phone and it had rung out loud and clear. But when she tried her friends again, there was still nothing. Whatever the problem was, it was not her phone. She kept her worries to herself.

Squinting through the rain, she was not inclined to conversation but was aware that the children had fallen unnaturally silent. And then something in her peripheral vision caught her eye. The man stood so still that she had almost passed him by unnoticed. But then he had lifted his placard.

"THE END IS NIGH! REPENT YOU SINNERS!" it proclaimed in large red letters. Unease squirmed in the pit of her stomach. She hoped the children hadn't seen him.

"It's not night, silly man," stated Katie.

"It said nigh, not night Katie," Jim-Bob corrected her and Georgia winced, suspecting what would inevitably follow.

"What does nigh mean then?" Georgia's fears were confirmed.

"I think he means we are all going to Hell," Jim-Bob supplied.

Katie burst into tears. "Are we Ben? Are we all going to Hell? Mommy says that's where the bad men go and I haven't been bad…"

Georgia felt as if someone were slicing little bits of her heart off at a time, just for the fun of it. "Of course not, honey. The man's wrong." She hoped it would be left at that, that the children would focus more on the idea of not going to Hell, than what was implied within it, like that they were all going to die.

"*Are* we going to die?" Ben asked quietly, so that the others could not hear. He had climbed into the front passenger seat so that he could give the others more room in the back and also so he could help navigate if necessary.

"No one is going to die on my shift!" It had been the war cry in paeds and was what she had always told herself as a young resident doctor. Whilst it had till now stood her in good stead, she could only hope that it would still apply in this ever changing scenario.

Ben accepted her response and did not ask for clarification. This worried her even more. For some reason she felt she would have been more comfortable, if he had demanded she back her statement up with a detailed plan. His quiet acceptance was at once a rebuke for thinking herself able to cope with the situation and an indication of how hopeless he himself seemed to view it. Or maybe it indicated an unswerving confidence in abilities even she was not convinced she possessed.

Quite frankly, whichever way she viewed it, the prognosis was not good. Unconsciously she stomped on the accelerator a little more than she had intended. The car veered slightly to the left, the tyres losing their former purchase on the road. A clammy sweat broke out on her brow and down the length of her spine, as she narrowed her concentration to bringing the car back under her control. How easy it was to lose a grip on things.

She chastised herself for the accident that she had very nearly caused. It never entered her mind to congratulate herself in avoiding it.

"WATCH OUT!" The shout came from Ben, who now covered his eyes with his hands. Georgia's head swivelled like it was on a stick, first of all to Ben, who had issued the warning and then back to the road, which seemed to be the cause of his alarm.

There was something on the road ahead. No, not some*thing*, some*one*. And they were right there in the middle of their path, the car bearing down on them as if he or she were suicidal.

Foot slamming onto the brakes, Georgia unconsciously pushed her arm across Ben's torso, holding him in place and preventing him from banging into the dash. Thank God she had made sure their seatbelts were all on.

The forward motion of the car, combined with the wash of water on the road tried to prevent the brakes from doing their job and for a moment the car slid forward towards the stationary figure, before it ground to a halt in a squeal of brakes.

Eyes downcast, averted from the car and its occupants, the woman was more than a little unnerving. Soaked to the skin, her clothes draped wet and bedraggled on her small frame, her hair hanging down either side of her face, hiding her features from view.

Heart still hammering from the car's slew towards the stranger, Georgia didn't at first recognise how bizarre the woman's behaviour was. Right up until, throwing back her head, which made the water spray off it in a dirty arc, the strange woman looked up.

With eyes that had sunken too far back into her skull, she gazed at Georgia dispassionately. Rain dripped from the ends of her hair, which Georgia knew in dry conditions would appear matted and unkempt. Dark hollows in her cheeks were the only colour in her pallid face, apart from the equally dark circles under her eyes. And somehow her nose looked distorted, like she had been in the ring with a heavyweight boxer.

Drug ravaged, the woman was ageless. Old crone or withered teenager, she could feasibly have been either, it was impossible to tell. In a way they amounted to the same thing…this aged being which was nothing more distinguishable than being merely female…was at the end of its life cycle. The drugs, to which the woman was clearly addicted, would make sure of that.

Paralysed by indecision, Georgia didn't know what to do. As a doctor, hell as a human being, she admonished herself internally, surely her duty was to help this stranger. But could she do that with three young children in the car? There was no denying there was something more than sinister about the woman.

Hand on door handle, Georgia still hesitated. The woman had not shifted her gaze and was now saying something. Georgia strained through the noise of the engine and the rain to hear, reluctant to abandon the children for even a moment. But the external noise was too loud. Georgia leaned further forward in her seat, straining to hear the woman's plea for assistance and yet her hand remained firmly on the door handle and she did not release the button, which had locked all the doors from the inside.

Something wasn't right here. Her mind was frantically trying to assimilate what was actually going on with what she *thought* must be happening and the two did not correlate. Belatedly she realised the woman was not really speaking to her. Admittedly the stranger was looking in her direction but it was more like she was *looking through* Georgia rather than at her, like her focus was on some far-away place, causing her pupils to be dilated but her gaze remain unfocused. In addition to that, her mouth was not opening wide enough to convey an audible level of sound. She was mumbling incoherently, by the look of the vague and somewhat undefined shapes her lips tried and failed to make.

Paranoid ravings. That was most likely what was going on. Delusions brought on by drugs and fuelled by a paranoia that meant the woman felt victimised, suspicious and distrustful. The woman was at best, a liability to those around her and at worst, dangerous. Georgia was willing to bet that the latter was more likely.

There was no way she could expose the children to the risk that this stranger would pose them. Nor could she just abandon the woman. Perhaps…

"Auntie Georgia look!" Jim-Bob's voice was full of fear and the hackles rose instinctively on the back of Georgia's neck. She glanced at him, expecting his attention to be riveted to the woman, who still stood ahead of them but instead he was pointing towards the back of the car and the trailer beyond.

Like a rat up a drainpipe, a man clambered up the trailer and onto the bow of the boat, his feet seeming to find ready footholds wherever they landed. Skinny and in wet filthy clothing, he was clearly a paramour and accomplice of the woman.

Georgia felt the hairs on her arms spring up erect in fear and her fight or flight response kick in. Whimpers from the back, reminded her of the presence and vulnerability of the children, should she have needed any reminder, which she most definitely had not.

Feeling her gaze upon him, the man deliberately paused, to flash her what had possibly once been a disarming smile but which now was filled with nothing more, than pure unadulterated malice. Rotten stubs of teeth lined gums which were raw and bleeding and already missing some molars.

And there was something else there, other than malice. There was a leer, a quick lick of scabby lips with a thickly mottled tongue, and a flicker of interest on his face, as she felt his gaze travel the length of her hair, down her neck and towards her breasts.

The feeling of violation that this produced was profound and unconsciously she shied away from his gaze, automatically facing forward again. Back to the druggie who now stood directly in front of the windscreen, having used the momentary distraction provided by the man, to sneak up on the car.

Having clicked back into the present time, for now anyway, the woman's smirk was knowing and evil. The whites of her eyes glowed a dull yellow and a greyish spittle congealed at the corners of her mouth.

Reduced to stark terror, Georgia watched as in seeming slow motion the woman reached her arm around the side of the SUV, trying to reach the handle without moving from where she stood. She seemed to believe that Georgia would not simply run her over in an attempt to escape.

And the stranger was absolutely right.

Georgia cursed herself at her inability to flatten this woman like a bug on the windscreen. But it was not in her personality to be able to harm another person. Until the woman laughed at her, eyes darting slyly between Georgia and the three children in her care.

It wasn't the derision that incensed her. It was the woman's willing abdication of the female role of nurturer and carer. Even more terrified of what this woman might do to the children, than she was at the implied lust of her male counterpart, Georgia acted purely on instinct.

Foot on the accelerator, she shifted gears cleanly. The car sped into reverse, throwing the man off balance and leaving him clinging desperately to the boat's weather shield, which now flapped loosely in places. The woman meanwhile, fingers tightly wrapped around the door handle of the driver's side, had fallen to the ground and been dragged backwards.

Determinedly showing no mercy, Georgia braked fast and watched as the man was catapulted away from the boat, still clinging to a piece of torn off plastic shield. He landed with a sickening thud on the wet asphalt of the road. Georgia didn't even look over to where he now lay. Wasting no time at all, she shifted into first gear and pushed the car's engine as fast as it could accelerate.

At no time did she look down to see if the woman was still attached or not. She was a cockroach, a mere plague on humanity and nothing more. It hurt Georgia to think in this manner but she accepted that sometimes bad things had to be done by good people. Unfortunately she had just had her turn.

Shaking now in delayed response to their peril, she glanced in the mirror at the children in the back and at Ben at her side. "Are you all ok?"

"That was cool Auntie Georgia!" remarked Jim-Bob, seemingly unfazed by their brush with danger.

"I'm ok," stated Ben a little too quietly and Georgia worried that he had realised more of what was going on than the other two, sitting as he had at the front. There were possible problems ahead there, she thought, as he struggled to come to terms with what he had seen. But now was not the time to try to deal with them, she decided wisely.

"Who were those people?" asked Katie in a voice which reflected her confusion over what she had just seen Georgia do.

"Bad people," Georgia looked at the kids in the mirror before she decided to elucidate further, "very bad people who wanted to steal our car and our boat." She didn't add what else she suspected would have happened to them all and especially to her personally.

"Bad people go to Hell, that's what mom says."

Georgia nodded silently in agreement. Trouble was, Georgia was beginning to suspect Hell was already full to overflowing.

The empty highway stretched in front of them.

Chapter 15

Jack drove back to the apartment without conscious thought. Instead, his brain planned what now had to be done and how he would achieve it. The Midwest was a big area and there was not much chance of him and Dan just happening upon the boy's parents. They would need to know more exactly where they were headed. But that had been information that Kevin hadn't known when they had spoken on the phone.

Jack could only hope that he would be able to get through to them later and that they would have more information for him by then. Until then, all he could do was carry on. Get Dan and get the hell away from this area which was about to be the next site of the storm's devastation.

The roads remained mostly deserted, with traffic only very light in both directions. Where were these folk going? Home? Work? Further into an area which would soon prove to be their personal battlefield?

He wished he could stop them. Stop every car that passed him and all those on the road behind him. But what would he say? What could he or they do? Only what he was already doing, gathering up the people important to him and keeping them together.

The idea of writing an article had been Ed Malone's ruse to get him to meet Sam White. But even if he were to write one… and just supposing there was time to print and circulate it, what then?

The reality is that there would be anarchy. In the panic and confusion the roads would become jammed, tempers would be frayed and there would be carnage. Not to mention the fact that all those people would be exposed directly to whatever the weather threw at them. There would be no shelter on the open road. At least this way, people had a chance.

It was a slim point of consolation but he worked it hard. This way, people would stay home, stay indoors and have some measure of protection. But like a dog with a cut, he couldn't leave it alone, worrying at the sore flap of skin he had created.

How would people know how bad it was going to get? How would they know to stay indoors? He reached for his phone.

The call was answered on the second ring.

"Hi Jack." No questions, no explanations. Ed Malone just waited for Jack to have his say.

"Ed, I've met Sam White and I know what's going on. But I've got a couple of questions for you."

"Fire ahead." Calm and patient, Ed was doing his best Wizard-of-Oz impersonation.

"Are you going on the ark?" Funnily enough, it hadn't been the question he had been about to ask, it just popped out. He wondered why he hadn't asked Sam White about that.

"Too old. Sam and I felt there had to be a cut off age. No point in us oldies trying to rebuild the world...and to be perfectly honest I kinda like the present one too much. I'd miss it, warts and all. So I've decided to just take my chances here." So matter of fact, he almost sounded chirpy.

Jack's breath was indrawn sharply. It hadn't been the answer he had been expecting. Flummoxed for a moment, he stuttered out his response.

"I'm not going either..."

"Now hang on a minute there!" Ed cut him off sharply. "You are exactly the sort of man they need on board!"

"Not for that reason, but because I have to leave now, I can't wait till the ark is ready to go."

"Oh, of course. Dan." Ed caught on quick.

"Yeah, my brother Kevin and his wife are ok at the moment. The army are moving them. I'm taking Dan to find them."

"Did Sam tell you where he's headed?"

"The Midwest. That's also where my brother is being relocated to. He's not sure where exactly but somewhere there," Jack realised how ludicrous it sounded, to be just heading anywhere within such a huge geographical area. But that was exactly how it really was.

Ed waited for him to say something more. The silence was deafening and profound. There was so much that Jack wanted to say but for once he was unable to find the words to articulate it.

"You will tell people to stay indoors won't you?" was all he managed.

"Yes. I'm approving the print run as we speak. The White House is no longer in a position to censor us. And even if it was, I wouldn't give a damn anyway. There's not much we can do for most folk, 'cept to tell 'em to stay indoors in as safe a place as they can find. The rest, I'm very much afraid, is up to Mother Nature and their own personal God."

Jack nodded, even though he was aware Ed couldn't see him.

"Take care Ed. It's been an honour and a privilege working with you."

"You too Jack. I am honoured just to have known you. Oh and one last thing Jack," his voice was firm and held Jack's full attention. "That political scandal that you blew out of the water, the one that lost you your career? That was the darndest, bravest thing, I have ever seen any reporter do. Don't you go forgetting about that, when your back is to the wall. Just think on that and know that you will get that boy through. 'Cos you are Jack Ryan, the best that ever was." There was a slight shift in the tone of Ed's voice and Jack knew that he was smiling.

"Now get going before anyone else hears me being soppy and I lose the ferocious reputation I worked so hard to achieve."

Ed laughed genuinely, as if he hadn't a care in the world. Jack hastily pressed the end call button, to cut the call before the laugh ended. That way, he would always remember the last thing he had heard from wise old Ed Malone was a joyous laugh. As good memories go, it was the cream.

Rain threw itself at the car so hard it was a wonder it didn't dent the metal. Pulling up outside his apartment he nearly didn't spare the time to lock the car doors behind him but some small worry nagged at his brain, till wrenching the building door open with one hand, he pointed the remote on the key fob back at the car and watched as the lights flicker in indication of lockdown.

What if he hadn't locked it and it was stolen? It was inconceivable that he could leave them stranded just because he had not bothered to lock the car on his exit.

Climbing the stairs as quickly as he could, he became aware that the light was periodically flickering. Not with any rhythm but rather spontaneously, as if it were seeking a time and tempo but unable to find one. It gave the stairwell a rather spooky, ghostly quality but was more likely the effect of a fluctuation in electrical supply or voltage. Jack didn't know much about either but he did know that it indicated there was an electrical storm on its way.

Jamming his key into the lock so fast and hard, he found that he couldn't extricate it from the now open door. He figured that was of no consequence any more. Once he had Dan and a few belongings, he would leave this place. It was unlikely he would ever return, he realised.

Struggling to remove the jammed key from the lock, the solution became obvious. Twisting the key backwards and forwards, he gave it a sharp and brutal thrust in the wrong direction and snapped it in half, flush with the door and with the broken off piece just jutting out of the lock.

Problem solved. He had opened the door and still had the rest of his keys, including the car ones on the fob in his hand. For a split second he stared dumbly at the remaining keys. There was a history there, which up till now had charted his life.

There was the key to the front door of the old family house, which his parents had given him responsibility for, when he had been just fourteen. There were the keys to this apartment and to his car. There were the keys to his filing cabinet at work. He wouldn't need those again either. And lastly there were the keys to Francine's flat. He had never been asked for them back when they had split up the previous year. Maybe he had believed that if they held on to each other's keys they would somehow drift back into each other's lives. Now she was married to someone else. He would never need those keys again either.

Grasping the keys for the car, he unhooked the others from the fob and left them lying on the floor as they fell and went in search of Dan.

The TV blared out from the living room but there was no other sound. Perhaps Dan was asleep.

On first impression it certainly looked that way. But on closer inspection, there was an unhealthy flush to Dan's face and a stillness to his body that seemed both unnatural and abnormal.

"Dan! Dan!"

There was no response. Jack gently shook the boy but it did not wake him up. Instead his head lolled oddly at a strange angle to his neck and with an unnerving flaccidity.

Images of flood wreckage filled the huge TV screen and Jack's mind whirled. The reporters were talking about the devastation the storms had caused, but to Jack it was all just noise with no discernible words, almost as if the reports were in another language. Unable to immediately locate the TV remote he pounded the power button till the TV became nothing more than a reflective piece of black glass.

Hurrying back to Dan, Jack racked his brains for what little medical knowledge he possessed. Had Dan choked on some small morsel of food? Lifting the boy's head a little off the sofa he cushioned it on his arm, prised open his mouth and peered into the dark recess.

He couldn't see anything there and anyway Dan was definitely breathing. It was shallow and quiet but didn't seem to have been caused by any kind of obstruction.

He placed his index finger in the hollow of where one day when he matured, the boy's Adam's Apple would be. Pressing ever so slightly inwards, afraid of what he was doing but also afraid of what would happen if he didn't do it, he watched as the pressure stimulated an automatic response in the boy to swallow. Jack was fairly certain Dan had nothing lodged anywhere in his throat.

Heat burned through the wet coat he still wore, where Dan's head rested against his arm. Had Dan drank something which had poisoned him? There was nothing in the apartment which could have caused this, no pills or drugs, but there were cleaning fluids of course. Would Dan have accidently drunk toilet cleaner? Jack couldn't see how this could have happened accidentally and he was certain that Dan would not have done it on purpose. And yet...the TV reports, the fear and worry about his parents...had Dan been pushed too far by it all?

Jack scanned the floor around the sofa and the low table which stood in front of it. There was nothing anywhere to indicate that Dan had tried to take his own life.

Mystified and no further forward in trying to identify the immediate cause, Jack considered calling an ambulance. But here was the Catch 22. If he phoned, the paramedics would come, they would save Dan's life and then they would admit him to hospital. And then the worst storm in the history of mankind would arrive in their little corner of the world. The storms that would rip some buildings and its occupants apart.

But if he didn't phone? If he didn't phone and Dan died…then he would have lost the boy he loved like his very own and he would have let his whole family down.

So the solution was to get Dan well, without involving paramedics and hospitals. Simple enough…on paper anyway. It occurred to him to check what other symptoms Dan was displaying. Examining his neck, he could see that the flush spread under the boy's clothes. Lifting his top he scoured Dan's back and stomach but there was no rash, just red hot skin everywhere.

The boy's hair was slick with sweat and the top clung to him in places. Whatever the cause of the fever, the temperature itself was now a danger to Dan. It was imperative that the boy's temperature be lowered as fast as possible, before it resulted in febrile convulsions.

Jack had a faint memory of being very young and of Kevin being ill. Kev had had a spiking fever which had resulted in him writhing about uncontrollably, incoherent and looking for all intents and purposes like an epileptic in the middle of a seizure. Their mother had been in a state of panic as she had tried to bring his temperature down. Jack racked his brains trying to remember what she had done.

Gently placing the boy's head back on the sofa, Jack dashed to the bathroom and placing the plug in the plughole, turned the cold tap on the bathtub on full blast. Leaving that to fill up, he hurried into the kitchen and tore open the freezer door. Grateful for the bag of ice, which sat unopened on the top shelf, he grabbed the bag, not bothering to shut the freezer door and headed back for the bathroom.

The water had already reached the halfway mark, so he turned the faucet off, lest he make it too deep and drown Dan by accident. Ripping open the bag of ice cubes he let these pour into the cold water, leaving the empty bag discarded on the floor.

Then he went to fetch Dan. Leaving the boy's tracksuit bottoms on, he decided to remove only the top part of his clothing. It would give him a wider area of skin to check for changes and also make it easier to check the boy's breathing by the shallow rise and fall of his chest wall.

Grasping the top by its hem, he shrugged/ wrenched it in combination, off of the still comatose boy.

Pulling it away and up from his nephew's body he released one arm first then levered the whole garment over the boy's head. But the other arm proved to be more troublesome, as if the garment was glued to the skin with sweat and grime.

Jack gave a tug and pulled the arm free. But the sight which met his eyes was not a welcome one.

Chapter 16

"Well?" She had come in so silently that he was only now aware of her presence.

"His situation has changed Sally. He had to leave now. Couldn't wait for us to be ready." Sam chewed on the stem of the pipe waiting for the inevitable questions.

"Did you tell him how dangerous it would be?"

"He's an intelligent man, he already knows the risks." He could have added more, that Jack had a mission of his own, but sometimes it paid to answer questions without elaboration, he had found.

"Hmm, I wish I had been here to speak to him now." Shoulder length grey hair feathered around her delicate features, Sally's face belied her inner strength.

"Even you could not have changed his mind my dear."

"Perhaps not, but I hate to think he will be struggling out there, alone, when we could have helped him."

Her sentence spoke volumes to him. Implied within it was the strength and loyalty he loved her so much for.

Not once had she doubted him, his decisions or his abilities.

Yet he instinctively knew the reason why Jack had declined the offer of a place on the ark. For Jack, the risk that something would go wrong, so late in the day, was a risk too great. To put the fate of his nephew in someone else's hands was incomprehensible to a man such as him. Ironically, if she had only known it, it would be this very reason that Sally would not rest, until Sam had tracked him down and convinced him of the error of his ways. If she had known there was the life of a child involved, nothing would have stood in her way.

He looked down into the eyes that even after nearly forty years of marriage, he never tired of gazing into. Arms outstretched around one another, he couldn't honestly have said who was doing the comforting and who was receiving it, where one body ended and another began. He felt deep down, that it was a completely reciprocal thing, that each gave succour and comfort to the other and had it returned tenfold.

"I guess we had better get on with the plan then?" Her raised intonation at the end turned the statement into a question.

"Yes, let's get on with the plan."

"Ok. We had the final consignment of the food and bottled water delivered yesterday…"

"And we already have the diesel on board, as well as blankets and the other necessary equipment," he mentally ticked off.

"We need to fetch the drugs and medical supplies now then."

Fleet of foot, she was already half way to the ground, impatient to take action.

Unmoving for a moment he watched her from the height of the deck where he stood. How small she looked from up here. He wondered, as he had a hundred times, no perhaps more like a thousand times before, how she would cope without him. And in a second of uncharacteristic selfishness he hoped that of the two of them, he would indeed be the first to die. Because without her, he was certain that *he* would not cope.

Shaking his head to rid himself of such draining negativity, he followed her to the truck, making sure to lock the strong warehouse door and padlock it against intruders.

The drive to the hospital was undertaken in an unusually quiet way. He used the cover of concentrating on the wet road, peering through the distorting translucency of the rain, to avoid conversation.

For her part, Sally seemed equally keen on keeping her thoughts to herself. He wondered how much Lucy had played a part in the decision to save the children in the hospital.

Lucy, who hadn't lived to see her third birthday. The pain that came with that thought, was still as sharp and keen, as it had been on the day she had died. Perhaps Sally had been right all those years ago. Perhaps he *should* have attended the support group for bereaved parents.

Sally had certainly found it a help. Run by Betsie Bently, Sally had found an outlet for her grief and made a life-long friend. And in time, she had seemed to come to terms with their loss. She had learned to accept it in a way that he knew he never would. Not that her way was right and his wrong. It was merely a different coping mechanism that each used. But in truth, he wondered as he drove along the rain-smashed highway, how much of the driving force behind him leaving and building his own ark was about his failure to save Lucy? His failure to keep his only child safe from harm.

Except it hadn't really been his failure. Leukaemia was indiscriminate in its choice of victims. He knew that. In his head at least. He just couldn't get that idea through to his heart, that was all.

The hospital car park was overflowing and cars were abandoned on any spare bit of grass or tarmac the desperate drivers could apparently find.

Sam drove past and headed for the loading bay. "Phone Bill now and tell him we are just pulling up," he instructed Sally.

Sally dialled Bill's number and passed on the message.

"He said he will meet us there." She kept her eyes forward as if avoiding his gaze. He wondered whether she was frightened of what he might see in her eyes, frightened that she might reveal how scared she was. Or was it the opposite? Was it that she was reluctant to meet his gaze because of what she might see in *his* eyes?

They hopped out of the truck and entered the hospital. Walking side by side, he was relieved when she sipped her hand into his. Her bones small and delicate, he wrapped his larger fingers around hers and knew that she took comfort in that.

Dr Bill Bently waited for them through the next set of doors.

"I can spare two orderlies who will help you load up the supplies and I have already given them a list of what you will require." He handed them a sheet of paper which listed everything from bandages to saline bags and the quantities required.

"It's fairly extensive...but it won't last forever..." Bill hesitated, "these children ...some of them are terminally ill..."

Sam felt Sally's hand tighten in his. "I know that Bill. But I can't just write them off!"

Without even having to look at her, Sam knew from the sound of her voice, that Sally's eyes would be bright with unshed tears.

"And if they are going to die, then it needs to be when they have their family around them, not alone and desperate, in the middle of a catastrophic storm."

"Just as long as you realise that you can't save them." Bill's voice was beyond wretched and Sam pondered how much of a personal toll, watching children suffer throughout the years, had taken on the other man.

"It's what having Lucy taught me." Sally's voice was quiet, sure.

Sam gulped at the mention of his daughter's name. Such a direct reference to the pain and suffering she had endured and they had had to endure with her.

"Yes, I believe you are right. And Betsie would have supported you in every way too. But there are some things we need to discuss."

Sam and Sally waited for Bill to elaborate. The orderlies brushed past them, boxes piled high on wheeled trolleys, taking the supplies out to their truck and returning with the trolleys empty ready for reloading. They watched this process a couple of times, before Bill led them over to a corner of the room, where they would not be in the way, or easily overheard.

"The children's families are being told to come in to see me early tomorrow and I have arranged for them to be transported to you in ambulances staffed with the doctors who will also be going on the ark." He paused and took a large breath before resuming.

"Georgia Wade will not be coming now however, so I have approached another doctor to take her place. He is not as well qualified or experienced," Bill sighed and Sam knew what overwhelming stress the doctor was under.

"But one of the over-riding factors in choosing a doctor, was that they do not have an extensive family which will need to be incorporated. This fellow is an only child and his parents are both deceased."

"But why the change of plan? Georgia and Bessie were close and I thought she was the natural first choice." Sally was puzzled, she had met Georgia a number of times at Betsie's home and thought her a most delightful young woman.

"As Sam had requested, I kept the ark a secret until it was necessary to tell Georgia," Bill explained.

Sally looked to Sam for an explanation.

"There was just an initial concern, that as an empathetic doctor, Georgia might let slip some of our plans to a parent, before we were ready," he stated.

Sally nodded her head in comprehension, "yes, I can see why that would be a concern. But why is she no longer coming?" she looked back at Bill.

Sam fished his pipe out of his pocket where he had deposited it on entering the hospital. The whole building was of course a no smoking zone, but as the pipe had never ever been lit, Sam figured that wasn't too much of an issue. He wasn't sure where the conversation was headed, or how the plans were about to change but he had a sudden bad feeling in the very pit of his stomach.

"That stuff will kill you." Bill attempted to lighten the atmosphere with the weak joke, knowing that Sam only used the pipe as a prop.

"Why is she no longer coming?" Sally repeated the question with an intensity that showed she was not prepared to be side-tracked. Every comment Betsie had made about Georgia, every time Sally had seen the two women together, had spoken volumes to her. She had seen the gleam of pride in Betsie's eyes when discussing Georgia's accomplishments, seen the motherly love the older woman had lavished on the younger one. And she had witnessed its return too, from Georgia to Betsie.

Indeed, there had been times when that love shone so brightly, that Sally had had to avert her eyes, had had to look away, lest she be reminded of what she had forever lost, when Lucy had been snatched away from her by fate.

"Her priorities changed." Bill stated it flatly, then realised how it must have sounded to the others. "No, that's not really true. The truth is, I changed her priorities for her."

Sam and Sally waited for him to find the words to continue in his own time. In silence, the three of them stood and watched the orderlies continuing to select and move boxes onto the trolleys, readying them for loading into their truck.

"She's looking after her friend's three children, from Seattle. It didn't seem fair to lump even more responsibility onto her. I couldn't ask her to also have the fate of a whole ward of sick children in her hands. I gave her my car and my boat and told her to head for the Midwest."

"But she's like a daughter to you…how will you get by, not knowing how or where she is…" Sally stopped dead, raising both hands in horror to her mouth as a sudden realisation washed over her.

"You are not coming either, are you?" Half whisper, half plea that she be wrong, her tone conveyed her shock and distress.

"No, I'm not, I'm afraid. Can't leave my Betsie here all alone," he smiled forlornly.

"But think of the children, they need you." It was the soundest argument Sam could think of to persuade Bill to reconsider.

"No, Sam, they need doctors, not me in particular!"

"But you are the best!"

"And I am too old! There's an age limit for usefulness remember!" he tried to compel them with logic to see his side.

"We fixed the age limit to consider propagation of the species, not for usefulness, as you well know!" Sam said bluntly.

"Well, see there's the thing. I'm not going to do any propagating, am I? So my place is better taken by someone who can, someone who can help build another generation. That's why I've chosen…"

"If we had thought purely like that, then we ourselves shouldn't be taking up places!" Sam still tried to beat Bill's logic with logic of his own. He and Bill had become more acquaintances, rather than true friends, through the friendship of their wives but there was respect on both sides and an acknowledgement for each other's intellect.

"But you have designed and built the ark and you are essential to its proper functioning. Who else could repair it, or modify it if those were to become necessary? So you see you are vital to the other passengers. I however, am not."

"Please Bill! It's what Betsie would have wanted," Sally beseeched him. Bill smiled sadly, knowing full well she was right.

"Yes, she would have made me go. She would even have given me her place if she could. But that is exactly my point." Bill looked at them both and the well of sorrow and heartfelt loneliness in his eyes was unbearable to behold.

"She is not here to make me leave her. And I cannot leave her. But you two have a task ahead of you. Save those you can ...and those you can't, give them some dignity in their death."

Accepting the finality of Bill's decision Sam placed both hands on the other man's shoulders.

"We will look out for Georgia and help her in every way we can," he promised solemnly.

"I know you will."

The orderlies approached the three people standing silently together.

"Truck's fully loaded," stated the smaller of the two.

"Thank you, that will be all for now," Bill smiled at them. "Now if you will excuse me, I have patients to attend to." Bill turned away from Sam and Sally.

"Bill?" Sally waited till he had turned back to her, expecting a last question or request, before planting a kiss firmly on his closest cheek. "That one was from Betsie," she said quietly.

Bill raised a hand to his cheek where the kiss had been planted, as if to nurture it and prevent it from fading.

There was no more to be said. Sam and Sally watched as Bill slipped unobtrusively out of the remainder of their lives.

Chapter 17

"I'm hungry," Katie complained querulously.

"Let's just go a little further before we stop."

"But Auntie Georgia you've been saying that for ages!"

It was true, she had been saying it for ages. Georgia looked at the clock on the dashboard. She had been driving continuously for hours now. Subconsciously, she was aware that she had been trying to put as much distance as possible between them and the two druggies who had tried to steal the boat. But she couldn't just drive on and on forever.

Her eyes were tired and strained from concentrating, constantly having to look through the wet windscreen and her back and shoulders ached with tension. It was as good a time and place as any to stop.

The road ahead and behind was deserted but she needed to find a safe place to pull over, just in case. Unable to clearly see the road markings due to the volume of water on the tarmac, she pulled right over to the side, before switching off the engine.

At once the thunderous pound of the rain on the SUV seemed more ominous and she reached for the radio knob. But right at the last moment she stopped. Were they likely to hear any good news on the radio? Unlikely. More likely they would hear things which would only frighten the children further.

Making a conscious effort to look bright and positive, she turned to the children. "Shall we find out what lovely food we have with us then?"

"Yes, yes! I want peanut butter sandwiches!" cried Katie.

"I want chocolate spread!" shouted Jim-Bob jubilantly.

Ben said nothing.

"Well I don't know what there is there but I'm sure we will find something delicious." She looked out at the torrential rain. "But you all need to stay here while I get the food, otherwise we will all be soaked."

Three heads nodded vigorously in her direction. Pulling her coat close around her, she opened the car door and swung her legs out. To her amazement, the whole landscape was water. It was like she was in the middle of a lake. Water was already up to the foot board of the SUV, any higher and it would be coming into the interior of the car.

With no choice but to drop into it, Georgia shivered as the cold water swished around her calves. She had been aware that it was no longer just surface water on the road but was surprised nonetheless at how quickly it was building up.

Sloshing around to the trailer whilst keeping her balance, proved to be quite tricky. There wasn't quite a current to the water but it did certainly seem to have a suggestion of ebb and flow to it. Perhaps it was just that it was settling, where it had been previously displaced by their passage through it. She reached the back of the trailer and began to climb up to the boat.

All of a sudden there was a huge lurch and a sliding sensation. Georgia clutched at the weather shield of the boat, memories of the man she had so recently ejected from that very same spot, echoing soundlessly around in her head.

There was a bobbing feeling to the boat now, as if the trailer it was still attached to, no longer had purchase on the road. With a burgeoning horror, she looked back at the SUV where the children still were.

Rain continuing to streak the outside of the windows, she still had no trouble making out their little horrified faces, mouths open in what appeared to her, to be silent screams. And once more the car lurched.

Clinging on desperately, she realised that what had appeared to be like a lake was most likely an actual lake. A terrible and cataclysmic error in her judgement had seen her drive too far off the road and onto the very edge of the water.

Now the car began to fill up on the inside. She could see it sinking deeper into the lake, water swirling around it like a ravenous living thing. Without any conscious thought, she launched herself into the water and swam back towards the car.

Her clothing pulled at her and tried to entangle her in its folds but she would not let herself be so easily defeated. Reaching the car she hauled on the door handle. But it would not open. The pressure of the water against it was too great to enable the door to be released.

Jim-Bob's hysterical face beseeched her to do something, anything to save them and Georgia's heart pounded with fresh adrenaline. The water inside the car was now up to his chin. The situation was desperate.

"Take your seatbelts off!" she shouted at them, trying to also mime the action to drive the point across, whilst still not daring to lose her grip on the door handle.

"Get your seatbelts off!" she screamed into the rain. She tried to look behind and beyond Jim-Bob, to check that Katie had managed this. Younger and smaller than the two boys, she would be the first to drown if still strapped in.

Kneeling on the back seat now, Katie was straining to keep her head above the water and only just managing to do so. The next part was the most terrifying bit and where it could all go horribly wrong but they had no choice in the matter.

"The windows won't open because they are electric! And I can't get the door open till the car is full of water." She knew that once the force of water inside and outside the car equalised, she would be able to open the door and help the children escape. But panicked and petrified, the risk of the children drowning in the meantime, was immense.

"Keep your head as high as you can and take a big breath before the water gets too high." Three pairs of impossibly huge eyes regarded her from inside the car, faces drawn and haggard, reminding her of images of children in war-torn countries.

The SUV sank a little lower in the water.

Sobbing now, she watched the car fill up, till the children were forced to crane their little faces into the very ceiling of the car, still attempting to breath.

"Take a big breath and HOLD IT. I WILL GET YOU OUT. I WILL GET YOU OUT!" repeating it like a mantra. As if some magical quality embedded within the words themselves, would act like a talisman, ensuring their safety, she repeated and repeated herself.

She saw them gulp huge breaths before they became completely submerged and unconsciously drew in a deep breath herself, holding it in sympathy with the children. Forced to wait until the car was completely full of water, before the door would open, she could feel her lungs burning, desperate for the release of the stale air.

Hauling desperately on the handle of the back door, she wrenched it open and dragged Jim-Bob and Katie out. Coughing and gasping they thrashed around in the water, arms and legs kicking, fighting to stay afloat. Georgia turned her attention back to the car. To the front door handle, behind which, Ben was still trapped.

Scrabbling at the handle, fingernails tearing across the paintwork and snagging on the key hole, she pulled hard. Unmindful of the splinter of pain which ripped across her finger as the nail was torn loose, she hauled with all her might on the handle.

And the door opened. Ben, his body slumped across the frame, tumbled into her arms. He had been trapped a little longer than the others had but there was no time to see whether he was unconscious or dead, all she could do was hope and pray that it was the former, rather than the latter.

Swimming towards the boat, half dragging half supporting Ben's limp body behind her, Georgia worried about the other two children.

"Swim over this way," she tried to call but her voice seemed weak and ineffective against the force and noise of the rain. Nevertheless, she was heartened to see that both children were attempting to reach her. But how was she going to get two young children and an unconscious boy into the boat?

Treading water, still holding Ben up, she realised she would have to let him go to climb into the boat. It was not a viable option. Neither was passing him to his younger siblings. There was only one way it could be done.

"Jim-Bob, get on the boat and then help Katie up!" she instructed. She watched the boy struggle to pull himself up, unable to aid him in any way. It took a few minutes before he was safely on board and able to help Katie, who by now was flagging.

It took an age for Jim-Bob and Katie to be both safely on board and Georgia herself began to wonder if she could stay afloat for much longer, with the deadweight of Ben still in her arms, weighing them both down.

"I'm going to pass Ben to you now. Don't try to pull him up, just hold him for me!" She was worried that if they tried to haul him up, the weight would see them toppling back into the water again themselves.

"Do you understand me?" she queried, needing confirmation that they knew what to do. Unable to talk through exhaustion, the children merely nodded silently.

It would have to do.

Using up what she felt was possibly the last reserves of her strength, she pushed herself and Ben half out of the water. Like a whale coming up for air, she thrust Ben at his siblings, noting how they latched themselves onto an arm each before she released him herself and sank below the murky water.

Energy reserves depleted, it would have been easy to just let herself sink away. But she could not do that, not when those children depended on her for their safety.

Forcing limbs that were leaden to work once more, she thrashed her way to the surface and around to where she could most easily climb into the boat. Like a zombie, she shuffled over to where Katie and Jim-Bob still clung to their brother who was suspended by his arms, half in, half out of the water.

A flicker of recognition ran through her mind. Head slumped onto his narrow chest, hair bedraggled and wet, his arms raised in a parody of supplication, Ben more than a little, reminded her of images of Jesus on the cross.

Grateful for her arrival, the other two children did not relinquish their hold on their brother, for which she was grateful, but instead helped her to haul his body onto the boat.

'Let him be alive! Let him be alive!" she thought to herself, banishing the image of crucifixion and all it implied from her conscious thought.

"I never believed in that 'suffer all the little children' stuff and I'm not going to start now," she muttered. She didn't know if she was saying it to convince herself or to defy any deity who might choose to be listening. Either way, right now she would put her faith in science and the tools of her trade any day before religion.

Cold fingers pressed to his throat, she felt for a pulse. Her own heart stilled and quieted till she found a response in him…weak and thready but there, most definitely there.

Deftly she flipped the boy onto the recovery position and helped him expel the filthy water from his lungs. Grey brown sludge poured from the boy's mouth, exploded out on a fit of coughing.

It only struck her now, now that the air was wracked with violent wracking of lungs, how quiet Katie and Jim-Bob had been whilst she had worked on Ben.

For the first time in several minutes, Georgia looked up and around her. There was something not right and her brain struggled to think what it was.

Katie sat on the deck of the boat, exactly where she had been when she had been holding on to Ben. Eyes red and swollen, she was crying. But this wasn't what Georgia fixated onto. The car was gone. Completely submerged, so that not even a hint of the roof was now showing above the water, it was easy to believe it wasn't even there.

Except that it was. And it was attached to the trailer upon which the boat was securely fixed! Her eyes swivelling rapidly back to Katie, Georgia noted with horror how the boat tilted at one end, as the weight of the car began to drag it down in the water.

It was only a matter of time before the boat sank too! She racked her brains to remember how the boat was fixed to the trailer. There were connections to the back and also the front of the trailer which held the boat in place. Without these being undone, the boat was on borrowed time. And so were they!

Pulling Ben into a seated position, she sent Jim-Bob inside the boat in search of towels and blankets. "Katie honey, come sit next to Ben and help each other keep warm for a minute."

It wasn't the real reason she wanted Katie to move from where she now sat but it provided a good excuse. The children were traumatised enough without having to worry whether or not she would drown whilst trying to separate the boat from the trailer.

Silently Katie moved to sit by Ben and Jim-Bob reappeared with a pile of dry bed linen.

"I need to get back in the water to undo some straps. Don't worry. It will take a little time but it will be fine. But I am going to need you to get inside the boat and find the box with the perishable food in it. Open it up and see what we have." She tried to keep her voice light as if what had just happened was an everyday occurrence. She wrapped the dry bedding around Katie and Ben.

Jim-Bob regarded her blankly but did as she had bid, carefully refastening the plastic weather shield back around the door frame behind him.

Taking a deep breath, Georgia slid off the side of the deck and back into the cold water. Limbs shivering uncontrollably, and rain continuing to pelt down on her head, she held the breath and dived.

Forced to open her eyes underwater, to locate the locking mechanisms, she tried to focus on how much depended on her success rather than the pain of stinging eyes and bursting lungs.

The straps at the back of the trailer were easy to undo but the locks at the front were more tricky, requiring her to surface several times for fresh air before re-diving to have another attempt.

For a while she began to think it was impossible, that something had caused the metal clasp on the safety chain to warp, so that it could not be unhooked. Fingers cold and raw with continued force being applied through them, she was required to think what would happen if she did not succeed.

Adrenaline flooded her veins and her heart accelerated so much she feared it would burst through her chest wall. But the adrenaline did its job. Hands working independently of her mind now, they twisted and worried at the clasp, pulling, teasing and manipulating it in every direction, shredding and lacerating the skin with abandon. Suddenly, just at the point where her lungs expelled the very last of her breath, the clasp gave way and the car and trailer continued on to their watery grave, leaving the boat buoyant behind them.

Like mementos in a coffin, the ruined photo of Betsie and now useless cell phone sank with the vehicle.

Lungs empty and devoid of both air and energy, Georgia was entirely spent. A blackness descended over her mind and her body became limp and lifeless. Slowly, her body floated to the surface.

Chapter 18

Jack stared in disbelief at Dan's arm. Swollen beyond its normal size, it was an angry shade of red and suppurating from a point just below the shoulder. Thick yellowy-green pus leaked from a blister about the size of a nickel and there was some dark red encrustation surrounding it, suggestive of dried blood.

The whole arm was discoloured and hot to the touch. What could have caused this? Jack racked his brains. He didn't possess much medical knowledge but he had heard of certain bugs and spiders which could cause such a reaction with their bites or stings. But those tended to be tropical creatures and not likely anything Dan would have come into contact with.

Something snaked through his brain, wriggling like an eel out of water. He tried to grab hold of it and shake it out for closer inspection. Something Dan had said. Something about his arm on the plane. What had it been?

The vaccine! He had been given the vaccine on the plane! And he had said his arm had been hurting since then. It was clearly a reaction to the vaccine he had had. Was this normal? Jack didn't know. He personally had refused the vaccine, so had no personal knowledge to fall back on.

Common sense spoke up. Surely if this was a normal reaction, it would have been common knowledge by now. There would have been some coverage of it on the TV surely and they would have covered it in the newspaper. Ok, so it probably wasn't a normal reaction then. So it was abnormal. But that didn't mean much either to him. Perhaps it was like when babies had the MMR vaccine, the one that covered them from measles, mumps and rubella? Some of them developed high fevers because their immune system was reacting to the vaccine, whilst others were completely unaffected.

But this did look a bit more serious, he had to admit.

Did he have the *right* to make the decision not to call an ambulance to take Dan directly to the hospital? Then again, did he have the right to commit Dan to staying in an area that would soon be wracked with catastrophic storms? Undecided as to the right thing to do, he hesitated.

Dan moaned, a thin stream of bile leaking from the corner of his mouth and pooling on the sofa. The sound was like a slap in the face to Jack and catapulted him into action.

Gently pulling off the remainder of the boy's top, he scooped him up in his arms and carried him into the bathroom. Poised above the bathtub he hesitated once more. What if plunging the boy into the freezing water did not have the desired effect of waking him and reducing his temperature? What if this action was too extreme and actually stopped his heart?

He couldn't be sure either way. But one thing was certain. Every second Jack hesitated, was another second closer to Dan's brains being fried by the temperature of his body. And then in an eye-blink Jack's whole life changed.

Dan began to violently buck in his arms, limbs jerking haphazardly, like those of a puppet on a string. Face contorted as if in pain, Dan ejected the partially digested pizza and other contents of his stomach all over himself.

The stench foul in his nostrils, Jack's own stomach recoiled but he held fast on to the boy. Nostrils flaring and brow wrinkled up as if in response to extreme pain, Dan was almost unrecognisable.

Jack knew that the moment of decision was upon him. What he chose to do now would set the course of his life forevermore.

He plunged Dan into the icy bathtub.

A scream, the likes of which he had never heard before, assailed his eardrums. Dan writhed and screeched and fought against his imprisonment in the tub like a wild animal. Eyes open but somehow appearing lost in some mist, as if Dan *saw* but could not comprehend what he was seeing, there was no recognition there at all.

Childish fingers tore at his hands and arms but he ignored them and kept his hands wrapped firmly round the torso of the boy, holding his body in the cold water. Just above the waterline, Dan's head thrashed from side to side and backwards and forwards. Jack wished he had had the foresight to wrap something around it, it cushion it from the hard metal of the tub.

A towel hung on the rail nearby. But if he were to reach for it, he would lose his grip on the boy, who would either drown or somehow launch himself out of the tub. He didn't dare reach for it.

Short fingernails embedding themselves in the fleshy part of his forearm, Jack gritted his teeth against the pain, and told himself Dan wasn't aware of what he was doing.

When the foul mouthed swearing began, it was almost a relief, providing a distraction as it did. Jack marvelled at the variety and ingeniousness of some of the profanity that Dan spouted. Always a polite and well-mannered boy, had he been the least aware of what he was doing, Dan would have been mortified. But this was the sickness talking. Feverish and delusional, Jack would no more hold this against Dan than he would an attack by a rabid dog.

Giving one final buck seemed to be too much for Dan, and once more his body became limp and listless. His eyes rolled up so that only the whites were visible and his face became slack and calm as he faded back into unconsciousness.

Supporting his body in the tub now as opposed to restraining it, Jack noticed how as the ice had melted and the water heated up, it had taken the heat out of the boy's skin. The infected arm was still swollen and discoloured but the rest of the boy's body now has the subtlest hint of mottled blue as it cooled and goosebumps were starting to break out on both his chest and other arm.

Sure that his temperature was for now under control, Jack lifted Dan from the tub and wrapped him in a large bath towel. Carrying him back into the living room, he placed him on the floor. He didn't want to risk putting him on the bed or the sofa where he might roll off and hurt himself.

Returning to the bathroom once more, he scanned the medicine cabinet for appropriate medication. Paracetamol, Ibuprofen and antibiotics were what he was searching for. He found them all but unfortunately not in liquid, powder or capsule form.

'Beggars can't be choosers!' he reminded himself tersely, taking the bottles into the kitchen area. He read the instructions regarding dosage and then set about reducing the correct amount of tablets to a fine powder, using the back of a small spoon to crush them. Scooping this powder into a cup, he then made it into what he hoped was a palatable paste by adding milk, sugar and cocoa powder.

Greyish-brown it looked revolting but he hoped it would do the trick of keeping the boys temperature down and fight whatever infection there was.

Then all he had to do was get Dan to swallow it. He raised Dan's head and held the cup to his lips but the unresponsive boy did nothing. Jack was sure that if he attempted to pour the liquid down him, it would either choke him or just be spilled and wasted, so instead he spooned the mixture gently into the boy's mouth, waiting till each one had trickled down his throat before lifting the next spoonful up.

It was a painstaking process and cost time, which Jack would have preferred to have used, to get them as far away from New York as possible. Once the cup was empty, he straightened Dan out on the floor once more and hurriedly began to pack.

T-shirts- tracksuits bottoms and underwear as well as some warmer clothes were all thrown into a bag. He tried to pick clothes which they could both wear, albeit with a little rolling up on Dan's part. He would have no further use for suits and smart trousers …or at least no use in the foreseeable future.

Clothes, shoes and toiletries sorted, he emptied the entire contents of the medicine cabinet into the bag. In truth it didn't amount to much – a couple of packs of indigestion tablets, some calamine lotion left over from some exotic holiday he had spent with some equally exotic ex-girlfriend, some Band-Aids, throat lozenges and a bottle of cough medicine.

From the bedrooms he packed the pillows, duvets and a few framed photos of his family. Next he raided the linen cupboard, selecting towels and sheets for them both.

After that, all that was left to pack were the medicine bottles he had taken into the kitchen and the contents of the fridge, together with whatever else he could scavenge from the kitchen cupboards and freezer.

Placing the bags together in a pile, it didn't really look like much. Not for a lifetime of living anyway, he thought. It certainly wasn't much to have accrued in the life he had lived up till now…and it wasn't much to take forward into whatever sort of life he was likely to have in the future either.

He figured there was some sort of philosophical teaching in there, but for the life of him he didn't know what it was, nor was he particularly inspired to care at that precise moment.

He had to get the bags and the boy into the car. He was loath to leave Dan for any length of time at all, but there was really no option, as he couldn't carry the boy and the bags simultaneously.

Unless he took the elevator of course. Moving towards the prone boy, he stopped only when the lights flickered not once, but twice in quick succession.

It would be just his luck if the power failed or shorted whilst they were in the lift. Was it worth the risk? No, he would take the stairs, taking the bags first, then returning for Dan as soon as possible, once the bags were safely stowed.

Grabbing the bags, he left the apartment and headed for the stairs. Going as fast as he possibly could, he was dismayed to be held up by trying to negotiate himself past the wide girth of Esme McGruder, inhabitant of the apartment directly opposite his.

"Goodness me Mr Ryan!" exclaimed Mrs McGruder, who was a stickler for formal speaking, "Anyone would think you were doing a moonlight flit!" She nodded her head towards the array of bags he was holding, but did not alter her wide-hipped stance, to help him get past her in any way.

Aware that time was of the essence, Jack could afford no delays. But intuitively he was also aware, that the making of polite conversation would delay him less here, than any brusqueness, which would merely result in this large woman planting her not inconsiderable bulk, directly in his path.

"Yes, it does look like that, doesn't it?" he agreed, striving to keep his face open and friendly. Esme McGruder's eyes narrowed. She had smelled a rat he feared.

"You seem to have everything but the kitchen sink with you there." She appeared to be waiting for some sort of explanation. Irritated now by the woman's perseverance and forwardness, Jack strove to stay calm and give an appearance of being relaxed.

"Well you know how it is. Sorry Mrs McGruder, I must dash!" and he half shoved, half squeezed past her. Up too close for personal comfort he was aware of the smell of her fetid breath and of how her fat seemed to squish into him as he squeezed past.

Not in the least offended, she wheezed, "yes of course. Hope you have an umbrella!" at his retreating back and continued on her way up the stairs. Once at the truck, he slung the bags onto the front passenger seat and used the pillows and sheets to line the footwells of the back seat. He would place Dan on the back seat where he could be kept from harm and supported by the soft materials.

Back inside the building he was more than a little disappointed to find his neighbour still huffing and puffing her way up the stairs, forcing him to squeeze past her once more. However, by the time he had reached his door, she was only just behind him, having somehow made better progress than he would have expected. By the time he had collected Dan, he was sure that she would be safely ensconced in her own apartment.

Unfortunately that idea proved to be wrong. Emerging from the apartment for the final time with the boy in his arms, he was disheartened to find Esme once more blocking the stairwell.

Bent over at the waist, she now completely blocked the stairs, forcing him to wait while she straightened herself up. Sensing his presence she spoke whilst still facing the ground. "Sorry Mr Ryan but I appear to have dropped my keys. I won't be a second."

Dan weighing heavily in his arms, Jack stood still and waited, his impatience creeping up through his body like ivy round a sapling, twining itself round and round, strangling the life out of the tree.

"Here we are," she said simultaneously straightening up. "Oh, my…what is going on?" Fat fingers clenching at equally fat florid cheeks, she once more dropped the keys she had just picked up.

"Excuse me Mrs McGruder!" Brusqueness just the right side of rudeness was as much as Jack could muster under the circumstances and he attempted to brush past the woman.

"Now you wait just a moment! Who is this child? And what are you doing with him?" Surprisingly deft on her feet in a way that Jack would never have thought possible, the woman moved to stand directly in front of him, blocking the stairs and the exit they promised.

Eyes now narrowed to suspicious slits, it was clear that his neighbour had put two and two together and come up with two hundred and two. There would be no getting passed her without her co-operation. Or without killing her. Right now, the way Jack was feeling, he would happily have taken the second option.

"He's sick. And he's my nephew. Remember I mentioned him the other day? And you asked to see a photo?" Enlightenment dawned in the woman's eyes. It would appear that she had remembered after all. Jack mentally thanked himself for humouring her request that day, it had been a blessing in disguise.

"Oh so I did! Poor chap, what's wrong with him?" Now just plain concerned and curious, she still hadn't moved out of the way.

'MOVE DAMN YOU WOMAN, MOVE!' Jack screamed internally but he worked at keeping the thought from his eyes and face, lest she become suspicious again and continued to bar his way.

"That's what I'm trying to find out. I'm taking him to the hospital and going to camp out in the car there, till he's better," he tried a forlorn and appeasing smile. It did the trick.

"Of course, of course. Let me get out of your way, and please make sure to tell me when he recovers. I'll be praying for you." And she moved, finally.

Grateful for the release, Jack bounded down the stairs and past her. But his conscience would not let him go that easily. Not bothered about the lies he had told her, for he had had good cause to do so, he was however, bothered that he had not given her warning of what was to come. As his neighbour and self-styled protector of children, didn't he at least owe her that?

He paused, one foot on a stair and the other foot a stair below, Dan's weight balanced equally in his arms and looked directly at this old woman, who had probably never done anyone any harm and thought how she might end her days alone and in terror.

"Mrs McGruder, there is a storm coming here. As big as the one which took out the Midwest and then the West Coast. Maybe even bigger, who knows."

He watched the look on her face change to one of abject horror. "If you can, get out of New York. If you can't or won't do that…find the people you love and be with them…" He turned on his heel and left.

She never spoke a word but he heard he fold her corpulent body to the floor and begin a soft barely audible keening. Gulping back his own emotions, he left the building and gently placed Dan on the back seat of the truck, ensuring that the boy was cushioned as much as possible.

He climbed into the driver's seat, his own words echoing in his ears. 'Find the people you love and be with them.' It was exactly what he planned to do.

Chapter 19

Neil Harris fidgeted with the pen in the top pocket of his pristine white coat. He wore the doctor's coat with pride but a definite lack of finesse. Shrugged onto his lanky frame it made him look no more worthy of awe and respect than the average dentist.

Years and years of school, college and finally medical school, had filled his brain with the wisdom and academic prowess his job required without ever boosting his self-esteem higher than that of the average bar-fly. He twiddled the pen a little faster, a little harder.

"You may wonder why I have called you all here." Dr Bently addressed the assembled crowd in front of him. The hospital lecture theatre was bursting at the seams with parents and brothers and sisters of the sick children in the hospital's paediatric wards. Unaccustomed to being on the small stage as opposed to sitting comfortably in the audience, Neil was finding it difficult to raise his eyes to the gaze of the overflowing audience. He glanced over to the other young doctor who flanked Dr Bently.

Dr John Stark was having no such trouble.

Full of confidence, he beamed his cosmetically enhanced smile out at the nearest of the audience. The man radiated self-assurance from every pore of his body. But Neil had always found something false in it. A bit like watching an actor play a part very convincingly, whilst still holding in your head the very realisation that it was a role being merely played out.

"There is a storm coming. A catastrophic storm which will devastate the area." Bill Bently's voice rung out with a crystal clarity even over the sudden gasp of indrawn breath from a multitude of bodies.

As if his neck was on a jerked chain, Neil's head snapped around to face the older doctor. In his peripheral vision he saw the fixed smile on John Stark's face falter for a moment, lips turning down at the corners as if the man were suffering a stroke. A little corner of Neil rejoiced at something wiping off that smirk before his consciousness reasserted itself and he realised he had bigger things to think about.

From sudden deathly silence to a barrage of noise, the assembled crowd erupted into near hysteria. Bill Bently merely stood still and waited for the inevitable to happen, for the people to finish their verbal rant and turn their attention once more to him.

Back ramrod straight, Bill waited it out whilst Neil worried at his pen, fingers pressing too hard at the nib, so that it broke off from the main stem. A dark blue ink pierced the fabric of the coat, the stain widening so that it looked like the bloom of blood, only darker. Mesmerised, Neil watched the stain spread across the left hand size of his chest, directly above where his heart rested.

'It's like someone shot me and I'm an alien, bleeding blue blood!' He was aware that it was a rather surreal thought but then again it was turning into a rather surreal day, after all.

"You must all be aware of the increasing severity of the weather and of the storms in other parts of our country and indeed across the world," Bill continued into the growing silence. But at the comment regarding the world, Neil noticed that there was a spike of dissention once again. Perhaps these people hadn't known that there had been storms in other places. Admittedly it had not been widely reported and even Neil himself had only heard very vague comments about it. In addition to that, these people's attention had clearly been focused elsewhere, on their very sick children.

"There is nothing that can be done to stop the storm or to protect your children from it…" Bill paused for breath. In the small silence which followed, the only sound which could be head was a quiet weeping. United in their shared horror and grief, mothers and fathers alike had unified into something resembling a single voice. A solitary note of desolation.

Even though a part of Neil's mind was shocked at what Bill was saying, it was also scrolling through a list of possible solutions for him personally, ways he could save himself. Now perhaps he was wrong, he debated with himself, but he was fairly certain that there were no such thoughts going on in these other people's heads. There was something almost bovine about them, he thought. Just like a herd of cattle, these people stood and awaited their fate, accepted that it rested solely in the hands of others and not their own.

"That is why I have called you all here and why I have arranged for you to be taken to safety with your children." In his desperation to give them hope, Bill had rushed his words. He listened to the echo carry itself across the room, resonating off each wall, before dying away to eventual silence.

The quiet was unnatural. A calmness born of despair and resignation filled the air. Bill knew they had not understood his last statement. He drew a breath and began again this time spacing the words more evenly so that they could be understood.

"That is why...I have called you here..." he made sure the echo of the last phrase died away before he began the next bit. It was harder than he would have imagined to do this, to relinquish control over the fate of the patients in his care. Even though it was in the best interests of his patients to do so, it was so diametrically opposed to his beliefs, it caused a very real pain in his heart.

"I have arranged for you...to be taken to safety...with your children." He stopped, expecting a volley of questions and demands for explanations but there were none forthcoming. A deathly hush had descended. Grey faces stared back at him, the many races and ethnicities which made up this audience blended into one shade, as shock took over their countenances. Shoulders sagging from the constant distress of seeing their children suffering, this information was nothing more than another nail in their coffins. He was reminded of photos he had seen of holocaust victims.

He turned to the young doctors at his side. "Doctors Harris and Stark will accompany you and provide medical assistance." He took in the blank stare of Neil

Harris in his ruined white coat and the ashen face of John Stark. He had never really taken to either man but they had proven themselves to have the makings of skilled doctors in the little time that he had known them. More importantly, both were from out of state, with no immediate family around them, to whom they might be inexorably tied. Neither had been his immediate choice but rather they had been his *only* choice, now that Georgia Wade was off the list.

Neil felt the weight of Bill's stare as the implications of what had been said began to sink in. He was to be saved! Administering to these families was to be his ticket to survival! It was certainly the strangest thought he had ever had. An unbidden image came to mind. His father standing in front of the huge stone fireplace which dominated the formal living room, one leg bent, foot resting on the marble hearth as he gave his solemn speech once more, the one about how it was fitting that Neil became a great doctor and did the family proud.

'Well I'll be darned!' he thought, aware that the use of the vernacular words and tone would have deeply offended his father to the core. He withdrew the ink stained hand from his pocket and ran it through his thinning hair, unaware that it left a thick blue streak on the tips of the follicles it passed over. 'I'll be darned!' he thought once more.

Satisfied that neither doctor had protested at this assertion, Bill turned back to the assembled crowd who seemed to be waiting for his explanation with no real expectations of salvation at the end of it.

"I have here a list of names and order of transportation. With the doctors' help, we will have you on your way as soon as possible." He passed a piece of paper to each of the doctors who took it without saying a word.

"One thing. For your safety and that of your children, it is imperative that you tell no one else what is happing." He watched their faces as this plea sunk in, watched them register what he meant and what he was asking of them.

"I know that you will all have loved ones elsewhere, who you would wish to say goodbye to. I cannot ask that you do not do this. All I ask is that you delay it until the last possible moment, until you are safely on your way." From the look of incomprehension on so many faces, he knew he had to explain.

"If you say goodbye too soon, if you give warning of what will come to pass, you will set up a chain of events which will make it impossible to save your children. People will panic, roads will become gridlocked and more people will die than might otherwise have happened. INCLUDING YOUR CHILDREN." He thundered the last bit out, needing to make dramatic impact.

In a way, it was immaterial to these families that their sick children currently residing in the hospital wards, were in some cases terminal, that the children already had a death sentences bestowed upon their heads. What mattered, was that they would not have to lose their child *this day*. For them, tomorrow, and their child's survival into that bright new day, was all that mattered. And Bill understood that sentiment. It was after all, exactly how he would have felt if Betsie had still been around.

"So unless there are any urgent questions," he paused just in case but there was only silence, "let's get started. Wait for your name to be called, then you will be taken to your child, who is already waiting for you in an ambulance and you will be taken to a secret location…"

"But what about Tia?" It was a child's voice, unsteady and unsure but spoken loud enough to be heard over Bill.

Bill scanned the crowd. A small boy, no older than six or seven clung to his mother's hand, face streaked by tears and nose running profusely. Bill tried to smile reassuringly. "I have made sure that all your immediate family is here so I'm sure your sister is somewhere in the crowd…" he scanned the rest of the audience, looking for a girl who stood with people not of her family. He didn't know why this girl Tia would not have stayed beside her family but it was not really his concern. He was eager to get started and this was just a delay.

"Tia's not my sister. She's my dog."

Bill shook his head. It made sense now.

"Well I'm sure she will be fine. Dogs are," he struggled to find the right words of reassurance here. "…very adaptable," he finished.

"I'm not going if Tia's not going!" The boy sat down, arms crossed and body huddled into itself.

"Now look here," Bill began before pulling himself up sharply. Who was he to be telling this child whether or not he should go? Who was he to be deciding others' fates? To be determining who should be saved and who should not? Deciding *what* should be saved?

He had never questioned his belief that a human life was more important than an animal's. That *humans* were more important than animals. But just because it was *his* belief, did not make it a universal truth. For this child, perhaps his dog was every bit as important as his family.

Perhaps it was his dog which gave him the courage and strength to face each new day.

"Ok, let's assess the situation. Please put your hand up if you have a dog at home you need to fetch." A show of hands came in at around twelve families.

"And now those of you with cats please." This time the count was nearer to twenty.

"Ok that's not too bad then!" Relief etched out a new tone of voice for him. There was a way around this problem if he did a bit of jiggling, he was sure.

"We haven't got a cat or a dog. Mommy says we haven't got enough time to give them. But we have got Hammy the hamster…" the little girl in the pink pigtails trailed off but already Bill knew where this was going.

"Show of hands please for other pets, hamsters, gerbils and so on." Thank God this was New York, there were unlikely to be any horses or potbellied pigs amongst the pets. Two hands were raised.

"Ok so we are going to have to make a little amendment to the plans then. If you have a pet to fetch, allocate one person now to fetch it." There was a flurry of organisation going on amongst those relevant families.

"Fetch the pet and some food for it and get back here as quickly as possible. Come to the ambulance bay at the front of A and E and we will get you to rejoin your families if they have not already left." Bill's mind whirred through what needed to be done and how to make it happen.

"If they have already left, you will join the family in the next ambulance going out. We will make this work. We have to make this work! Now go!"

He watched silently as husbands turned to wives and kissed them like it was for the last time, before kissing each of the children and departing. In every case, the husband had nominated himself to fetch the pet, leaving the wife to care for the children, he noted. Funny how in times of stress, the human race sometimes became the most noble they could be, rising above petty mindedness and ideas of equal rights and sexism. Sometimes people just did what had to be done.

Bill turned to the junior doctors beside him who had so far been silent. "Do you understand what is being asked of you?"

"Yes, I do and I accept the challenge!" John Stark's usual confidence had been returned and Neil was sure his chest jutted out even further than it had previously.

"Yes." Spoken quietly but with a firmness which he told himself showed he was also fully up to the challenge, Neil tried and failed to look Bill in the eye.

"It is a lot to ask, to have the welfare of so many people in your hands. And there are others too." He watched as both men were noticeably surprised at this comment. Taking this opportunity he tried to explain the situation as succinctly as possible.

"There is a boat. Styled like an ark, it has been specifically designed and created to save mankind from extinction. It can take approximately four hundred and fifty passengers." He was aware of how short and undetailed his sentences were but he was eager to get going. Words were only words after all, and they would all see the reality of the ark for themselves very shortly.

"That number has been made up by the children in the paeds wards at this hospital, their immediate families assembled here, you two doctors, some selected paramedics, the ones doing the ferrying back and forth obviously and some other members of the public, chosen by the ark's creator and engineer."

Bill indicated the lists they held. "Family by family we need to get the people on this list to the ambulances provided. Medical supplies, food water and all necessary equipment are already on the ark and it will leave within twenty-four hours of now. I am not at liberty to give a destination or furnish you with more detail than that. We need to get started now."

Stark was nodding his head vigorously as Bill talked, as if he was already aware of all this, and Bill had a sudden urge to knock it off his shoulders. The guy was just so smug. Perhaps he had been the wrong choice after all.

Then again, there hadn't exactly been a huge shortlist, as most of the other doctors had extensive families. Nonetheless, perhaps it had been a mistake to overlook those doctors. But it had been what he and Sam had initially agreed, that they should chose doctors without families of their own, so that these very sick children were their priorities. Doctors they may well be, but it was human nature to put the welfare of those you loved first, and everyone else second.

Of course if he hadn't chosen to stick to that agreement, then he would never have sent Georgia off in the first place. The truth was, it was a dilemma for which there was no comfortable solution. And now they would all have to live, as best they could, with that decision.

Chapter 20

It was cold. She was cold. And numb. And wet.

These realisations came one at a time, uninvited and unwelcome, like strangers at a party. Opening her eyes didn't help that much either.

There was no comfortable bed, no bedroom, no walls, neither familiar or unfamiliar. Instead there was water.

Held in an upright position by the lifebelt positioned around her upper body, all Georgia could see was water all around. But there was a rope tied to the belt which was pulled taut. Surely it had to be tethered to something on the other end?

Limbs stiff and unwilling to do what was requested of them, she worked her body round to face the opposite direction.

The boat!

Like a veil being lifted from her eyes, she suddenly remembered everything. The car sinking in the water, with the children trapped inside. Getting the children to safety...had she done that bit? Fear seized her heartbeat from her. She couldn't remember! One of the boys had been drowning, she remembered that...but had she got to him in time?

The absence of her own heartbeat, somehow made it strangely harder to hear anything else. It was so quiet. So *deathly* quiet. There was no sound coming from the boat at all.

Heartbeat returning with a painful rush, she grappled with the lifebelt, trying to disentangle herself from it. Thrusting it aside, she dragged her heavy limbs to the side of the boat and pulled herself up.

The weather shield seemed to be trying to resist her and her fingers slid over its smooth surface, failing to find any strap or anchor to hold on to. Slipping down into the water once more, her index finger caught in a tiny hole in the shield. It was enough. It *had* to be enough. Pushing her finger through, she grabbed on to the shield and used it to lever herself up. Mindless of how and where it ripped, she pushed herself up and onto the boat.

Shoulders stooped and back hunched, she didn't have the courage to look inside the boat for a moment. She gazed at the shiny wood of the deck, reluctant and fearful to look up. What if? Whatever she saw or didn't see now, she knew she would have to live with for the rest of her life. Deliberately she straightened her shoulders and looked up. There, just inside the boat and clearly visible from where she stood, were three children, curled up on the benches, fast asleep and safe.

Georgia's knees buckled with relief. Choosing to sit down before she fell down, she took a look at their surroundings. They had been driving on a road when they had decided to pull over for something to eat, that was the last calm memory she had. Everything after that, was like one long stream of continuous horror, where one fear and fright, turned and morphed into some other terrifying and perilous situation, going on and on, escalating till it reached a crescendo.

They had slid off the side of the road into a flooded lake and presumably that's where they had stayed. She tried to think logically. How far had they travelled from New York? How long had they been in the car? Hours. She had been driving for literally hours and hours. The children had been hungry and she had been stiff and tired but she had been determined to put as much time and distance between them and their attackers, as she possible could. The people who had attacked them, the drugged up couple she had mistakenly tried to help, were far, far behind them.

They had to be out of New York State by now. That much was surely certain, even if their actual location was still a mystery. And at least it had stopped raining. For now anyway. Either that or they had driven out of the storm area. She cast a glance at the sky. Grey and heavy with rain clouds, it was a looming threat and one which was unlikely to just go away.

A small shuffling noise from within the plastic shield alerted her to the fact that the children were awake.

"Auntie Georgia!" A chorus of voices rang out and three bodies launched themselves into her arms.

"We thought you were dead!" Katie's face seemed even smaller and younger than before.

"I told you she would be fine," Ben reassured her. Uncaring as to whether he considered himself too old for those sorts of things, Georgia pulled him closer into a hug. Tears welling up in her eyes, she fought them back. The children had been through too much in the last few days to dwell on it all. What was needed was a bit of levity right now, she decided. Grappling round the trio like an octopus she tickled them all mercilessly, till they were begging her to stop.

"Do you want to know what happened?" asked Katie breathlessly, sitting cross-legged on the deck next to Georgia.

Georgia hesitated but something about the shine in Katie's eyes told her the girl wanted to tell.

"Go on then, tell me what I missed," she poked Jim-Bob in the ribs and ticked, before he managed to wriggle away.

"Well, you were floating in the water. I saw you and I thought you were dead but Ben and Jim-Bob jumped in to save you." The note of pride in her voice at the bravery of her brothers, tugged at Georgia's heart.

"They couldn't get you out of the water though, so they put the beltlife…"

"*Life*belt," Jim-Bob corrected automatically.

Katie rolled her eyes at the interruption. "*Lifebelt* around you, then we tied it to the boat really goodly."

"You can't say 'goodly', its bad grammar. You have to say 'really well'." Jim-Bob instructed her.

"If it's the end of the world, then I can say whatever I like!"

Georgia was disappointed to realise that the children had remembered the man who had stood with his placard at the roadside the previous day. But she had to admit that Katie had a point.

"Well what a brave bunch of children! I am so lucky." She had been about to say that their parents would be proud but had thankfully managed to stop herself in time. She offered them as genuine a smile as she could muster.

They were all alive. They had a boat, food and fuel. Those were the obvious positives. It was the negative aspects of the situation which were causing her so much trouble. They had no idea where they were or which way they should be heading. The map had been in the car and was now gone, along with her cell phone and any other means of navigation.

Except that wasn't there a compass in the cabin? She was sure there was! Getting to her feet, she decided to try to keep the conversation as light as possible.

"So did you have a feast for dinner last night?" Moving into the cabin she saw the opened boxes and empty packets scattered in and around the makeshift beds the children had made.

"Well it was a little bit sensible," Ben confessed sheepishly. "Katie only wanted chocolate and Jim-Bob wanted potato chips, and anyway we didn't want to cook anything so we had potato chip sandwiches and chocolate bars for afters."

It was as good an explanation as any, Georgia thought. She silently blessed Bill for putting the sort of food that kids liked into the boat for them. Thinking of him brought another lump to her throat and she quickly pushed him to the back of her mind. There would be time in the future to grieve for all their losses but this wasn't it. This was the time for survival.

"So how long was I unconscious?" Georgia asked but from the pounding that was now evident in her head, she would have guessed quite a long time.

"Well after we got the belt around you, it seemed to get dark quite quickly. We tried again to get you in the boat but when we couldn't we made sure the rope was as tight as we could get and we took turns to watch over you," Jim-Bob explained

Georgia was touched by their concern.

"But when it got too dark and stopped raining we decided we should get changed into dry clothes, have something to eat and get some sleep. So that's what we did." Ben finished off the tale.

For the first time Georgia noticed the children were wearing different clothes to the day before.

"I guess I should follow your example and get into something dry then," she replied, indicating her still wet clothes.

"Ok, we will wait outside," Katie said, sounding very grown-up.

Thankful for the privacy she had been offered, Georgia closed the cabin door and peeled off her wet clothes. Throwing them onto the bundle the children had already made of their discarded things, she located a towel and dried herself off, before donning fresh clothing from the bag she had brought.

Bundling up the sleeping bags, she took a moment to organise the cabin so that it was tidier and more normal. She wasn't really sure why but it seemed important that things be as orderly as possible.

"Ok, come in now kids," she called.

There was some fun opening up the boxes and seeing what was inside. It was obvious that they should eat the perishable food first, but for the sake of allaying her own fears, she wanted to see what the other boxes contained.

Bill had done them proud. There were tins and tins of all sorts of food, many of which didn't need much, if any, cooking. Tins of ham and beans and fruit were great. Versatile, nutritious and long lasting. The supply was plentiful but even so, Georgia was reluctant to use too much. There was no knowing when or where they would get another supply of food from. This would have to last indefinitely.

"What do you fancy then? What about bacon sandwiches?" The mere thought of the smell of frying bacon had her mouth watering.

"Yes, yes, yes!"

It was a unanimous decision. The children sat in the cabin, whilst she cooked on the little stove. The warmth from their bodies and the cooking lifted their spirits and they talked animatedly about things they liked and disliked, both to eat and to do.

Several times they laughed uproariously and Georgia almost forgot about the predicament they were in. There was something so normal about being with them like this. Even though she normally didn't have that much contact with them, they were always so easy to get along with that they tended to pick up on one visit, where they had left off from the last.

But of course this was very, very different. And yet…there was a feeling of such ordinariness of them all being together like this, laughing and making light of things…such a lack of strangeness to it…that it was eerie.

Placing the sandwiches on the table in front of them, she was gratified when they insisted that she chose the first one as they had at least eaten whist she had been unconscious in the water.

Playfully grabbing at the top of the stack she laughed as they copied her example and dived in at the food. It was good to see them so full of life after what had happened. Perhaps that was the key to their very survival now, to take life as it came and enjoy the precious moments when they could.

But as if her thoughts had been relayed to the children on some invisible thread of communication, the mood abruptly changed. Jim-Bob had been talking about his prowess as sports when he mentioned a little thing his dad had said to encourage him on.

That was all it took for the flood gates to open. Eyes fixed on the next sandwich she was in the middle of picking up, Georgia didn't see the emotion creep up onto his face. But she heard it in his voice. Strained as if he was forcing the words out of a closed throat, the boy stuttered out his dad's comment before bursting into wracking sobs.

Dropping the sandwich, Georgia pulled the boy towards her and cradled his head in her arms.

"It's ok to be upset. Your mum and dad love you very much." She was aware she had used the English word 'mum' rather than the kids customary 'mom' but she didn't think they would mind. "Just as much as you love them. And once the floods are gone, we will search for them. They will be looking for us too, so we will find each other." She hoped what she had said was true.

Jim-Bob continued to sob, although he didn't fight against her or refute her comforting words. But there was another sound now which demanded her immediate attention. The trained doctor in her recognised it, even as the woman in her struggled to place the sound and where it came from.

A sort of high pitched wheezing interspersed with an attempt at a cough. Panic seized Georgia's heart. As if in slow motion she turned her attention to Ben. No not him, he was fine, except for the puzzled look on his face which was partially turned away from Georgia. Seen in profile, he looked absolutely fine and so her gaze followed his...

Katie!

Little Katie, with a face that was turning purple. Eyes bulging, her mouth wide open, she struggled to eject what was lodged in her windpipe, the remnants of the half eaten sandwich strewn on the table in front of her.

As if she were in a never ending nightmare where the laws of time and distance do not hold true, Georgia saw herself in slow motion, as she reached across for the girl. The whole situation and all its intricate possibilities were laid out in her mind like a banquet, from which she was cruelly not permitted to choose.

On the verge of swallowing a bite, the girl had been overcome by her brother's grief and subsequently her own. In that nanosecond of fate, she had not swallowed the morsel, but instead had *inhaled* it and now she was choking.

Life, death and all the infinite possibilities between these two states, now lay in the hands of fate alone. Too far down to been seen from the girl's open mouth, the only options were removal of the morsel by surgical instrument, or the successful use of the Heimlich manoeuvre. Lacking any surgical instruments in their current situation, Georgia had no choice and no time to waste.

Grasping Katie in the correct hold, she thumped twice in the middle of the child's back, hoping that this would be successful. Still, the food refused to be dislodged, so she enfolded the child in her arms and jerked sharply upwards and inwards, forcing the trapped air out of the girl's lungs and finally dislodging the obstruction.

Coughing and gasping for air, the large chunk of undigested bacon sandwich flew from Katie's mouth and landed somewhere unseen on the floor behind them.

Together, Georgia and Katie sank back onto the bench seat and held on to one another. Without a word the two boys moved to flank them. Squashed together, all four were wordless and emotionally drained.

As one, the children wept for all that had happened to them in the past few days, for what had *nearly* happened and for what they feared might *yet* happen. Bodies limp and bent, they cried and cried and cried. And Georgia joined in with them. And from outside, the insistent pitter patter of rain began once more.

Chapter 21

There was a kind of rhythm to it. The rain drummed heavily on the windscreen and tyres sloshed through rainfall which now noticeably deepened on the road with every passing hour. And overriding this was the intermittent but pitiful moan from the back seat.

Even from the driver's position, Jack could feel the heat which Dan was generating. Like having your own private radiator which had a broken thermostat, the boy was being consumed by his own fever. The tablets Jack had given him, seemed to have worn off within the first hour and wary of overdosing the boy, Jack had decided to stick to the intervals suggested on the dosing instructions. But it was yet another hard decision to make.

Jack lowered the car windows, hoping that the temperature outside would cool Dan but it seemed only to cause he to moan louder and shiver violently. Reluctantly, Jack rolled the windows back up. He wasn't sure what he should do. In fact, had he made any decisions that were right at all yet? Should he have taken

Dan to the ark after all? Should he have just picked him up and headed to hospital? Should he even be attempting to get Dan back to Kevin? Or should he just be trying to get Dan to safety?

All these questions and others ran through his head in a never ending litany. What was he doing out here on a deserted highway, with a sick boy in the back, on a road that was fast becoming a river? 'Cos, see there is the real thing,' he admonished himself. 'This truck will soon be out of its depth, literally and figuratively too.'

Out of the centre of New York, he would perhaps miss the full show of the storm but could he get far enough away, fast enough, to ensure their survival? He really didn't know. And even if he did, his plan to *drive* into flood devastated areas was nigh on impossible. At some point he would have to ditch the car and find a boat. The question was really how long before they got to that point?

Grimacing, he shuffled in the seat, keeping his legs extended, not daring for even a moment to take one foot off the accelerator, or rest the other from hovering over the footbrake. It was too big a risk to take. Every muscle and bone in his body ached. He knew he had been driving solidly for hours but had no idea of the distance he had already travelled. It was dark and he was tired but he would not let himself rest just yet.

Another half an hour and he would stop. It would be time then to repeat the paracetamol but he would not give it early. He shook his head and rolled down the driver's window. Cold wet air thrashed his face and hair and rain sprayed over him, helping him to stay alert. He stuck his head out of the window and continued to drive. It reminded him of a scene he had watched in a movie once. The hero had been celebrating something and had done this very thing in the spirit of exuberant adventure. It struck him as ineffably sad. That way of life was gone.

It hadn't been the kind of life he had subscribed to...fast living and fast cars...but it had been there if he had wanted to choose it. But what sort of world would there be for Dan? A world where survival was the only aim? Where each day was a fight against nature till, finally you gave up and nature won? Because nature always won in the end didn't it?

The silhouette of a tree, trunk wide and planted firmly in the ground appeared at the side of the road. Fingers tightening on the steering wheel, he thought for a moment of altering the path of the truck. Just the slightest nudge in that direction would take them into a head-on collision with the tree. It would be fatal and brutal but it would be quick. One instant flash of pain then eternal darkness. It had a certain appeal.

Grasping the wheel, he made his hands keep their true and steady course and turned away from the tree. Branches bowed in the gale, it seemed to call to him, demanding that he return and meet his doom in the kiss of its coarse bark. The descending gloom and the storm had combined to make the tree appear sinister and strangely sentient, like it was a conscious being trying to lure him to his death.

But the thoughts had been his and his alone. And they were selfish thoughts. Who was he, to think he could make a decision for Dan? To decide whether the future was going to be too hard to cope with? To decide on Dan's behalf to end it all? Because that exactly what it would have amounted to.

And it would all have been for nothing then. All the suffering and the anguish that his parents had gone through in sending him away, all the effort the soldier had made to get him on the plane...everything would have been in vain.

Jack slowed the car to a halt and pulled over on to the side of the road. Cogs on a wheel. That's what it all was. Cogs on a wheel. Everything that had occurred, every action and reaction by every person both Dan and Jack had encountered in the last thirty-six hours, had inevitably led to this one moment in time. The one defining moment in Jack's life.

With a sudden clarity, he realised that the most significant moment in his life, was not the writing of an expose which had blown apart his career...it was this...right now! It was having the courage to face whatever the future brought, with a commitment to make it the best he could, for this young boy.

Locating the medicine he had brought, he climbed out of the car, so that he could administer it to Dan more easily. Closing the car door behind him he hesitated a moment, one hand still resting on the panel of the door, metal cold and wet against the palm of his hand.

There was a noise that didn't belong to the storm and the night. Rain desensitising his hearing by its heavy pounding everywhere it fell, he strained to pick out the false notes.

There! And there again! Caught up in the fury of the storm it would have been easily missed if he had not been seeking it out. With a glance to check on Dan, who's condition seemed no different to how it had been for the entire journey so far, he was compelled to seek out the source of the sound.

He waited a life time to hear it again and had almost come to believe that it had never existed, that it had been purely a figment of his imagination. One heart beat passed, another and another, ten and then twenty…and then yes…there it was again.

Calf deep in water, he half trudged, half swished to the other side of the road and the field which lay beyond it. The source of the noise was somewhere there, hidden in the swathes of long grass or grain which bent in the gale, backwards and forth as if beckoning him, just like the tree had.

Unseen but no longer unheard, the whimpers were more apparent, more compelling and more urgent in their appeal. Someone was hurt there.

At the very last moment before he launched himself into aiding this unknown person, a little flicker of doubt entered his mind. What if it was a ruse? What if an unknown attacker lay there, ready and waiting to dispatch him and steal his car? What if that person then threw Dan out into the middle of the road?

And yet, weren't these just ridiculous thoughts? Who in their right mind would just lay here in the hope that an unsuspecting person would come along, try to rescue them and thus provide them with a free ticket to ride as it were?

Mid-stride, the arguments for and against were equally persuasive and unable to stop himself from investigating, he at least congratulated himself on taking the sensible step of using the remote on the key fob to lock the car against intruders.

Satisfied at the responding flash of headlights to indicate the operation of the locking system, Jack turned his attention back to locating the source of the noise.

Trying to fade out the rain, he focused on tracking the sound across the field, ignoring the way the deep mud sucked at his feet with every step taken. Again, again and again, the sound came, each step bringing him closer and closer.

Pushing through the stalks, he found there was a little clearing where someone had already trampled the vegetation down. A body lay prone on the ground, silent except for the wordless cries of pain and desperation it still emitted.

From the size of the body, Jack judged it to be a teenager or perhaps a small woman who lay immobile there. It was too dark to see anything except the vague outline of a shape and Jack couldn't even tell which end was the head and which the feet. All he knew was that there wasn't enough length in the body to be a fully grown man.

How was he going to get another unconscious person in the car, even if it were another child? How was he going to be able to look after another sick person? The back of his mind told him he should be wondering where this child had come from. He had passed no houses for many miles now. But that was of no consequence in a way. It didn't really matter how this person had come to be here, did it? What mattered was what he could do to help.

"My name is Jack and I'll try to help you. I have a car over on the road, do you think you can walk there if I help you?"

There was no response, not even the whimpering from before. Was the person unconscious? Had they not perhaps understood? He was unsure. Unwilling to just take them by force, he tried to explain his actions and reasoning.

"I am going to pick you up now and carry you to the car," he braced himself and bent his body closer to the ground. There was a funny musky smell he noticed and wondered how long this person had lain there unattended. "When we reach a house we can stop and see if you know the people there." It sounded kind of lame but he didn't relish the idea of just forging ahead with this child, irrespective of what had happened to him or her.

Arms extended, he slipped them under the cold, wet body...and whipped them out again as if he had been electrified. Thick, wet matted hair covered the body. It was everywhere!

Images of a werewolf or horribly mutated child filled his mind briefly before reason set in. It was an animal! Not a human which lay prone before him! Tentatively in the concealing dark, he reached a hand out and placed it on the flank of the creature.

Stroking it softly, produced the most pitiful whimpers and he could tell from the way the fur ruffled in one direction and smoothed in the other, that he was facing the animal's head. It was a dog. He was sure of that. A large, relatively long haired breed. And it needed help.

There were no longer any questions in his head. Scooping the animal up in his arms, he was surprised at the lightness of the creature. He had thought by the sheer size of it, that it would be at least twice the weight it was.

It crossed his mind that he could yet live to regret his actions but it was even less in his nature to leave a wounded animal, than it would have been to leave a wounded human. He reckoned that probably said something about him that wasn't particularly sociable but those things were no longer relevant in this newly developing world anyway, he mused.

Silent in his arms, he was surprised when the dog responded by licking the length of his face with a hot tongue. Warm dog breath filled his nostrils but it wasn't repulsive at all. It was the smell of gratitude and of life and he felt his lips curl up in a faint smile.

Reaching the car, he had a moment of fumbling, trying to hold the dog in one outstretched arm and wrestle the car keys from his pocket, with the other hand. Almost dislocating his shoulder in the process, he managed to balance the dog on his elbow and bicep, freeing that hand to locate the key.

It was only when the door opened and the little illuminating bulb above it lit up, that he saw the full condition of the creature he held in his arms.

A young German Shepherd breed of dog, it was in an emaciated condition, far thinner than it could have become over the space of a few days. Depositing it gently and carefully on top of the bedding in the foot space at the back, Jack took in the sharp jut of ribs and hip bones, through fur which should have been thick and luxuriant but instead was matted and dull.

"What's happened to you fella?" Jack asked sadly. His question had not been loudly or sharply voiced and yet he saw the dog noticeably flinch at the words. Sad, miserable eyes gazed up at him, and he felt an uncontrollable rage against the person or persons who had treated this animal so badly. "Don't worry fella, we are all gonna look after each other from now on in," he promised.

Closing the car door softly, lest the animal take fright and suddenly find the energy to bolt, however unlikely that was, he went in search of what he needed. Medicine for Dan and food and water for the dog.

Forcing the medicine down Dan's throat, and washing it down with some water, he hoped he would not have to repeat the process before he saw some improvement in the boy.

The dog was easier to treat. Wary of overloading its empty stomach, he decided the best thing was to give it food little and often. That said, there was the other problem of what and how to feed it. He had no dog food, so clearly it would have to have human food. Ripping slices of cold meat into chunks, he hand fed the animal. The dog, its hunger and desperation outweighing its fear, took the food delicately and gently from his hands. With kind words of encouragement, Jack offered the last scrap of meat and patted the dog on the head.

It was time to restart their journey.

Soaked to the skin and exhausted and yet with a strange sense of exhilaration and renewed purpose, he switched on the engine and steered the car back into the middle of the lane.

He had taken on even more responsibility and yet he felt unquestionably lifted, as if this dog was going to share some of the burden rather than increase it.

His eyes strayed to the rear view mirror, which he had repositioned so that it showed Dan lying unconscious and feverish on the back seat. But the reflection was not what Jack had expected to see.

The boy was still out cold but he now had the fingers of one hand entwined in the coat of the dog who lay beside him, snuggled into him as if it was finally in its rightful place. As though sensing it was being watched, the dog lifted its eyes to the mirror, meeting Jack's gaze, before lowering its head once more, resting it on the chest of the sick boy.

It was only then that Jack noticed the boy's fingers working the dog's fur and realised that neither boy nor dog had cried out in pain since they had been together.

'Maybe there is hope for us, after all,' thought Jack, as the first rays of dawn light swept away the dark and the rain.

The highway stretched before him, grey asphalt with looming thunderous grey clouds above.

Chapter 22

"A dog! No, not even that! *Dogs*! With the emphasis on the plural!" Sam paced up and down one of the smaller cabins, hands and arms jerking every which way in frustration.

If it hadn't been such a tense situation, Sally would actually have found it rather funny. "We will make room. And anyway, it's not as if there are a hundred cats and dogs..."

"No, it will just feel that way!" He was in full exasperation mode now. As if on cue, a low whining began on the other side of the cabin door. Sam yanked the door open so hard, the hinges creaked and Sally feared the door would splinter off the frame.

A little terrier sat on its hind legs, begging attention. It was so cute, Sally had to stop herself from bending down and ruffling the soft spot behind it ears. Its attention and focus was not on her. Its eyes were riveted on Sam. For some reason she had yet to comprehend, animals loved

Sam. All animals! Not that he ever seemed to go out of his way to attract them. They just did.

Without taking its eyes off the object of its adoration, the little dog's body quivered in anticipation, as it gathered up its energy before springing into the arms of the man who stood before it.

Reflexes working on automatic, Sam's arms closed around the little creature, catching it and holding it gently, before replacing it on the floor. "Be off with you! Go find your family!" he admonished it. But Sally's ears, so finely tuned to all the moods of this man she had known for over forty years, detected an almost reluctant note.

Perhaps they had been wrong to never try to become a family again after Lucy. Perhaps they should have adopted a child or even just had pets. Instead they had remained a couple, relying only on one another, comforted only by one another. It was a great position of honour to hold, that of sole consoler of life's ups and downs but it was also one of unique responsibility and pressure.

Sensing that it had outstayed its welcome, the little dog turned around and started back up the corridor towards the stairs which led to the upper deck. But at the foot of the stairs it paused. One paw on the bottom step, and tail tucked despondently under its body it turned round to give a last beseeching look.

"Perhaps we had better check on how things are going up stairs," pronounced Sam, heading through the doorway as he spoke. Bemused, Sally followed in his wake, noticing how the dog waited till Sam caught up with him, wagging its tail furiously at their approach.

Sally also noticed the furtive pat that Sam gave the dog, under the pretext of checking his laces were done up.

"It's just that we don't have food for animals." His protests were getting weaker she noticed, as they climbed the steps. "They brought pet food with them and after that...well we will have scraps to give them anyway," she countered.

"But there isn't enough room for them!"

"They will sleep in the same cabins as their owners."

"What about when they need toileting?"

She had to admit that was the trickiest problem. "We could cordon off a small area on the top deck for their use and then swill it down daily." It was as good a solution as she could find.

"I suppose so," Sam tried to sound more reluctant that Sally thought he actually was. They had reached the main deck where John Stark was welcoming aboard yet another family. And their cat.

"Welcome, welcome aboard. I am Doctor Stark!" he gushed at the bewildered family, beaming a smile at them which would have been more fitting on a TV game-show host. A small needle of unease roiled in Sam's stomach, watching the scene without becoming involved in it.

"I have assigned you the use of cabin number 15. We will get you down there and comfortably settled before we show you around..." Like he was welcoming them aboard his own private yacht, there was a smarminess about John Stark, that Sam could not ignore. Something about the man rankled him. He was sure that he was an excellent doctor, Bill had in fact assured him of that very thing...it was the *man himself* Sam was concerned about. That sense of self-importance and high ego. He had seen that too many times already in his career – usually from the people who put their own self-worth before the good of everyone else.

"He will bear watching, that one," he murmured to Sally, aware that her grip on his hand had tightened as they watched Dr Stark at work. Forty odd years of marriage had twined them so close, that sometimes thoughts did not have to be voiced. Sally was aware of the potential danger posed by this young man too.

"And let me introduce you to Sam and Sally White," Stark indicated them by a sweeping gesture of his hand. Sam wondered how long Stark had been aware of them standing there, watching him. He also wondered what was about to be said and whether or not it was for his benefit. He wouldn't put it past this man to be false to his face, there was such a persistent unease in Sam's heart.

"Sam built this ark," again the big flourish of arms and theatrical tone. But inside of all that bluster, Sam noticed that he had referred to him by his first name, omitting the title of 'Doctor'. Yet he had clearly referred to himself as 'Doctor Stark'. Granted Sam's doctorate was in the field of science as opposed to medicine but he still held the title by rights. The needle of unease sharpened itself on the walls of Sam's stomach.

"…and his charming wife Sally has helped him fix it up and make it comfortable…" Stark managed to make Sally sound no more intelligent than a seeing-eye dog and Sam bristled on her behalf.

"Well I did what I could but Sam did all the real work," supplied Sally ingeniously, taking the focus away from Stark and his 'damned by faint praise' attitude. The family at once turned their attention towards her.

The girl, barely ten years old by the look of her, was thin and gaunt, her face pale and drawn. But her eyes radiated hope. Sally took in the way the girl's skin hung loose and marbled white from her bones and the incriminating bandana, spun too, too brightly, around the girl's head. The garish yellows and greens of the material vied for the eyes' attention and did nothing to enhance the child's delicate features.

Like a mask, the bandana's sole purpose was to allow the wearer to hide away, but just like a mask, what it did in reality, was draw attention to itself and the disease it hid. Her mother and father were also pale and gaunt but for them, there was no hope radiating from their eyes.

"Cabin fifteen wasn't it?" Sally checked.

The mother nodded, eyes brimming with tears.

"I can't thank you enough…both of you…" she began, clutching at Sally's arm with a grip like steel pincers, one tear rolling down the hollow of her cheek.

"To just be given this chance…thank you," her husband attempted to finish the thought for her but he too was emotional.

Sally felt the need to come up with some profound words of wisdom to offer them hope and light their way. But none were forthcoming. She recognised the cruel signs of this child's illness, she knew the statistics and she had had personal experience of them. And yet…

And yet, such a powerful light shone from the girl's eyes, it was like watching a whole galaxy come to life. As if she had journeyed to another world, held in the child's open and wondering gaze, Sally heard words come out of her mouth without her consciously intending to say them.

"Fate has brought us together and fate has its own reasons and purpose." To her ears it sounded like some New-Age tosh but it seemed to help these people and the woman offered her a wide if rather shakily conceived smile.

"Ah Harris, there you are!" Stark's tone was jaunty and jocular but neither Sam nor Sally missed the omitted title of 'Doctor' once more, nor did they miss the way Neil Harris seemed to nervously twitch at the other man's voice.

"This family are for Cabin…"

"It's ok, *Dr* Harris," Sally hadn't intended to, but she unconsciously put emphasis on the word 'doctor' as if to invalidate any subliminal signals Stark had already put in place, "I will show Mr…" she waited for someone to supply her with the right names.

"Mr…" the man stopped to correct himself, realising they were past being formal with each other, "Greg and Olivia Collins," he put a hand on his daughter's shoulders, "and our daughter Lucy."

Lucy. Another Lucy. Who was also sick.

Sally's world rocked.

Just for a moment, she felt the deck sway under her feet, as if the ark was actually afloat and not still landlocked. She could not look at Sam, aware that he was as affected if not more than, she was.

She fixed a smile on her face. If she could hold it for long enough, perhaps it would just stick there. "Let's get you to your cabin then." To her own ears she sounded falsely bright but no one else seemed to notice. Apart of course from Sam.

"Why don't you stay and supervise here, dear?" Sally gave Sam's arm a comforting brush. Her suggestion had several reasons. Firstly she wanted Sam to curb John Stark's sense of importance, secondly she knew how upset he now was and wanted to divert his attention elsewhere and thirdly because she really didn't need his help to show these people around.

She couldn't admit, even to herself that there was a small secretive and selfish part of her, which wanted to be as alone with *this* Lucy as possible. It wasn't *her* Lucy, it would never be her Lucy. That child was gone, turned to a fine pale dust by time and tragedy...but for just one moment she could *pretend* couldn't she? Pretend that Lucy hadn't died, that she had been here all along...

And yes, *there* was the road to madness. To watch another child with the same name, the same illness, weaken and die all over again. What was it she had said to them earlier? That fate had brought them together? Well if it had, it was a mocking fate.

One hand on the balustrade, she led them down one level to the deck below. "Here is our day area. We have comfy seats and toilets and a kitchen here."

"They are like cinema chairs, wow! All that's missing is the popcorn," laughed Lucy, her eyes dancing with delight.

"Yes honey, all that's missing is the popcorn," agreed Sally. How intensely sad, that this child who had never known normality, other than having medicines and injections on a daily basis was now being thrust into a world where normality was being turned upside down and shaken hard. And she still managed to find pleasure in it.

"Your cabin is on the deck below this." She led them down the next flight of stairs and onto the deck below. "Here we are. Its small I'm afraid but space is at a premium as I'm sure you are aware." Throwing open the door she revealed four bunk beds with a narrow central isle. A small chest of drawers was the only other furniture. And above it was a hook, already fixed with a saline drip, ready for emergencies.

"I'm afraid the bathrooms are communal but there are several on this level."

"What's below us?" asked Lucy.

"Another deck but that one is more like dorms, with some more bathrooms." She didn't add what remained unspoken, that severe as Lucy's condition was, it was inappropriate to put her and her family in the dorms with other families. The terminal cases had all been given their own cabins to preserve their dignity as much as possible. Lucy was terminal. Even if Sally had been unaware of that from looking at the girl's thin and wasted frame, she had known as soon as John Starkey had said 'Cabin fifteen'.

The cancer was the girl's death sentence, the cabin her cell. Sally wished fate and destiny were tangible things, things that she could squeeze and beat and *force* to change. But that was not the way it was.

"How long will we be on this boat then?" Lucy seemed to need to ask all the questions her parents could not ask for themselves.

"I don't know. It depends on what we find when we get to where we are going. But there is plenty food and water and everything we will need, so don't worry."

Lucy beamed at her. The smile stretched impossibly wide across her little face and Sally realised that the girl would be a beauty when she was older. If she survived that long. Unable to talk any more, Sally turned away from the family. "When you have unpacked, feel free to have a look around but please do not leave the ark, for your own safety." All three people nodded their understanding and acceptance.

"Mrs White," Lucy had one final question.

"What will happen to me when I die?"

It was so unexpected it provoked a shocked gasp of breath from Sally and both of Lucy's parents. Sally's mind almost unravelled itself. What was the girl asking her? What would happen to her body if she died? Would she be in pain? What would happen to her parents if she died? Whether or not there was a Heaven for her to go to? Sally didn't know if it was one of these questions, all of them together or something completely different.

She looked to Olivia Collins, seeking help but found none. Like her daughter, Olivia seemed to have relinquished all responsibility for herself, relying instead on Sally's decisions and care.

Falteringly she began, "well I'm sure that won't be for a very, very long time..." but was cut short.

"That's not what the doctors at the hospital think!"

Sally was inspired by a thought which just popped into her head. She grabbed onto it. "No, maybe not, but then again you are on an ark, about to sail down the middle of New York and I bet they wouldn't have thought that possible either!" It was evading the question and they both knew it and yet like a secret between them they both held it close.

"Are there really animals on board too?"

Sally was grateful for the change of subject matter. She thought about the little dog which had accompanied them up the stairs, before disappearing to find its family.

"Yes there are." She had a brainwave. "Would you like to see them?" Lucy's eyes shone. "Oh, yes, please."

"Come on then." Closing the cabin door, the four of them made their way down to the lower deck and the dorms there.

Sectioned into several large rooms, all of which had their doors wide open, the sound of children's laughter echoed out from one room and blended with the next. Children dashed from one room to another, meeting friends, making friends. And alongside several of these groups, dogs of all shapes and sizes bounded. Pack creatures by nature, the dogs were loving the noise and attention and so were the children.

Looking at them now, it was hard to believe that the children were ill and of course some of them weren't. Some were merely the siblings of children who were ill. And of those who *were* ill, many were on the road to recovery or not that seriously ill to begin with. The terminal cases, not *cases*, *children*, she reminded and reprimanded herself, had been put on the deck above, in the cabins.

"Mom can I join in?" Lucy asked, spotting one group of girls fawning over a little fluffy dog.

"Your medicine makes you prone to catching bugs easily. I don't think..." Greg Collins began. But he was halted by the pressure of his wife's hand on his arm and the look on her face. 'Let her go,' said that look, 'let her have some *fun* in her life'. Sally saw it plainly. In protecting their daughter, in prolonging her life, they had been having to deny her the very thing that life for a child should be all about. Discovery and fun.

Greg Collins swallowed hard.

"Course you can Lucy. Go and have some fun."

Sally watched just long enough, to see Lucy bound over to the group of girls. Body stick thin, she was a sorry sight amongst the healthier looking girls but she held her head erect and there was a glow to her cheeks which hadn't been there just a moment before.

Sally turned away and headed back to find Sam. Perhaps the thing about having pets on board was going to be the best thing they ever did.

Chapter 23

Filled with inertia, Georgia had allowed the boat to drift for quite some time. There was too much of a sense of inevitability of outcome, in whatever she tried to do.

They had escaped New York in a car…which then almost became a watery coffin. Then on escaping the car and freeing the boat from the trailer, she had almost drowned. Now Katie had almost choked to death just by eating a bacon sandwich.

In a way it was ludicrous – that life should turn on such a small circle of fortune – but as far as she could see, it was certainly true. She remembered a newspaper article she had read some time ago about a man who had survived a huge fire in his apartment block. The firemen had been amazed that the man had been entirely unscathed, particularly when it was the untenanted apartment directly below him, which had proved to be the source of the fire. The fire had spread upwards, consuming all in its path and rendering the man's apartments uninhabitable –yet the man who lived there had emerged without a burn, wheeze or even smear of soot on his forehead.

The next week, exactly seven days after the blaze, the man stepped out of his *new* apartment on the other side of town, slipped on a pile of wet leaves, fell down, banged his head on the sidewalk and died. Just upped and died. Just like that.

Had his time been up, she had mused, as she had read the article with a growing sense of wonder. Was there some celestial being with a clip board and a list of names, watching and waiting, making sure that each individual only used their allotted time span?

It did sometimes seem that way. And if it were true, what then? Did it give her the right to hold her hands up and say 'ok, take us now'? It was a repugnant idea to her but there was more to consider too.

What if they were in search of something which was no longer attainable? The way of life they had known was gone, replaced by something that had yet to take shape and form. But what if that never happened? What if there *was* no future for these children? No future except to scavenge for food. No future except mere existence? Was it enough to go on for?

The rain continued to fall, as Georgia and the children sat inside the boat, huddled together and silent. Cut off from the outside world, she tried to piece together what she knew of the situation, with what she understood of human nature.

The storms which had spread across the continent were generally catastrophic. And yet there were survivors everywhere. There had been pictures on the TV of people being air lifted to safety, or collected on boats and in those areas already affected by the storms, the news reports had suggested that the flood water had been beginning to dissipate. But many buildings had either been battered beyond recognition by the storms or too water damaged to be of any future use.

Industrial, commercial and domestic properties had been ruined. People's livelihoods, businesses and homes had been destroyed and many people had lost their lives. In a strange way it was not unlike the aftermath of a war. Like nature had waged a war upon mankind!

It was a strange thought but also rather fitting. Just like after a war, people would have to try to piece their lives back together, because really, what was the alternative? To just give up and let the war claim yet another victim? This American nation was built on the blood of pioneers, she told herself. And all those things and places which had been destroyed, had once never been there in the first place anyway.

And if somewhere deep, deep inside of herself, she couldn't find even the tiniest grain of pioneer spirit, of the kind that many other English people all those hundreds of years ago had demonstrated, then she should never have taken on the task of protecting these children. Surely she was built of sterner stuff than to just lie down and accept what fate threw at her?

She was *not* the man in the newspaper article and neither were these children. Fate did not have an allotted timespan for them already set out, she was sure of it. Their safety and their futures were in *her* hands and hers alone. So she had to take action, not sit there pondering the meaning of life, she told herself.

"Come on, let's get this show on the road!" she declared brightly. The children looked up at her, eyes dulled by too much trauma.

"Who wants to steer?" she tried to make it sound exciting but the three faces which regarded her remained blank and disinterested.

"Kids I need your help," her tone was beseeching and it was the last thing she wanted to do, but she had to make them snap out of their apathy. It worked.

"I will help you," Auntie Georgia, stated Ben and the others echoed his remark. The children had already been through so much, that their loyalty and bond with her and each other, had been forged in steel and strengthened with iron. They could no more refuse to help her, than they could wilfully stop their hearts from beating.

"Right then, I will give you all a driving lesson," she smiled at them. Pulling the spare engine key off the hook where it always hung, she held it aloft in the air, like a magician demonstrating a trick, before inserting it into the slot on the engine.

"This is an inboard motor, which means the engine is inside the hull of the boat," she explained, "so we need to make sure we press this switch before turning on the ignition, that way we won't be choking on fumes." She scolded herself for using the word 'choking' but the children didn't seem to notice and were actively engaged now.

She pressed the switch and turned the key in the ignition and held her breath. It had never occurred to her to doubt that the engine would start first time. But it occurred to her now. Thankfully it purred into life straight away. A smooth and rhythmic thrum reverberated through the cabin of the boat, juddering through her body in a not unpleasant way.

She had never had any training in driving the boat but she had watched Bill do it often enough and once she had had a go herself for ten minutes or so. It hadn't been particularly difficult to do but it had required attention to both the steering and the throttle and she thought it too big a task for one child alone.

"The steering wheel is only to guide the boat in whatever direction it is going. The speed is controlled by this lever here, called the throttle." The boys watched her, rapt with attention.

"How do you boys fancy doing that between you? One of you could steer and the other keep our speed steady and then you can change around?"

"Yeah, that sounds great. I want to steer first!" Jim-Bob was jumping up and down with excitement and Georgia couldn't help but laugh. It was just what they needed, something to lift their spirits.

"What will we do?" asked Katie.

"Ah, well we will have the equally important job of navigating to where we are going," smiled Georgia. But the mood was ruined by Katie's next comment. "Are we going to fetch mom and dad?" she asked eagerly.

It was Ben who came to her rescue. "We are gonna have an adventure Katie," he stated, eyes a little bit too watery but tears bitten back for his sister's sake. "And then we will get mom and dad," he finished, turning his face away as if the throttle required his full attention, even though the boat was not yet moving.

"Ok Captains, let's get underway!" cried Georgia, desperately trying to keep the tone light. She looked at the compass to check which way they were facing.

Luckily they appeared to be pointed in the direction they wanted to travel in.

"Head out that way," she pointed ahead. "Don't make any big turns of the wheel Jim-Bob, just little correcting movements when you need to. And Ben, keep an eye on the speed. We don't want to dawdle but we don't want to speed either. Just keep it steady."

She turned to Katie. "Right, you and I have some navigating to do." There were spare maps in one of the drawers under the seats. She remembered putting them there herself long ago, when she and Betsie had accidentally both bought identical ones. Perhaps a map wouldn't be much help but at least it was something.

It occurred to her, that as it was flooded ground they would eventually be travelling over, there may well be obstacles hidden under the water, which would damage the boat. But she didn't know what choice they had in the matter.

There was also the question of how deep the water was and what they would do when eventually it was not deep enough for the boat. Would they be able to travel on from that point on foot? What would they do about the food? There were too many questions and none of them answerable, so there was really no point in worrying about them. 'One day at a time', she thought, 'one day at a time'. That was all she could deal with and all she had to work with.

Using the compass and the maps was harder that she expected it to be. The day was still gloomy with rain and although it was not intense enough to warrant being called a storm, it was most unpleasant. In addition to that, there were no obvious landmarks to follow. It was like a new land had been carved out of this waterlogged landscape. Field merged with river and road, so that there was no discernible end to the panorama of water.

Georgia and Katie sat inside the cabin on the bench overlooking the front of the boat. There was some flotsam in the water, the odd bit of fallen tree or floating debris but between them they had managed to spot them all so far and thus avoided barging in to them. Probably the little bits of wood wouldn't do any damage to the boat anyway, but it was safer and wiser not to take the risk.

"Hey look Auntie Georgia, you are on the map!" exclaimed Katie excitedly, her finger poised over the State of Georgia on the map in front of them.

"Well actually my real name isn't Georgia, at all," she informed them. It had never occurred to her before that they hadn't known this.

"You mean your name isn't Georgia Wade?" Ben's voice had gone up an octave in his surprise and Georgia laughed despite herself. Both boys had now turned to face her, eyes wide and waiting for her response.

"Are you in disguise? Like a trained assassin ...or a spy...a spy from England?" Jim-Bob's imagination was firing up to full steam.

"No, nothing quite so exciting, I'm afraid," she laughed. "My *real* name is Georgina but I never liked it much. Then when I met your mother she used to tease me about an old song we both liked called "Midnight train to Georgia" and the nickname "Georgia just kind of stuck," she explained. "So now I am Georgia Wade. And I like it."

"How old were you when you met mom and what's the song like?" Katie asked.

"Well I met your mum when I went to college. My dad's firm moved him out to America from England for a few years, so my mum and I came with him. But when they moved him back to England, a few years later, I was already in medical school and training to be a doctor, so I stayed here." Giving them the explanation brought home the realisation that she would probably never see her own family again, never know if they had been saved or not.

It was a hard thing to come to terms with, so she pushed it out of her mind for the time being. She knew she had a sweet voice and had always enjoyed singing yet it seemed strange under the circumstances. Then again, everything was strange under these circumstances. The circumstances themselves were strange.

"The song goes like this," she cleared her throat and in a quiet but assured voice she sang

'L.A. proved too much for the man,

So he's leavin' the life he's come to know,

He said he's goin' back to find

Ooh, what's left of his world'," she faltered here. The words struck her as so poignant and way, way too close to the mark. Like the songwriter had been clairvoyant, she realised the song could be taken to have been written about the precise moment in time they now found themselves in…a world where they had no idea what was going to be left unaltered.

"Go, on, go, on, that was really good," urged Ben. Three pairs of eyes regarded her with a star struck expression. She forced a smile and carried on to the chorus, so they could see how the nickname had stuck.

"The world he left behind

Not so long ago.

He's leaving,

On that midnight train to Georgia,
And he's goin' back
To a simpler place and time.
And I'll be with him
On that midnight train to Georgia,
I'd rather live in his world
Than live without him in mine." She cut off the next verse and built her voice into a crescendo for the abridged finale.

"And I'll be with him
On that midnight train to Georgia,
I'd rather live in his world
Than live without him in mine."

Rapturous applause filled the little cabin.

Everyone's attention diverted elsewhere, no one at first noticed the increased amount of flotsam in the water, heading directly towards them, as the boat pushed further and further into the area that had until recently, been the very eye of the storm.

Chapter 24

I t was a strain to open his eyes. Sleep had a vast appeal and Jack clung on to it with all his might. There were things in the waking world that were too hard to deal with. Decisions to make, actions to take and repercussions to live through. For just one minute longer he wanted to evade these things. To flit unfettered by the constraints and difficulties of the waking world, into a dream landscape, where even the darkest demon could be conquered by a blade of steel and a blood-sucking vampire slayed, by a timely shaft of light.

Daylight bathed his face with an insistent brightness and he knew he had to open his eyes and face up to his responsibilities. The sun was high in the sky, the day well underway, he could tell that by the quality of the light which shone on him. But he kept his eyes closed a few moments more. He had to think a plan through, before being confronted with whatever the day had to throw at him. Because the minute he opened his eyes, he would be overtaken with so many facts and problems to overcome, his mind would become immediately overwhelmed and any decision he reached would be influenced by what he *felt* rather than what he *knew* to be true.

He had been an investigative reporter once upon a time and he knew that it was important to acknowledge the facts in any decision making process, even if you then decided to turn them on their head. So, what were the facts here? He had driven on for as long as he had been able, before exhaustion had overtaken him and he had begun to swerve dangerously on the road. Then he had had to stop and sleep.

So far he had taken a high route out of the New York area, keeping as far north as possible, where the storms had not yet fully wreaked their damage. It had crossed his mind that he had chosen to believe Sam White without benefit of any real evidence or proof. What if the man had been deluded, or even worse, criminally insane? What if he had put Dan at risk for no real reason at all? Except he knew this wasn't the case didn't he? He knew Ed Malone did not suffer fools and it had been that great man himself, who had steered Jack in Sam's direction after all.

And yet the lure of remaining on their present course was undeniable. Here was an area, which although rain lashed, had not been devastated by a giant storm. Yet. Because if all that Sam White had said was true, it was only a matter of time, before the storm hit any area it had not previously visited. He had no choice but to eventually go south into the Midwestern area, if he was to avoid immersing them into the rage of a full out storm.

The question now, was whether or not he could continue heading across the country for a while, before dropping down towards the south. To make *that* decision, he needed some facts about their present location and status. He opened his eyes.

A fine misty rain fell outside the car. Too fine to almost be seen by the naked eye, it was there nonetheless and sent a chill down his spine. It was a precursor of what was to come, he felt, a warning from nature that this was just the beginning.

With his peripheral vision, he scanned the backseat area. Afraid to turn his full attention to Dan and the dog, he held tight to some notion that he would see some movement there to indicate that all was well. Reluctant to face his fears, he stared straight ahead and strained at the edges of his vision to see something, *anything* which would give him hope and eradicate this dread from his heart. But there was nothing.

No movement, no sound, nothing came from the backseat at all. Unconsciously holding his breath, Jack sat up straighter and turned to face the back of the car.

Dan and the dog were snuggled together and the boy's face was pushed so far into the thick fur on the dog's chest, that with each inhalation and exhalation he took, the dog's hair ruffled gently in the breeze. And there seemed to be an evenness to it, that hadn't been there before, Jack noted with relief. Dan's breathing was no longer rapid and shallow, with an irregularity that sliced fear into Jack's heart. Instead it was smooth, measured and calm. Gone too was the deathly pallor, replaced now by a warmer, more healthy skin-tone.

Just like before, the dog seemed to become aware of his attention and lifted its head. Tongue lolling from a corner of its mouth, and large white teeth on show, it looked as if the dog was grinning at him. And perhaps it was, he thought. He couldn't help grinning back. In the midst of all this danger and unknowable fate, there was such a feeling of destiny playing out, that he found himself questioning his former disbelief in providence. Who had *he* been, to say that there was no such thing as fate? He certainly would not be so sure in the future, that much was certain.

"Where are we?"

He had been so engrossed in the dog, that he had not noticed Dan open his eyes. Now the boy's voice startled him. The dog however seemed completely unperturbed and turning its attention away from Jack and back to Dan, it swept the boy's face with a huge wet lick.

Far from being distressed or even repulsed at finding a huge unknown dog at his side, Dan merely giggled. Jack felt his face crack into a wide grin. Things were going to be ok.

"Oh that's …" he tried to think of a good name for the dog but his mind was almost completely blank, "Fella!" It was as good a name as any he supposed.

"Hello Fella," Dan kissed the very tip of the dog's black nose.

"Come on, let's give the dog a toilet break, have something to eat and be on our way again. You gave me a real scare you know!" He hopped out of the truck, dismayed to find the water level was now up to his ankles. Luckily the truck bed was high and the water level would need to rise quite a bit more before it would begin to seep into the inside of the car.

"I was sick wasn't I?" Dan began to remember the previous day's events and frowned in concentration.

"Yes, you were." Jack was unsure how much to reveal to Dan. He didn't want to unnecessarily frighten the boy. But he did need to have a look at Dan's arm. Unconsciously his gaze drifted to Dan's shoulder and the boy cottoned on.

"It was the vaccine that made me sick, wasn't it?" He flinched when he tried to rub the arm and pulled up his sleeve to investigate. The material was matted and stained where the infection had run from the injection site and Jack could see that it was still stuck to the wound.

"Don't yank it off. You will pull off any scab that has formed. Here let me help." He opened up the car door and let the dog out before sliding into the seat next to Dan.

Gingerly he teased up the sleeve and was relieved to see that the swelling and inflammation had now gone, even if the injection site itself did look less than normal. Dan looked briefly at his arm then turned his head away from the grisly sight. He watched the dog find a piece of grass outside the car to perform his toilet. He laughed as he watched.

"Think you better change the dog's name 'cos Fella's a girl!"

Jack cast a glance over at the dog, who sure enough was squatting as female dogs did to urinate. He laughed too. It had never even entered his mind that the dog could be a girl.

"Hmm. I think you are right about that. Any ideas for a name then?"

"Where did she come from?" Dan asked.

"I don't really know. I just found her in a field. I don't know how long she had been there but she's clearly not been looked after." It wasn't much of an explanation but it was all he had.

"Roxie. I like the name Roxie. And she's not wearing a collar so we have to name her something." He called to the dog, "come on Roxie." Furiously raking up muddy waterlogged earth to cover her toilet, the dog pricked up her ears at the sound of her new name, almost as if she had always been called it, and hastened back over to the car.

"Ok, we will have something to eat and be on our way again." Jack pulled out food from the bag and shared it out equally. From the very corner of his eye though, he could see Dan donate some of his own share to the hungry dog. Jack didn't interfere for now but he was aware that it was something he would need to keep an eye on.

Meal and toileting over, it was time to hit the road again. "Could you put the radio on please?" Dan asked.

"I tried earlier but it there was only static." When they had first left New York the radio had been working. There had been reports of heavy rainfall and some localised flooding but no real panic. After a while the broadcast had broken up. He hadn't been able to tell if he was just moving out of range of the station or if it was affected by the weather. Changing channels and frequencies hadn't helped either.

He switched on the radio once more and was surprised to hear a voice clear and sharp. "...has worsened. Reports suggest that the freak weather experienced by New Yorkers today, is indeed set to continue and some predict that New York may see its own Super Storm, the likes of which has already devastated large parts of our nation..."

He depressed the off button, muting the report.

"No, no leave it on please Uncle Jack. We need to know what's happening." And of course Dan was right. They did need to know what was happening. Jack switched the radio back on.

"...Office has been strangely silent about expectation and weather forecasts but this reporter has it on good information that...now wait just one second..." the reporter's voice changed dramatically and despite himself Jack slowed the car's pace, while he waited on the edge of his seat for the man to continue.

"We have a report that's just come in and hot off the press so to speak. A major New York newspaper is warning residents to stay indoors. It is suggesting that the wider New York State area is in for a storm, the likes of which it has never seen before. The wording of the article is severe, let me read it out loud..." there was the sound of a newspaper being folded and papers shuffled. "In capital letters, the headline states 'NEW YORK SET FOR DEVASTATING STORMS,'" the reporter paused for breath. "This newspaper has been informed by an unimpeachable White House source, that the storms which overwhelmed the Midwest and the West Coast areas of America have now moved on to New York State. These storms are extremely violent and catastrophic and chances of survival if you are caught out in them are extremely low...' Whatever you are doing listeners, stop now and *just listen,*" the voice advised, the man's tone grave and forceful.

The report continued on, advising people to stay indoors, preferably in buildings which were higher than two stories but less than ten. Jack blessed Ed Malone for his perspicacity. Ed had known exactly what to print. A clear set of instructions to minimise the death toll and give everyone the best chance of survival. Get above the flood water he was saying, by being in a building which had at least two stories, but not one which was top heavy and liable to collapse in the rage and power of the storm.

He wondered briefly about Mrs McGruder and whether she would heed the warning. He hoped so. Crazy as New York City was, he corrected himself, *had been,* impersonal and anonymous as it had tended to make its citizens be with one another, it had also been a vibrant and exciting place to live. And if it had been in his power to individually save all its weird and wonderful residents, he would have done so. He turned the radio off.

Dan remained silent in the back, lost in his own thoughts. "I tried to phone your dad again whilst you were asleep but there was no tone, not even a ringing sound." He would have preferred not to have told the boy this but knew it was only a matter of time before he asked anyway.

"There were reports on the TV last night," Dan stated quietly. Jack remembered the blaring TV screen and the fear that Dan had deliberately done something to himself. "Things are really bad, aren't they?" The tone of his voice left no room for denials, for evasive comments or even downright lies.

"Yes Dan. They are really bad." Jack halted the car for a moment. They had reached a crossroads. A decision was called for now. Did he carry on straight ahead, keeping to the northern states, perhaps even eventually climbing into Canada, or did he stick to his word and take the fork which led south? It was a big risk either way. But for Dan, if not for himself, he was committed to trying to find Kevin and Stacey. Dan had to at least try to find his parents because if there was any hope for him at all, then they had to give it their best shot.

"Uncle Jack?" Dan's voice betrayed his nervousness. "We're going to find mom and dad, aren't we?" A quiver in his voice suggested he was aware that Jack was having to make a conscious choice about which road to take. Because whatever path Jack chose now would alter the course of their destiny, for the rest of their lives.

The fork in the road seemed so innocuous and yet a world of decision and consequence hinged on it.

Foot on the accelerator he wasn't even aware of making a decision but suddenly he was moving again. Driving down the fork which led to the south, as his tyres swished over the wet tarmac and the road wound unendingly on, he hoped not for the first time, that he would not live to regret what he was doing.

Chapter 25

It was a lot harder than Sam had imagined it would be. On paper at least, it had seemed relatively easy. Get the ark built and equipped. Get the medical supplies, the food and fuel in and stored away properly. Then get the allocated passengers in. After that, all there was to do was wait until the time was right to sail away. That was where the problems lay, right there in the waiting to sail away part, he thought now.

He had tried to account for everything. But what he hadn't accounted for, what he had been unable to account for was the grief. Grief at abandoning family and friends, work colleagues and even in some cases, hated jobs and bosses. The adult passengers milled around, eyes red rimmed with crying and faces swollen and puffy and they waited for the time to leave. Rain lashed the roof and sides of the warehouse but the structure held.

Conversation was virtually impossible because of the noise of the rapidly approaching storm but the vocal silence was a killer too. The air was thick with tension and Sam was eager to be gone. Looking through one of the large warehouse windows again, he checked the level of flooding outside. The sky was a dirty grey and the sun was completely absent.

Men and women bustled past him. Forced to manufacture something for them to do, anything which would take their mind off things, he had allocated small jobs to them. The men were putting another coat of tar onto the base of the boat to make it more waterproof and the women were varnishing the rest of the wooden exterior.

They were completely unnecessary tasks. The ark was as water tight as was possible but it gave them something to do with themselves. It had been Sally's suggestion of course and therefore a wise one and he had followed it unquestionably.

A man brushed brusquely against him, causing Sam to stumble and bang painfully into the window frame. But instead of offering an apology as Sam would have expected, the man merely glowered at him. If looks really could kill, Sam would have been flat out on the ground, all life extinguished from his finished body.

He tried to smile at the man. It was after all a very tense situation. But the look of pure hatred and venom which radiated from the other man, made Sam's blood run cold. Why should this man hate him so? Was he not aware that Sam was trying to save his and his families lives? That he was being rescued when others were set to die in the storm that raged outside? Was he not grateful? It certainly didn't appear that way.

Moving out of the man's way, Sam went in search of Sally. Looking in their cabin first, he found it empty. He knew where she was likely to be. Cabin 15. With Lucy.

Knocking softly on the cabin door, he waited till it was answered, rather than just barging in. Sally opened the door herself. Beyond her he could see Lucy sitting up in bed, reading a book, whilst her mother sat beside her, just watching the girl.

On seeing it was him, Olivia came over to the doorway. I have just been saying to Sally how grateful we are that you have given us this chance to be with Lucy," her voice broke, "however it turns out."

Sam placed a comforting hand on her arm, "I know my dear, I know you are." He turned his attention to his wife. "Unfortunately not everyone seems to feel like that!"

"Will you excuse me please Olivia, I have to have a word with Sam." Sally smiled a farewell at Lucy and stepped through the doorway and into the narrow gangway, closing the cabin door behind her.

"What's wrong? What do you mean?" she asked, worry furrowing her brow. Sam wished he hadn't had to be the cause of her worry. Hadn't this woman had more than her fair share over the years already? Since the very first time he had laid eyes on her, all he had ever wanted to do was shield her from pain, from the misery that happens in the midst of every life and make her laugh and smile. But of course that was not what had happened. He sighed.

"There are some people on here who seem to be angry at me. It's almost as if this storm, this whole situation is my fault! And yet I am the one trying to help them. I just don't understand!" He hated the fact that it came out as a barrage of gripes and he felt that he sounded like a petulant child.

"It's not you. It's the situation. People are having to leave their families behind. To an almost certain death. They can't *not* leave because of their children...but equally how do they reconcile themselves to the fact that they are leaving their mothers, fathers, brothers – the entire rest of their families? It's an almost impossible choice and yet really it's no choice at all."

She drew him into an embrace, eager to comfort him. "They *are* grateful to you but in general they can't show it. Because to show it would mean they have accepted the chance to live, even when others in their family will surely not survive. Can you imagine how soul destroying that must feel?" she looked solemnly into his eyes.

"Yes, I guess I can." He was saddened that it had taken her to explain all of this to him. But then again she always had been more intuitive about people than he had been. He thought about Bill Bently and the decision he had made, not to leave with them.

There had been a time when in the middle of building the ark, it had occurred to him that Sally would not be prepared to leave, because of the very same reason that Bill had refused. They too had someone they had loved, interred nearby. But even the pain of being unable to visit Lucy's final resting place any more, had not deterred Sally from their mission. Instead she had focused on the fact that they were trying to *save* other children. Other children who were *still alive*, who still had a fighting chance. It was exactly this which had motivated her and in the end, motivated him too.

"SAM! SAM, WHERE ARE YOU?" Neil arrived in front of them before his voice had stopped ricocheting around the gangway walls.

"What is it?" From the colour in the young doctor's face, there was clearly some cause for concern or excitement.

"The water is starting to come in now. It's already ankle high and rising fast."

Sam gave Sally a quick peck on the cheek. "Stay with Lucy and her mother and I'll come find you later, ok?" He smiled at her, trying to reassure her that now the time had come, all would go smoothly.

"I love you." She stated it simply and turned away.

"We need to get everyone back on board." Sam moved rapidly to the stairs and began to ascend, Neil following at his heels.

The atmosphere on the top deck had changed. Now it was charged with a feeling of electricity. Brushes and tins were abandoned as men and women fled back to the safety of the ark, huddling together and waiting for instructions on what to do next.

"Ladies, if you can please go below and calm the children, that would be good. It would also be a good idea to make sure there are no items which could do damage or injury to anyone it they fall off a shelf or anything. Please ensure that all heavy items are stowed away in the drawers and lockers and that everyone remains in their allocated cabins or dorms."

It was of course all common sense stuff but he realised from years as head of a body of research scientists, it was often the common sense things which got overlooked. And it was often these silly little things which caused the major problems in the end, he had found in his experience.

He waited till women were out of sight before continuing with the men. "I am going to need some help.

The process is largely automated but there is a lot to do. For those of you who have been assigned cabins," he avoided implying that those who had terminally ill children would be needed elsewhere, "it might be best if you helped out below decks." A small band of men departed, without argument or debate. More than two-thirds of the original number remained on deck.

"When the water level outside is high enough, for the bottom of the boat not to scrape its way up the road, we will use a series of winches and pulleys to get the ark out of here."

"Scrape its way up the road?" The speaker's tone was incredulous and Sam turned towards the voice, eager to explain and allay any fears. Dr John Stark stood before him, mouth still open and with such a look of derision on his face, that Sam was instantly worried. There was something about this man – something deeply untrustworthy, doctor or not, that made Sam's flesh crawl. Sam tried to shake it off and appear unperturbed.

"The boat will sail up the road, there is no other way. It is reinforced with steel and will not leak even if it gets scraped by cars on the road, however it is sensible to take a course of prevention rather than correction of any problems don't you think?"

Silence met his reply and he couldn't gauge how well this information had gone down. Sam couldn't help himself from continuing on, "surely as a doctor you would agree that prevention is better than cure?" It was completely the wrong thing to say, but unfortunately he only understood that in hindsight. John Stark's face darkened. The doctor's heavy features seemed to grow tauter under his skin and his complexion darkened to match the sky outside. The knot of unease in Sam's stomach tightened.

"Are you telling me we are going to lift this boat out of here?" The words were almost spat out, such was the venom in the other man's tone. White teeth flashed as Stark spoke and they put Sam in mind of a panther as it prepared to pounce.

Silence all around, as the other men present, stood and watched this confrontation take place. "There is no other way." Sam pulled himself up straight and locked eyes with the other man. There was a challenge going on here, he realised. He had to win it, or none of them had a chance of surviving.

"Sure there is another way, a better way! We can open the doors and let the water lift the boat up." Sam was saddened to see several of the men nod their agreement of this suggestion.

"That won't work for several reasons. First of all," he stopped as there was a sudden crack of thunder and hail, the size of golf balls, rained down on the roof. They could clearly be seen through the reinforced glass panels on the ceiling. They landed with such force that even though the glass was industrially strengthened, small cracks were beginning to appear in it. It would not take long for the water level to be high enough for what they needed to do.

"Time is of the essence now," he changed tack and tried to rally them round. "If we do as you suggest," he directed this at Stark, "you must be aware that the ark will not fit through the doors, even the industrial ones. And if we wait for it to be high enough to take us out through the roof, we will be waiting in the eye of the storm for too long."

"My way is safer!" Chest puffed out, John Stark displayed his teeth again in what Sam could only think of as a show of dominance. How could Bill Bently have got this man's character so wrong, he wondered. Then again, Bill had only seen him in the hospital environment. Things were not quite the same now.

"Your way will see us all killed!" It was a more direct comment than he would have liked but he hoped it would do the trick. "You are a doctor. But I am a scientist and an *engineer* and I *built* this boat." It was a necessary statement of dominance and Sam hoped that it put the man in his place without robbing him of respect. The assembled men seemed to turn away from Stark and towards Sam, looking at him as if ready to do his bidding. But John Stark burned with fury. Like an actual heat, he could feel it radiating off Stark, directed like a solar flare in Sam's direction.

Right now, Stark was not a problem he was going to be able to resolve. Without moving an inch, lest he appeared to be turning his back on Stark, he spoke to the other men. "I need two men over there by the winch controls, and two men stationed there, keeping an eye on the water level." He pointed at the men and where they should go so that no more time would be lost.

"Everyone else needs to untie the lines that bind the ark to its supporting cradle and then secure the ropes so they are not trailing or tangled." He purposely kept his voice calm and measured. They were fast approaching a time of grave danger and concern but it would not do to have these men worked up, or more anxious than they already were, for that was when they were more likely to make mistakes.

From the corner of his eye, he saw Stark turn abruptly on his heel and stomp off, below decks. Unable to take command, he was clearly unwilling to do anything required of him. There was a hideous feeling of childish temper tantrum about the man, Sam decided. It was not like the ignorant stupidity and pig-headedness of some of the general population that Sam had from time to time encountered in his life. This was a more dangerous insolence, he felt.

Born not of ignorance, but instead a cunning intelligence, it masked a giant ego and a possible personality disorder. Sam was no psychiatrist, but he would have staked his life on that belief. He hoped Sally was safely tucked away in a cabin, well away from where Stark stormed off to. The problem that was Doctor John Stark had only just begun, he feared.

Sam wished he could risk the time to check on Sally but he knew his duty was to get the ark launched. "Could you check on the occupants of Cabin 15 and ask my wife if she is ok?" he asked one of the men discretely, reassuring himself that all would be ok. The man finished tying off the rope he held and hurried off.

In the rush of all the activity, Sam realised that he had forgotten about the noise of the hailstones. It hadn't disappeared or stopped, it was more like he had tuned it out, raised his voice above it and ignored it, as if it were nothing more than 'white noise'. As if nature abhorred this disregard of its very worst outbursts, it seemed to step up the size of the pellets of hail and the violence with which it unleashed them from on high. Huge balls of ice, some the size of small oranges, smashed into the tempered glass above their heads, starring it so that it began to appear milky and opaque.

"The water has reached the level," called one of the two men monitoring the gauge, which electronically informed them of the flood level outside the building.

"Pull the levers to start the winches," he instructed the men, stationed at the other side of the ark. The men did as requested and there was an immediate explosion of noise as machinery cranked into life. A judder ran through the boat and was answered in a rumbling in Sam's bowels. Here was the moment of reckoning, he thought.

"Everyone below decks, hurry! Find your families and stay with them!" he shouted, above the racket of the storm and machines. He watched them flee to the relative safety of below decks. He himself stood firm above deck, as the ark began its slow ascent, through the retracting ceiling and into the full fury of the storm.

Chapter 26

Georgia thought there was an almost majestic quality to the debris which floated towards them. Serene in its movement, it glided on tranquil waters which ebbed and swirled around their boat. Little bits of things; a piece of wood, a rubber wheel, a piece of fabric that looked like it might have been a curtain. All these things and more passed them by.

Like a strange conveyor belt, the water carried the items along, seemingly passing them by the boat for inspection. The rain had stopped or once more they had drifted out of its range and it was easy to spot the various floating items as they passed them by. But it was a weirdly eerie guessing game to play.

There were no landmarks to indicate where they might be, only the insistent arm of the compass, showing direction. One thing was very clear however – they were in an area which had already been flood devastated. In theory therefore, they ought to be safe from other storms.

The only problem was – and she had to be honest, it was a biggie – there was no dry land in sight anywhere. How long would it be before the water started to dissipate? How long before they came upon some people? Because surely there were some survivors? There had been rescue operations, she knew that but surely *somewhere* here there would be other people, wouldn't there, she wondered.

The boat moved slowly onwards, its speed restricted by the need to be careful and also a desire to be economical with the fuel supply. Something a dark fuchsia colour attracted her attention ahead and she focused on it, trying to identify what it was. Narrowing her concentration, she knew there was something familiar about its size and shape but still identification evaded her. Other objects drifted around the thing but she paid them no heed, they were darker coloured and had not captured her interest in the way the brightly coloured thing had.

Away at the back of her head a little voice insisted that she should look at the bigger picture, rather than on one little pixilation of it. But she ignored the insistent voice. So much had happened over the past day or so, that her mind sought just a little refuge from the constant barrage of problems.

"Watch out for that log!" Katie called to her brothers, calling their attention to a particularly large obstacle, directly in their path. "Oh!" The sound was wheezed out of the girl, carried on a breath which had no power.

The sound brought Georgia's attention sharply back into focus. The log to which the girl referred was not a log at all. It was a body.

Water bloated and face down, it was impossible to tell how old the person was but from the short hair which slicked to the head and the style of clothing, jeans and man's shirt, it was clear that it was a male.

And that bright pink thing? It came clear into view and Georgia's stomach churned at the sight. A doll. A little plastic baby doll wearing a bright pink dress, unblinking blue eyes staring into the sky, pink rosebud lips pursed in a permanent kiss.

Georgia grabbed Katie and pulled the girl tight into her, burying her face away from the awful sight. Katie had already seen the man's body and had recognised it for what it was but it would be too much for her to see the doll. To make the connections she would undoubtedly already make in her head. Georgia looked across to the two boys, who continued to steer and control the speed of the boat.

Faces ashen they turned to her, tears stinging their eyes. "Go to Georgia, Jim-Bob," Ben instructed. "I can do the speed and the steering for a while," he insisted.

Georgia would have loved to have wrapped them all up in cotton wool. Saved their delicate hearts from these sights but it was not possible and it broke her own heart. She noticed the omission of the title 'Aunt' in Ben's instruction. It was an indication of how he was trying to adapt, to be more grown up, to deal with the situation and protect them all.

But that was her job. She looked back through the window. There were other bodies, or at least she suspected that's what some on the things which floated towards them now were. It was after all, an educated guess.

"Swap with me Ben. You navigate and I will steer and Katie and Jim-Bob can have a rest." It wasn't much of an improvement for Ben, he would still have to see the bodies but at least he didn't have to take the responsibility of trying not to hit them with the boat.

"Can we…?" He was unable to finish the sentence but she knew what he was trying to say. "No, honey we can't help them. It's too late for them." He nodded his acceptance and kept his eyes fixed firmly on the water.

Deeper and deeper they ploughed through the bodies, sometimes missing them altogether and sometimes bumping into them with a jarring motion, when the bodies flowed too thick on both sides to be completely avoided. Each time it happened, her stomach lurched a little and she found herself silently apologising to the spirits of these unfortunate people. Perhaps in reality it didn't matter anymore. Their bodies were mere vessels anyway and their need for them was gone…and yet, it felt like an affront to the people they had been, to treat them as irrelevant.

Roofs of buildings came suddenly into view, their walls and structures still fully submerged. From what she could see it had been a smallish town, perhaps not more than a few hundred people. How many of them had survived she wondered. And how many had cowered in these very buildings, hoping the storm would just die out? But it hadn't.

"We will have to be very careful now Ben," she slowed the boat right down till it was only a fraction off stopping. Her natural inclination was to get the kids the hell out of this place but she had to curb it. If they tore through here, they could well damage the boat and then

....well that train of thought was better left unfinished, she thought.

Seeming to be unable to talk, Ben merely nodded his agreement. She wondered what damage this was doing him psychologically. It was not something she could prevent but that did not make it any less worrying.

"We need to avoid the buildings...even if that means..." what was she supposed to say? 'Even if that means running over the dead people?' It was an impossible situation. "Even if that means going through some other things," she gulped out. *'Other things.'* What a terrible way to refer to these bodies, these corpses which had once been someone's mother, someone's father, someone's *child*. She couldn't stop a shiver going down her body. Was Ben thinking about his parents? Was he worried that they too floated somewhere just like this?

She blinked hard, trying to clear her head and concentrate on the present predicament. Steering hard to the right, she slid the boat through a narrow gap between two buildings, only just missing one by a hand span.

"Left, left, hard left!" Ben shouted too loud for the close confines of the cabin in his fear. Georgia looked right. There only slightly to the one side of them, protruded a spire, the likes of which are often found adorning the tops of fancy temples and churches. It stuck out above the waterline, as if to show that God and nature's wrath had not been confined to the unrighteous. That this time, all of humanity had been judged and found wanting.

A small stained glass window overlooked the flood. Smaller than one she had ever seen before, it seemed somehow more intimate, seen from this close up. From the fact that they were virtually level with the window,

Georgia could determine that it was an image of The Virgin Mary, cradling her child to her bosom, protecting it from harm. She hoped it was a good omen.

Pulling hard to the left as Ben had directed, moved the boat away from the temple before it collided with it and Georgia watched the coloured glass move further and further away, losing its clarity of image as it became more distant.

She let out a sigh of relief and watched as Ben did the same. The water ahead was free of protrusions or floating debris. They had navigated the town and come through the other side.

But just as she had that thought, there was a huge grinding sound and the boat listed to one side. A tremor shook the boat and like a deliberate strike on a tuning fork, travelled all the way up her body till it reached her teeth, where it ended in a clash of upper molars with lower ones.

Something which lay hidden underneath the water had banged into the bottom of the boat and from the feel of the collision, it wasn't going to have caused no damage.

She held her breath. Eyes wide, she looked at each of the children in turn. It was too much. Too much for them all. And yet they were going to have to deal with whatever fate threw at them once more.

A trickle of water appeared below her feet. In horror she fell to her knees and cupped her hands, scooping it up and trying to stem the flow. More water seeped through and the boat gave a little lurch sideways. It wasn't much but it catapulted the children into action. Grabbing cups and bowls they tried to bale the water out, but as fast as they scooped it out, it came back.

Sweat soaking into her top, Georgia stopped a moment and tried to assess the situation objectively. The hole that had been torn in the bottom of the boat must have been getting bigger, as water seemed to be filling the boat faster and faster. They couldn't mend the hole. They couldn't just drive the boat away, it would just fill up with water and sink. They couldn't abandon the boat.

Except that they had to do exactly one of those things. There was nowhere to go to. Only the rooftops they had just passed. A picture came into her head then. An image of a brightly clad woman and child, the shades picked out in vivid tinted glass. The church or temple, whatever that building actually was, would have to be their salvation.

A flicker of double entered her mind. What if there was no level high enough to have escaped the flood, within the building. She scoured her memory for her insignificant architectural knowledge on places of worship. The last time she had been in such a place had been at a colleague's wedding. The memory did not help much as she was sure its steeple was much smaller than the one she had just seen.

Perhaps some churches had bigger steeples than others, perhaps some of the steeples had their own floor, above that of the church itself. Georgia did not have a religious bone in her body but she prayed now. She prayed that there was a floor there which was untouched by flood.

"Leave it. We have to leave the boat."

The children all looked at her as if she had gone stark raving mad.

"What do you mean, we can't *leave* the boat?" Ben shrieked at her, terror making him able to challenge an adult in a way he would not have dared before. Katie and Jim-Bob watched silently, their eyes moving from their brother to Georgia and back again.

"We don't have much time and we will have even less if you don't listen!" Her voice was firm and commanding. There was no good appealing to his common sense, he was too terrified for that to work. All that would work now was to override him, to make him aware once more that he was the child and she the adult. It relied a lot on the fact that he was a good and respectful boy and generally did as he was told. But it would take a toll on both of them, she knew. For her it would be a guilt trip, to manipulate him in this manner and for him, it would be a slap in the face after all the responsibilities he had so recently shouldered. But once more, there was really no choice.

"Help me get this off!" She hauled at the ripped and torn weather shield, pulling it off the boat and into the cabin. Ben's eyes remained riveted on the water, which continued to pool on the floor.

"Ben! Help me!"

Finally he turned and did as he was bid.

"Get the light boxes onto here and help me wrap them up so they will stay dry and float." There weren't many boxes they could save. Most were filled with tins and heavy items which would cause the whole package to sink.

"But the boat will float, won't it? It's made of wood." Jim-Bob seemed to be struggling with the idea of the boat sinking.

"When there's too much water on board, I think it will just sink. So we need to get out what we can first." She finished tying up the bundle and bound it firmly with a rope. She then tied the other end of the rope around her middle.

Grabbing the lifebelt she had previously been saved by, she hooked it around Katie and gave the girl a kiss.

"What about our clothes?" the girl asked her.

"I think it's more important that we save ourselves and as much food as possible," she explained. "We are going to swim back to that church tower we passed. Is everyone ok with that?" she saw the doubt in their eyes and remembered the last problems they had had with being in the water.

"Hold onto the rope around me, and we will stay together and help each other ok?" They all nodded fearfully. Together they slid the food parcel into the water then slipped into its cold murkiness one by one.

The spire was about the same distance away as the length of two Olympic swimming pools laid end to end. It was quite a distance for them to swim, but once again they had no option.

Huffing along slowly, the children splashing ineffectually at her side, she worried that they would expend all their energy before they even got halfway there. She kicked out hard with her legs and forced her way through the water, trying to drag them on faster, in her wake.

'Please don't let us bump into any bodies,' she begged in her head, keeping her eyes on the stained glass window as it came closer and closer and closer into view.

Chapter 27

It was Roxie who noticed it first and for some strange reason that didn't strike either Jack or Dan as being the least bit unusual. A sharp series of barks and an almost comical turning of her head to indicate which way they should look and they almost had no choice but to do as the dog wanted.

A little shack of a shop, it probably hadn't been used as a shop in many a year. The door stood slightly ajar as if inviting them in. The hinges were rusty and the door itself was swollen by water damage. The door would never be any good again but even so, it took some shifting to get it open enough for them to enter.

"Gone away on vacation," Dan read the weathered sign still pinned to the inside of the glass panel on the door.

"Must have been one heck of a vacation," Jack laughed, "cos it looks like they never came back!"

"Do you think…?" Dan's face reflected his fear that the shop owners would be inside, their bloated corpses all maggot and fly infested.

"No. This shop was deserted long before the floods came." He was sure of that. He indicated back towards the open road beyond the doorway. "Probably just not enough business around here anymore. I would imagine it was run by an old couple who went on vacation and just couldn't find the will to come back."

Dan nodded and turned his attention to Roxie who was busy sniffing everything vigorously. Shelves lined every wall and there were two isles down the middle of the shop. The items on the bottom shelves were clearly rotten but there was a variety of thing on the higher shelves which although dusty and grimy, looked otherwise unscathed.

A hammer and a set of pens sat side by side; it was the most incongruous grouping of items Dan had ever seen and from what he could tell, the whole store was the same. Bin liners sat next to a few dusty novels which in turn, rested against a packet of stainless steel cutlery.

"There won't be any food here. Or at least if there is, I don't think it would be safe to eat. But there may be other things we could make use of." Jack thought of Dan's bad arm and quietly scanned the shelves for any medication he could find.

Something caught Dan's eye. A hardback lined notebook. Reaching impulsively for it, he brushed away the dust from its cover and opened it up. Pristine white pages overlaid with faint blue lines met his eyes and it was a wondrous sight. He knew instinctively what he would use it for. He tucked it under his arm and returned to where he had seen the pens.

"What you found?" enquired Jack.

"Just a notebook and some pens…oh!" Turning into the next isle, Dan was surprised at what he found there. Jack followed behind. "What is it?" The anxious tone back in his voice, he followed Dan's gaze to the top shelf above him.

"Hmm. Now there's an idea." Jack seemed to be talking to himself and Dan wasn't inclined to butt in. Instead he continued to gaze at the beautifully polished mahogany wood of the coffin which rested on the highest shelf in front of him.

Roxie came round the aisle, tail wagging and feet swishing noisily in the water. Seeing the two humans whose attention was so focused elsewhere, she cocked her head sideways and waited to see what was so interesting.

"It's a coffin." Immediately the words were out of his mouth, Dan felt foolish. Of course it was a coffin, that was obvious, wasn't it? Then something else occurred to him. "There isn't a …"

Jack cut him short. "No, no, there's no one in it."

Dan wondered how Jack could know this for definite as even he could not see into the inside of the coffin from where it was stacked, its base level with his eyes.

"Help me get it down from there."

The request surprised Dan. Why would they want a coffin? What good could it possibly be to them? He was reluctant to even touch the thing. In a way it was irrelevant that it didn't contain a dead body. It had been crafted and built exactly for that specific purpose and that was creepy enough for him.

Pulling over a small ladder, Jack waited till Dan had climbed up, before he reached up and grabbed his end of the coffin. From his added height, Dan was relieved to see that the lid was firmly on and that no gruesome discovery awaited him.

Putting the book and pens he had found on a shelf once more, he reached out his hands but couldn't quite bring himself to touch the smooth wood or the cool metal of the shiny brass handles. He recoiled from the coffin, jerking his whole body away so fiercely, that the ladder clattered noisily against the shelves and Jack had to catch him and stabilise him, otherwise he would have fallen.

"Sorry," he looked apologetically at his uncle.

"It's ok Dan, these are weird days and we are gonnna have to do equally weird things to survive." It was a rather cryptic comment, but Dan wasn't inclined to ask for elaboration.

Mustering up his courage he thrust his hands against the handles. Cool in his hands, they neither burned him up on contact, nor self-detonated to spew foul contents all over him. He took a large breath and shouldered the weight of his end till Jack could manoeuvre himself into the middle of it and hoist it onto his shoulder.

Dan climbed off the steps and watched the coffin being carried carefully to the old serving counter, before picking up the book and pens once more.

"Clean and not too fussily lined, thankfully." Jack seemed pleased by what he had found on opening the lid. He replaced it over the casket and carried it out to the truck.

Dan used the time he was gone to search for dog food. There were a couple of cans lurking on a shelf and he snatched them up. Arms bulging now with items, he realised he would have to find something to carry the things they took in. There would surely be bags behind the serving counter?

There were. But unfortunately they were all of the paper variety and had long succumbed to water damage and just rotted away. But there was something else there too. A rag, bundled and scrunched up, it was hidden behind a load of miscellaneous stuff, just discarded behind the serving area. From the look and feel of the material he recognised it as oilskin cloth. He pulled it out of its hiding place and smoothed it onto the counter before piling all his finds on top of it.

"Woof, woof!"

He walked over to where Roxie's attention was fixated on a small furry toy cat. Dan smiled and tossed the toy in the air where it was deftly caught by the leaping dog. Dan grinned and ruffled the dog's shaggy mane of hair.

Jack watched unseen from the doorway. To be able to take each moment of life as a present, was a real gift. To be able to live for the here and now and not in the past or the future was a real blessing and Jack hoped that Dan would long be able to continue to do so. He had no idea what lay ahead of them but one thing was for sure, it was not going to be an easy ride. He had hoped they might find a boat here, a dingy or something but there had been none. But they had found a coffin and beggars could never be choosers he reminded himself.

"Anything else worth having?" he asked the boy.

"Couple of tins of dog food which I think should be ok as there is no rust on the tins. Other than the notebook I found, that's about it. I've put the stuff on the counter in a waterproof rag I found."

Jack nodded his approval. Walking slowly around the aisles he satisfied himself that there was nothing more they could make use of. He picked up a torch but on examination found that the metal bits inside had corroded away. He replaced the torch carefully on the shelf. He knew he could just have dropped it at his feet but that wasn't the right thing to do. For some reason it was important that he maintain the veneer of civilised living for as long as it proved possible to do so. He wasn't sure if this was for Dan's sake or his own, but he felt it was true.

Finally, bundle secured under Dan's arm, they left the shop as they had found it, even taking the time to shift the swollen door back to where it had been when they arrived.

Back in the car, the mood was lighter than it had been. Jack thought that was mostly due to the antics of Roxie who continued to chomp and chew on the furry toy and every so often to toss it in the air before collecting it again in her big teeth, making Dan laugh with delight.

Jack was glad that Dan was otherwise occupied. It meant that he was less aware of the worsening conditions they were driving through. It was raining, neither heavily nor lightly. Instead, it lingered in between those two states. But the water which lay on the road was becoming deeper and deeper and there were places now where at times he wasn't sure if they still travelled on the road at all, or were merely travelling alongside it.

Stomach tight with apprehension, Jack kept driving onwards, straight on and on, round bends and over crossroads, each twist and turn bringing him closer to his destination - and it crossed his mind, more than once - closer to their possible ruination.

Turning a sharp bend with care, he slammed on the brakes as the road ahead came into view. The car slewed a little and Dan looked up from petting Roxie.

They had been climbing a hill. Slowly but surely going upwards. The gradient had been negligible and neither of them had noticed the ascent. Now at the very top of the hill, with a sharp drop ahead of them, it was more than obvious.

But what made the very pit of Jack's stomach squirm, was the condition of the road at the dip at the bottom. Like a huge swimming pool, the road was completely submerged. No road or markings could be seen at all.

To make bad things even worse, there was no way other than this road to get to where they were going. Barriers lined both sides of the road, a sheet of mountainous rock on one side and what looked to be a sheer drop on the other. Nor was it an option to just backtrack to the last fork in the road. This was the way they had to go. No choice.

'Besides,' Jack told himself, 'this is what it's gonna be like everywhere from here on really!' He steeled himself for what he was about to do. "Get in the back." He turned off the engine for a moment and climbed out. Dan and Roxie followed.

Unhooking the tailgate, Jack lifted the dog into the back of the truck and helped the boy climb up. "Wait a moment," he said and pulling the fabric bundle out of the car, he opened it up and piled all their remaining medicine and food into the centre of it, alongside the tins of dog food and notebook. He tied it back together again as tightly as possible.

"The bag is not waterproof, but this is, so it will do a better job," he explained. Dan wondered what the better job was but dared not ask. "Come on we need to hurry!" Jack jumped into the back with them. He was parked at the top of a blind bend. Irrational as it may have been since they hadn't seen a single other vehicle in over a day, he had this fear that another car or truck would come along behind them and not see them there, till the very last moment, just before it crashed into them.

He could dismiss the fear in his head as ridiculous but his heart would not let it go. He pulled the lid off the coffin and watched Dan's face turn grey as he confronted the white padding and satin lining. "Climb in!"

"WHAT! YOU HAVE TO BE JOKING!" Dan could not help it from coming out as a shout, he was so stunned.

"We don't have a boat! The truck can't get through that, it's too deep," Jack pointed down the hill, "everywhere from here on in will be flooded and the box is made of wood. It will float." He had had to make a careful effort to substitute the word 'box' for 'coffin'.

"But...but it's a coffin." Dan protested.

"No, it was *going* to be a coffin," Jack worked hard to build an argument because this just had to be done, "but now it's *going* to be a boat!" He patted the inside of the coffin and was relieved when Roxie jumped straight in without hesitation. Dan followed more hesitantly.

"Put this on the space between you and Roxie and hold on tight." He handed Dan the bundle. "We will be going down the hill slowly but when I hit the water I will have no control over what happens next."

"But what about you?" Dan's face showed his horror. Jack looked at the boy and dog sitting in the coffin. There was hardly enough room for the two of them, let alone him as well. And then there was the weight to think of. The coffin by itself would float, but laden with too much weight, it would in the worst case sink and in the best, lie extremely low in the water. How much weight was too much? Well that was probably a question that he would soon have an answer to.

"The tailgate will have to stay down. You won't fall out of the back because we are heading downhill but when we get there it will level out and the box should be able to float away." It certainly sounded like a good plan to his ears.

"I will keep my window down and when we hit the water, I'll climb out and join you in the makeshift boat." He smiled, hoping that and the idea of an adventure would be enough for the boy.

"There's no other way, is there?" Dan asked hopefully.

"There's no other way."

Dan nodded slowly and turned away to look at the dog for a moment. When he turned back Jack was sad to see that his eyes were shimmering with tears. "You know I love you, right, Uncle Jack?" It was gulped out.

"I know. But it would be really great if you could tell me that again tomorrow and the next day," he smiled at the boy, ruffling his hair and trying to make light of the situation and provide some reassurance at the same time.

"Yeah, I will," spoken gruffly, Jack was struck by how Dan was having to grow up before his time. It was a sad, sad thing. Jack climbed back into the truck.

Heart hammering against his ribcage, he switched on the ignition and slowly moved down the hill. On the verge of entering the water he had to stop himself from slamming on the brakes and instead try to gently ease the truck into the water. As if in a dream, he watched the water rise inside the truck, felt the weight of the vehicle shift and then settle. It didn't take long for the water to be swirling around his hips and still he sat, watching it as if mesmerised.

"UNCLE JACK! UNCLE JACK!"

The shrieks brought him out of his trance-like state. Fumbling fingers found the seatbelt release button and then the open window beckoned. It was a tight squeeze but he was through the window without too much trouble.

And then the truck was gone. Almost fully submerged, all that could be seen of it was the roof. And where was Dan? Frantically he scanned where he thought the truck bed ended. Had the coffin sunk, after all? Jack felt his heart seize in fear and a blinding pain shot across his head from temple to temple.

"UNCLE JACK OVER HERE!"

Jack swivelled in the water. Taken by the current, the coffin had already floated off some way. Jack struck out strongly, helped along by the flowing water, in the same direction the boy was travelling in.

Reaching the boy took the very last of his energy. He grasped the side of the coffin. Reacting to his weight, the coffin tilted dangerously towards him, threatening to overturn at any moment.

"We will lean this way till you climb in," Dan seemed to have worked out the dynamics of the situation and pulled himself and the dog as far towards the water on the other side as was possible so as to reinstate the boat's equilibrium.

Jack found the strength to pull himself up and in. The coffin sank a little lower in the water but did not sink. Between them, they shuffled themselves into some kind of order, sitting cross legged so as to take up as little space as possible.

They drifted.

For a very long time, they let the boat take its own course.

Then for a very long time afterwards, Jack wished they had had some way of changing course as one after another, rotten bloated corpses began to float past them.

At first both he and Dan had heaved into the water, emptying their stomachs of any nourishment it had been able to have recently. After a while, the sight no longer affected them. And in a way, Jack though that was the worst thing of all – that they had almost become immune to it.

Roofs, the houses below completely flooded, passed them by and Jack began to despair.

There was nothing here.

Nothing and no one.

Until a barely seen face appeared at a broken window, in what appeared to be the spire of an old church. And until a barely heard voice beckoned, "over here! Come over here!"

Chapter 28

S am knew it was madness to stand there, alone on the top deck as the winches raised him directly into the fury of the storm. Hail pounded through the open skylights, as the ark headed slowly but surely up and through the opening. But miraculously he remained unscathed. As though blessed with divine protection, the hailstones vented their wrath on every side of him and yet none came near enough to bruise, let alone harm him.

He was aware that what he was doing was unnecessary; he had built the ark so that it could be steered and completely controlled from within its hull. And yet here he was, compelled for some reason to be out in the elements, seeing first-hand that everything was working ok.

In a way it was logical. Indeed wasn't it what was expected of every Captain? But these were not normal, logical times. He hoped Sally was ok. He had not had time to have the man report back to him about that.

Then again, Stark didn't strike him as the sort of man who would do anything openly. He was much more of an underhand sort of man than that, Sam thought.

Through the skylight now, the ark hovered mid-air with only the winch to support its vast weight. The sky was black as night, all daylight eclipsed by the ferocity of the storm. Like a scene from a nightmare, shards of lightning struck at buildings in a seemingly random manner and spirals of smoke from all directions, indicated that many buildings were now ablaze.

Sam tried but could not look away. From his position he felt like he was on top of the world, watching humanity's demise. Watching civilisations crumble.

And like a wrathful God, he was now going to throw his little bit of destruction into the pot as well. He had lied to these people. Not fully, just a little and for their own protection. But a lie was after all, still a lie.

The ark swung sideways, throwing him off balance and he staggered before finding his footing again. He took a small remote control device from his pocket, and as the ark began its descent, he pressed the control button. A judder passed through the boat and he knew that the caterpillar tracks were being lowered from where up till now, they had been hidden inside the very bottom of the hull.

It had always been unlikely that they could have merely sailed out of New York. Not only was the flood water unlikely at this stage to have been high enough as to have lifted them above the levels of cars and trucks, but the ark was several levels high and heavy. Its water line was positioned so that at least one level would be below water and whilst it was true that the hull was unlikely to ever be breached, it could easily be grounded or stuck in place.

Hence the need for the caterpillar wheels. They would literally just roll over everything in their path, till that was no longer a necessity and they could then be retracted. That was where the lie lived. To have misinformed these people that they were going to sail out of here, when in fact they were going to half sail and half crush over everything in their path.

He wasn't proud of the lie but he had learned that sometimes hard decisions had to be taken by one, for the good of the whole. And that was what he had done.

Alone on deck, he watched as the ark settled itself on the flooded road. Only the odd car roof could be seen now ahead. But others were covered by the flood water already. Did it matter how the ark got over these obstacles? Whether it sailed over, or drove? He knew in his heart that it did matter. That it mattered very much. Regardless of the fact that any occupants of these cars were undoubtedly deceased already, the idea of just rolling right over them and crushing them in the process was repugnant. That's why he had kept the wheels a secret, even from Sally.

A shard of hail struck his leg hard. He winced. Perhaps his divine immunity had ended, with his decision to use the wheels at whatever cost to his soul. It was perhaps a fanciful idea but he could not shift it from his mind. Hands raised over his head, he moved towards the refuge of the inside of the ark.

Grasping the handle of the doors, he pulled but they resisted. He pulled again and heard a faint clatter from the other side. The bolt was engaged! He was locked out! He thudded on the door, terrified that the pounding of his blows were being masked by the general pounding of the hail all around him. And still the door remained locked.

★★★

"Georgia, there's someone out there." Ben's voice cut through her exhaustion. She had been trying to figure out what they did next. The boat was useless now and although they had some food, it would not last forever. The floods were still high and it pretty much looked like a waiting game.

"Ben it will be more…" how she was going to finish the sentence, she had no idea. By explaining that there would probably be more and more bodies as time went on, till finally the flood washed them all away and the water went down? She sighed, defeated.

Ben continued to look out of the window. A rectangular box floated closer and closer to them and he was sure there were people in it. Three people! No, that was wrong…two people and a dog. Undeterred by Georgia's assertion that there was no one alive nearby, he decided to call to them. "Hello!" he cried as loudly as possible. There was no reaction. Neither of the people looked up, even the dog didn't seem to notice.

Cupping his hands around his mouth in an attempt to amplify the sound, he tried again. "Over here. Come over here!"

This time there was a reaction.

★★★

Sally felt the juddering of the ark as it was moved outside and into the storm. There was a strange rumbling too but she dismissed this as part of the operational sounds of the boat moving.

An urgent knocking alerted her to the fact that someone was outside of her cabin. She hurried to open the door.

"Sam sent me to check you are ok. I was told to go to Cabin 15 but they told me you had already left and where you would be," the man panted.

"Yes, I am fine," Sally's brow furrowed at the man's obvious anxiety on her behalf. "I will find Sam now and tell him myself. Thank you." She smiled in a placatory way.

"He's on the top deck."

It was said as a statement of fact but something about the way the man's eyes shifted away from her as he spoke, let her know how dangerous he considered that to be.

"I wouldn't have thought so now. The ark is outside," she indicated the small porthole, set so high up that all that could be seen from it was the dark grey sky, "and it is moving, so he must be in the control room, sailing us."

"I don't think so…" The man was more than hesitant, she decided now, he was positively doubtful. Sally's breath caught and without further ado she flew from the cabin.

★★★

Was it some sort of hallucination, brought on by exhaustion and fear, wondered Jack or was there really someone up there beckoning and calling to them?

"Dan, do you see what I see?" he asked tentatively.

Dan followed his gaze. "What...oh...there's someone up there! THERE'S SOMEONE UP THERE!" he bellowed the second time, in his excitement. He tried to stand up, frantically waving his arms back and forth.

"DAN. STOP. You are making us wobble too much and we will capsize!" Jack urged.

Dan stopped moving and instead sat very still. "Hello up there!" he called, excitement making his voice a little higher pitched than usual.

Jack laughed. In a way it was all so surreal. Corpses floated around them in every direction and they seemed to be exchanging salutations back and forth from a coffin to a church spire. How weird things had gotten.

***

Sally entered the control room in a flurry of expectation but she drew herself up sharp at the sight of John Stark at the controls.

"Oh it's you," she struggled to keep the emphasis off the word 'you'. "I thought Sam would be here," she looked around the confines of the small room as if it were possible that she had just failed to spot him. He was nowhere to be seen. "Where is he?" she asked lightly, wondering if it were possible that he had gone to look for her, just as she came to him and that somehow they had missed each other.

"Search me!" Stark replied.

It was delivered so flippantly, so almost sneeringly, that Sally immediately knew something was severely wrong. She thought back to Sam's last known position. The top deck! Was it possible he was still there? In the storm? She cast a glance through the large front windows at the view which had previously only been glimpsed in disaster movies, never before in real life. Was it possible that Sam was out there in all this?

She threw herself out of the room and ran towards the stairs leading to the upper deck. The bolt was drawn tightly across the doors which led to the outside, locking them firmly from within.

She drew back the bolt.

★★★

"It is! There are people out there! And they have a dog!" Ben was almost leaping up and down, shaking the thin floorboards on which they all sat, huddled together.

They were safe here, even if there was not that much room and the foul dank smell of the water which had flooded the lower levels of the building, still made them sneeze from time to time. But was there room for more people, Georgia wondered. *And* a dog? No point in worrying about it really, for there was no choice in the matter. Besides which, if both or even only one of the other people was an adult, then they would surely be of help to each other.

She jostled with the children for a view from the window. They crowded round, willing the occupants of the wooden box to come closer and closer.

With a sharp intake of breath she realised what the wooden box actually was. A coffin! What sort of people took refuge in a coffin? A little pulse of worry threaded itself around her heart.

★★★

Sam could see Sally. In fact Sam could see three lots of Sally. Problem was, he didn't know which one was the real her. He tried to raise a hand to stroke her soft hair, touch her warm cheeks but although he thought the movement clearly out in his head, his hands and arms would not respond.

"Rest darling. You need to rest," Sally brought her three faces down to kiss him but only one of them did. He felt her lips brush his head and linger a moment as if she could impart some of her strength into him. Sam drifted back into unconsciousness.

Sally crept out, leaving one of the paramedics in charge of her husband.

"Who locked those doors?" she demanded of the men assembled in the gangway, outside the cabin. She had called together every man who had been on deck with Sam before he had sent them all below. All denied locking the doors.

It could of course have been any one of them. They had no reason to do so but it could merely have been a simple mistake. But she had a feeling that wasn't the case. It wasn't any of these men here. She knew who it was. And she knew it through pure intuition, the way that a person can sense when he is being watched or followed. Something about the way the hairs felt on the back of her neck whenever she saw John Stark, told her it was he who had locked the doors.

She sent the innocent men away, back to their families and went instead to find the man who was proving to be her nemesis. John Stark.

★★★

"Put this round the dog and we can haul it up," instructed Georgia, throwing the lifebelt carefully out of the window, so that it remained in reach of the man but didn't hit anyone. She held firmly onto the end of the rope which let from the belt.

From the size of the other person with the man, she judged him to be a teenager or possibly a pre-teen. Anything else was impossible to tell as he sat with his back to her, unable to turn around lest it capsize the coffin he shared with the man and dog.

The dog was thinner than it should have been and the lifebelt was loose around its middle. The man bound it in, using some of the slack from the rope. "She's ready," he called, "but take her in easy. This girl has had a hard time of it."

Georgia prepared to let go of her initial anxieties. A man who was this concerned about an animal could not be all bad, she reasoned.

Finished tying the dog into the lifebelt, Jack gave her a kiss on the forehead and told her, "don't worry Roxie. You are gonna be just dandy soon." He couldn't really see the woman, all he could determine was that she had long dark hair and a voice that sounded as if she knew how to cope in an emergency. He watched the dog being hoisted up and taken in through the small window.

"Do you want the belt sent back out?" The woman's face appeared at the window again but this time she was leaning out, offering him a good view of her features. She was stunning. What were the chances of that happening? Perhaps fate was stepping in. On the other hand, since it seemed to be the end of the world, perhaps he just thought she was beautiful in the absence of other women to compare her to?

"Do you want the lifebelt, Dan?" he asked, eyeing the rough stone and figuring that the woman had probably had to climb up there herself using the stone as handholds.

"No, I'll climb up." Dan shuffled to the side, preparing to begin. Jack kept his arms paddling in the water, attempting to keep the coffin as close to the window as possible.

But in that moment of turning towards the wall below the window, Dan glanced up.

"Georgia!"

"Dan!"

The exclamations came simultaneously. Uttered on a gasp on both parts, they ended with laughter, Dan laughing with joy so hard that he nearly lost his balance and ended up in the water.

How did these two know each other? Jack racked his brain. Then the answer came to him. This was 'Aunt Georgia', the aunt of the children Dan had befriended. Jack took a good look at the woman again. She had a face that could easily have graced a glossy magazine. *This* was Aunt Georgia? Wonders never ceased.

Chapter 29

He had been out cold for a long, long time. He could tell that both by the stale taste in his mouth and also by the way his limbs and head ached as if they had long lay immobile.

He tried to stand but found that his legs were not yet ready to support him.

"Get back to bed, Sam White!" Sally's voice was strong but it did not have that worried tone in it anymore he noticed. That had to be a good sign.

"How long have I been out?" he asked.

"A whole day. But everything is fine and you needed the rest. You are lucky to be alive!" she softened her tone, "*I am lucky* that you are still alive. What would I do without you, Sam?" He wasn't sure if it was a question or a ticking-off. He made another attempt to stand, this time his knees did not feel quite so weak as before.

"You were out in the storm. Lord knows how many giant hail stones hit you but you were unconscious when we got to you."

He picked up the slight hesitation in the words 'got to you' and wondered what she wasn't telling him. His memory of what happened on deck was as like a block of Swiss cheese – full of holes.

"Who has been sailing the ark?" Even as the question left his mouth, he knew the answer.

"John Stark."

He knew by the way she said it that the idea horrified her even though she was loath to say so. "He seems to be doing a perfectly fine job and we are well out of the storms now."

"Help me up," he asked her, knowing that she was reluctant but that she would help anyway. He held out his hands to her and she took them and helped him stand. She knew better than to try and change this stubborn man's mind.

Slowly they made their way to the control room. He was surprised to see so many people buzzing around, sorting this and that. Everyone he passed said hello and wished him well. Everyone seemed to have a smile on their face.

It was the strangest thing to behold. As if they were aliens, unable to comprehend the disaster they had just evaded, the passengers seemed to be behaving as if it was the most natural thing in their lives, to be living here, on board an *ark*. Looking blankly at the twentieth person who enquired after his health, Sam found himself speechless. He turned to Sally for an explanation.

"I guess it's human nature dear. The mind just has to accept situations sometimes or go insane. At least they are getting on with looking after things."

Even in the communal area, there was the sound of laughter and of excited raised voices. Sally smiled at him.

"Whatever happens, just remember you gave these people the ability to feel like this again."

He didn't know what to say to that, so merely nodded mutely. They reached the door of the control room. Apprehension gripped him as he swung the door open. John Stark sat on the seat, staring at the view ahead, one hand resting on the steering wheel, the other on his thigh.

"Ah, I see the patient is feeling better!" he exclaimed, in a way that was a little too jovial for Sam's liking.

"Yes, much better, than you. And I thank you for taking charge in my absence." A vague memory came to him of the narrowing of Stark's eyes, the last time they had had contact. And then Sam had been alone on the deck. With the door bolted from the inside. It didn't take a mathematician to put two and two together.

"But I am back now. And I shall resume control, if you don't mind."

"Ah but I do mind. I mind very much indeed." Stark did not move a muscle but a little twitch started in the corner of one eye. Sally could just make it out, pulsing away. It wasn't a good sign of things to come.

"Well I'm afraid whether you mind or not, is actually irrelevant to me. I am this ship's Captain." Once again, Sam was aware of how he had pulled rank on the other man. He stood over Stark, looking down on him and refusing to back away.

Stark's twitch became more obvious and he seemed to wilt under the older man's gaze. And yet he did not stand or move away.

"If you could kindly vacate the seat please and be on your way…I'm sure there are patients who need your assistance..." Sam made it painfully obvious that Stark was no longer welcome in the room.

The doctor leapt up at the remark, as though the chair was suddenly on fire. His thick lips were pulled together in a tight line and sucked inwards towards his teeth. But once again, it was his eyes which gave the truest indication of his inner feelings, as he attempted a false smile. "But of course," he sneered at Sam, as if he had never intended to stay.

Sally breathed a huge sigh of relief when Stark left the room. There was a bitter acrid scent in the air and Sally thought it might be the smell of self-aggrandisement and inflated ego.

Sam settled himself onto the Captain's chair with a sigh of relief. "That was rather unpleasant," he commented.

"Yes it was," she agreed. "Let me go and get us some drinks and we can sit together." And she was off without waiting for his reply. He looked out of the windows at the landscape. So different after the floods to what it looked like before, he was saddened that so much natural beauty had been wiped out in one fell swoop.

They were well on their way towards their destination. At least Stark had done a good job navigating the boat. There was that to be thankful for. And the caterpillar wheels had been retracted he noted. The button which would have been lit when he pressed the remote control was now dark once more, its light extinguished when the wheels were no longer in use. So Stark knew about the wheels. He wondered if anyone else had been told and if they had, what their reaction had been.

Outside, there was only water to be seen. Water and some trees, their branches breaking through the water and reaching to the sky as if to ask forgiveness for some crime they believed they must have committed. It was a sorry sight alright. Where was this brave new world they were to forge? And what were they to forge it with? Perhaps Bill Bently had had the right idea after all.

Sally came back in, a mug of hot coffee in each hand. No. Bill had it wrong, he decided. There was never a reason to give up hope. Just as he had that thought, there came a tentative knocking on the door. He looked at Sally, who shook her head and shrugged her shoulders to indicate she didn't know who it could be.

"Oh hi Sally…Sam," the woman spoke freely to Sally but hesitantly to him. Sam figured that he had missed a lot of interaction between his wife and these passengers when he had been unconscious.

"The rain has eased off and a group of us were wondering if we could go up top and get some fresh air. We have been cooped up for so long it seems…" she tailed off, aware that she sounded rather apologetic for the request.

"Sam, this is Lindy," Sally supplied, expecting him to give the go ahead or not. Sam looked out through the window then back at the two women. There was not much to see that was inspiring but he guessed fresh air sounded like a good idea.

"I guess there's no harm in it."

"Great. Thanks!" Lindy beamed a big smile at them both and departed.

"You could be doing with some fresh air too," Sally suggested.

"I'm fine. Anyway, don't want to give that Stark another reason to get in here," Sam stated.

"Hmm you are right, I suppose." Sally sipped some of her coffee and watched him as he steered around some obstacles sticking out of the water.

Suddenly the door was yanked almost off its hinges and a very flustered Lindy rushed in.

"There are people...other people...out there!"

"Slow down Lindy. Other people out where?" Sally tried to calm the woman and make her coherent.

"Out there!" Lindy pointed beyond the windows, "outside. They are in some kind of building!"

Sam and Sally looked at each other. It had always been a possibility of course, that they would come upon survivors, but having looked at the devastated landscape, Sam would not have though it very likely to have happened where they currently were.

"You have to come and see!" Sam cut the ignition and weighed anchor, then as one, he and Sally followed Lindy up the stairs to the main deck. Several people grouped together, all facing the same direction. Sam and Sally joined them.

Off to their left, a church spire could be seen. If there had once been a window there, it was gone now and in its place a man held aloft what appeared to be a piece of paper. He was waving it like a white flag and shouting something indiscernible to the crowd aboard the ark.

"I'll bring the ark closer to him." Sam hurried off back to the control room. In a way there was no rush, it wasn't as if the man was going anywhere. And yet there was the biggest rush in the world. To save at least one more person from this watery landscape, to have one more victory against Mother Nature, was the most gripping thing that could have happened to them.

Sam lifted the anchor and turned the ark in the general direction of the man, bringing it alongside as close as possible without causing a collision. That done, he hurried back on top, to find that it was much more crowded now, news of their discovery having spread like wildfire.

"HELP US," was the simple sentiment written large on the sheet of paper which still fluttered from the man's hand. Unshaven for a while and with eyes that reflected all he had no doubt been through, the man seemed somehow out of place here. And there was something familiar about him.

Sam looked through the stubble and the exhaustion, to the features which lay beneath. Jack Ryan! Who would have thought it possible that they would meet again?

"How can we get to them?" asked someone in the crowd. Sam didn't see who, so he just gave his answer to the people in general.

"There's a bridge …hang on a moment." His mind was racing. Jack had been looking after his nephew and although there was no sign of the boy, the sign clearly stated 'us' so presumably he was there too. His mind still formulating a rescue plan, he untied the wooden bridge from its constraints and carried it over to where the ark was closest to the tower. He slid one end towards Jack, watching as he hooked that end over the window ledge and then Sam hooked the other end over the bars on the side of the deck.

"Is it just you and your nephew?" he called. If he had ever been told the name of the boy, he had forgotten it.

"No, there are others. Altogether, two adults, four children and a dog," Jack shouted back.

"Don't try to come across yet. We have to fix guiding ropes in place first," Sam called.

"What do you think you are doing?" A cold steely voice just over his shoulder, Sam knew without even looking it would be John Stark.

"We are saving these people, that's what we are doing." Sam thought that was pretty self-evident.

"There's no room for them!" Stark stated angrily.

"We will make room!"

"There is not enough food or water for more mouths!" Stark was adamant.

Sam cast him a withering glance. "There will be enough, because there has to be." Leaving one end tied to its post, he picked up a rope and quickly coiled it up in his hands.

"It's not up for debate!" Sam stepped onto the bridge and began to carefully sidle across towards the tower, playing out the rope as he went and creating a handrail along one side. There was a bounce on the bridge which was unexpected and he looked behind him to see the reason why. Sally was following in his wake, holding another coiled rope and making another handrail.

"Can't let you out of my sight for a moment. Who knows what trouble you will get yourself into without me to watch over you," she grinned at him. Sam looked over her shoulder, back at the crowd who watched them with baited breath. Stark was gone. He was nowhere to be seen.

Chapter 30

Carefully they eased their way over, Sam in the lead and the woman following close behind, both of them creating handrails.

"When I saw the ark, I knew it just had to be you!" Even to his own ears, Jack sounded almost jolly, *too* jolly he felt, considering all they had been through. Except that now they were being rescued. He moved aside to let Sam and the woman enter through the window.

"Sam! Sally!" Georgia was shocked as she instantly recognised the couple. All eyes turned in her direction.

"What...how...oh!" Suddenly the puzzle connected up in her head and she saw a clearer picture. Sam, Sally, Bill's talk of saving the children in an 'almost biblical way', the boat or ark as Jack had called it...she joined up the dots and made a leap of faith. "And Bill?"

Sally shook her head sadly. "He would not come."

"Oh!" Fresh tears welled at the corner of Georgia's eyes but she figured she already knew the answer to her next question. Bill had made her a promise and she knew he would have kept it. "The children are safe? The hospital patients I mean?"

"Yes they are safe. Them and their families and even their pets! We have two doctors on board as well as other medical staff..." Sally moved over to embrace Georgia, so pleased to see her again.

"We have been trapped here for..." Georgia looked around at the others, but no one helped her out, "at least a day, I guess. I've lost track of time." Something else occurred to her then, that she had almost not picked up on. "Which doctors?" she wanted to know.

"Let's talk later and just get you on board first," Sam interrupted the two women. He looked at the four children all standing watching the adults' interaction, not one of them making a sound.

"I'm Sam and this is Sally, my wife," he introduced them to the silent children. "Now *you* missy," he bent down to Katie's level so as not to scare her, "must be the youngest here..."

Katie nodded, her eyes huge and a little scared looking. She held one of Georgia's hands and rested the other on the head of Roxie who seemed to have accepted all these people, as well as the new arrivals, as instant friends.

"I'm the littlest," Katie agreed solemnly.

Sam smiled and Roxie, who seemed to find the situation not in the least bit disturbing, began to wag her tail.

"Well as the littlest, I think..." Sam didn't get to finish what he was about to say. Suddenly there was a sound of splintering wood and of many voices calling out in alarm.

"What the blazes...?" Sam looked to Sally and as the noise continued, found his gaze drawn to the window. Hooked over the rim of the stone sill, the bridge strained against its attachment there. For one long moment, the wood seemed to actually stretch itself, elongating like an elastic band, before snapping and splintering off, shards of wood spraying into the air. The sound was louder than Sam would have expected snapping wood to make and for an instant, he was so focused on the enormity of the sound, he couldn't quite figure out the significance of it.

"The bridge is gone!" Sally cried, leaping to the window, heart afraid of what her intuition was whispering in her mind. "The boat is moving away!"

"Moving away?" Sam felt as if he were in a bad dream. Was it possible that he was still unconscious and that all this was just a fantasy, an illusion of reality? One look at Sally confirmed it was a nightmarish reality without a shadow of a doubt.

Face deathly pale, she turned to him and blinked. A whole world was conveyed to him in that closing of eyelids and reopening. Stark! Stark had taken control of the ark and was moving it away!

Sam rushed to the window. Sure enough the boat was twice the distance away it had been a few minutes ago. He could still see the faces of the people on deck though, enough to make out their features. Most of them were strangers, but one he recognised, the woman called Libby. 'No, Libby wasn't right, *Lindy*, that was it. *Lindy*.'

Hands cupped over her face in horror, he saw her try to call something to him. Sam leaned further out of the window, straining to hear.

"...locked himself in the control room...try to get him out..." Sam was catching only some of her words now but he caught the general gist of it.

"...come back for you..." She was too far away now, receding into the distance.

"They won't let him leave us!" Sally half-stated, half-posed as a question.

"No, of course they won't," Sam assured the little group of people who stood, shoulders slumped before him. The scent of despondency reeked within the close confines of the small area. Even he did not believe what he had just said. Even if the men on board managed to wrestle the control of the ark away from the doctor, there was no guarantee that they would not be so far away, as to be able to find their way back to them.

They had been abandoned.

Dan watched and quietly listened as the adults told each other their stories. Most of it he already knew and what was new to his ears, didn't really do anything to boost his faith in mankind. He stroked Roxie and thought about the book he had liberated from the shop, along with the pens. He had torn a page out of the back of it for Jack to write on and wave out of the window but otherwise it was intact.

If they were all going to die here, trapped in this flooded place, then the least he could do, was leave some record of what had happened and why they had taken the decisions they had.

In a way all of it would be irrelevant 'cos dead is dead after all', he debated with himself but it would be *something*, not like a legacy or anything quite so grand...but...At school, the previous semester he had studied the book made of the diaries of Anne Frank, the girl who had lived cooped up with her family in an attic, whilst they tried to evade the Nazis of World War II. His situation was different – and yet it was exactly the same – just a slow wait for the inevitable to happen. He picked up the notebook and selected the red pen.

To Whomever Comes After :

A Brief History Of Mankind To The Year 2050

he wrote on the cover, using his very best handwriting. He thought hard. It was important, what he was doing, so he had to do it right. He put the lid back on the red pen and selected the black one. Hand poised over the top line, he began to write.

I hope that someone is alive to find this book and can take some comfort from it.

The situation has gotten desperate. Apart from the people we saw on a big boat, we may be the last people left alive in the world. I really hope that's not the case. I hope that somewhere my mom and dad are sheltering, just like us here and that they are safe. Maybe one day I'll find them and we'll all be together again.

And just in case it is you mom and dad, who find this book...if I am already dead, please know that I don't blame you for sending me to Uncle Jack's when all this began.

You weren't to know that there would be as much danger there, as there was at home. I just wish that you had come too, that we were all together now, at the end.

We can't survive much longer. Our small supply of food is running out and we have no source of clean drinking water.

Uncle Jack says it's called 'irony', the fact that we are trapped here by flood water and yet we have no clean drinking water.

I guess he's trying to keep me amused but I wish he wouldn't. We passed lots of dead bodies before we got here and somehow it doesn't seem right to not be sad for them as well as ourselves.

We are trapped in this temple. The water is too high to leave here and there is no way of knowing if we can last out till it's gone, or at least low enough that we could travel on foot. And anyway, I think I'd prefer him to just tell the truth. If I'm going to die here, I want to die with the courage of a twelve year old...

I don't want to waste your time, whining about how this all came about, no doubt if you do survive your story will be similar to our own. However on the chance that we are the last human survivors in a world where nature has become angry AND you are some future visitor from another world, I would like to put us down for posterity.[I think that's the right word — I always used to get it confused with prosperity.]

My name is Daniel Ryan [although I prefer to be called Dan] and I am twelve years old. I live...

Carmen Capuano

He didn't live anywhere now. He didn't cross it out, he just moved on.

I **lived** in Seattle with my dad, Kevin and my mom Stacey, till the storms started.

When the storms got really bad in Seattle, dad decided to send me to stay with Uncle Jack in New York. At the time, there was no sign of how bad it was about to get...and that it would spread across America. [Uncle Jack says it's actually happening all over the world!]

I begged them to come too but dad said he couldn't leave his clients, that if he did, when the storms were over, he would have no business left to run.

But why would anyone have needed the services of a lawyer in the middle of a flood? I still don't get it. Anyway, mom stayed to look after dad. She said he'd never cope on his own.

When things began to get really bad in New York too, me and Uncle Jack started to make our way to where we thought my mom and dad were...but we never got there. We only got this far. [Oh and I was unconscious when we started the journey – and we found a dog on the way, called Roxie. Well we don't know what her real name is, so we called her that but she seems to like it.]

There was an ark, but a mad doctor called Stark ran off with it [funny how that rhymes isn't it? Ark and Stark. Almost like it was meant to be!]

278

Dan stopped for a moment, wondering what to put next. The other children were grouped around Roxie, stroking the dog, who was enjoying all the fuss and rewarding them with big licks from her long pink tongue.

The adults were huddled over the other side, close to the window and deep in conversation. Dan looked back on what he had written. It didn't seem particularly clear or concise and in fact some of it was in the wrong order but it was his first attempt at writing a memoir after all, he told himself. He wasn't sure how he should carry on. Perhaps he should explain who was there and what they were like? He began to write once more.

Uncle Jack is great and he's good to be around but he's never been married or had children and sometimes I think he forgets what to say to me or how to be with me.

That's why I was so glad we found Georgia. She's a paediatrician; that's a special doctor for sick children and she's really great. Maybe if her and Uncle Jack had met under different circumstances, she would have been my auntie.

[They think I don't see the looks that pass between them, the same kind of looks that mom and dad used to give each other. But I do. I do and I'm glad, cos there's no room in the world anymore for anything other than love and peace...]

There was nothing more for him to say. He didn't want to be the one who had to do all the explaining and he wasn't even sure if he could do that anyway. But he knew a man who could.

"Uncle Jack," he called.

Jack came over, his face worried and drawn looking. Dan passed him the book. "I thought we ought to leave something to remember us by." The lump in his throat was hard to talk around and he suspected that if he carried on much longer, he would cry big wet hot tears all over his writing.

"Could you carry on for a bit? Please!"

Jack knew it wasn't something he could refuse the boy, even if he had wanted to. And the idea did have a certain appeal after all. He watched as Dan wrote a final few lines before holding out the pen and book to him.

I'm gonna pass this book over to my Uncle for a while. He used to be a reporter at a big New York newspaper so he's better at explaining things than I am, even though I can beat him hands down at computer games any day! So bye for now. Dan.

Jack took the proffered pen and book and read what Dan had already written. He knew what to do. He had to tell their stories but in a way that was not just facts. In a way that revealed who they were as individuals, what they believed in, what their hopes and fears were – he had to give the real essence of what lay at the very heart of each and every one of them.

If fate decreed that they died here, in this place, then what had started as their shelter would become their tomb and his words – and those of Dan – would be the only memorial they would ever have. And the person or persons who found the book, after they were gone, would be their only mourners. He took a deep breath and began to write.

Hello, Jack Ryan here. I've read what Dan has written so far and I won't contest any of it, even the bit about Georgia Wade!

Georgia has with her three children. Ben, Jim-Bob and Katie Collins. They are the children of a friend of hers and were sent to Georgia by their parents, when things got bad in Seattle.

Also here are Sam and Sally White, an older couple who tell me they have been married for nearly forty years and are clearly devoted to one another. So that's us. A little group of eight people and one dog, who time and fate and circumstance have brought together, to be trapped in the spire of an old church. I don't know if we are going to survive this but I do know I will never give up hope.

Humans are a strange and varied species and I can't tell you how they have fought and quarrelled since they emerged from caves millions of years ago but one thing I can tell you, is that they are strong and tenacious and always fight back.

When the storms first began, raging in localised areas of the Midwest, there was fear and apprehension. But there was no real panic. Preparations were made, areas evacuated and life went on everywhere else, pretty much as normal.

But things soon changed. The storms, instead of dying out, became more widespread and ferocious. The West Coast was the next area to be affected. That's when Dan was sent to me for safe-keeping. There were some indications that it was happening around the world but reports were strangely subdued on this matter.

The government, realising I guess that there would be panic and mass suicide if news got out, tried to keep a lid on it all. And mostly succeeded.

But there were some who suspected. Someone once said 'just because I am paranoid, doesn't mean they are not out to get me!' And I guess that's probably the truest thing I ever heard.

*The paranoid members of our society and the conspiracy theorists kind of had the jump on us. They already suspected the truth was being hidden from view. So, of course, "The End Is Nigh" weirdos went immediately overboard but most of us sane [as it turns out actually deluded] folk were watchful but not **too** concerned in truth.*

We still thought the storms would dissipate, burn themselves out, as it were.

As the days went on however, things rapidly and dramatically changed. Whole towns were being flooded and many people drowned or were killed in collapsing buildings. First in the Midwest then the West Coast. And then pretty much everywhere else as far as I can gather. Here in America, at least. And I suspect, worldwide too.

Death was everywhere. It was on the TV and on the streets and there was no escaping it.

He paused for a moment. It was incredibly hard to write like this, knowing that he was possibly writing it for someone who would read it after he and Dan and everyone else here was dead. But Dan was right. Somehow it was the right thing to do.

So now you know the background, I guess I had better tell you how this little group of people all came together and how our fate became decided. We

A strange phut-phut noise sounded in the distance. From the corner of his eye he saw Georgia throw herself towards the window.

"OVER HERE! OVER HERE!" she screamed, waiving the white paper out of the window as he had done previously.

Jack dropped the pen and the book on the ground and rushed towards Sam and Sally, who were crowding around behind Georgia, yelling and waving their arms in an attempt to be noticed by something outside.

"It's a boat! It's a boat!" Georgia cried breathlessly. "And they've seen us!"

Sure enough, the noise from the motor did seem to be getting louder, its thrum reverberating closer and closer.

"Swap places with me!" Georgia urged Jack. He slipped into the space she vacated and carried on waving the sheet of paper. Georgia gathered the children round her.

"This boat is a lot smaller than Sam's was and I think we will have to jump from the window to get onto it. Do you understand?" she asked, her voice high and urgent.

It was Jim-Bob who answered. "Us boys will be fine but Katie and Roxie…" he let the sentence hang.

"We can pass them down I think, don't worry." Georgia reassured them.

Jack watched with a grin on his face, as the boat pulled up directly below the window. Smaller than Sam's ark, it was not level with them but instead sat a little way below.

A large man with the rosiest complexion Jack had ever seen, stood at the helm. Lumberjack shirt stretched taut over his heavily muscled torso, he grinned widely at them, guilelessly revealing several gaps in an otherwise fine mouthful of teeth.

"You all getting in or not?" he drawled, like it was the most everyday occurrence in the world.

The boat appeared to be some strange amphibious sort of craft, like a cross between a big truck and a boat. Perhaps ex-military, it looked as if it might have been decommissioned many moons ago and yet been maintained extraordinarily well. 'God Bless America and all the darndest-fool-crazy people in her,' thought Jack.

"We sure are!" he grinned right back at their saviour, "we sure are!"

He turned away from the window for a moment. "Sam it's best if you go first, then Sally and Georgia. And I will go last, so I can help pass the children and the dog down to you."

"Fine by me," Sam agreed.

There were no questions posed, no explanations given and no one seemed the least bit worried about it.

"Name's Seth," their rescuer held out his hand to Sam.

"Pleased to meet you Seth. Very pleased indeed," grinned Sam, pumping the man's hand for all he was worth.

Quietly, as one by one, they left the temple, Dan stole a last look around. What should he do with the book? Take it with him? In a way that didn't make sense to him. Something told him they were on a cusp of a new world and to take what was now a record of *their past*, into it, just didn't feel right. In writing it, he had thought that he was writing about the end of the story of his life. Now he saw that it wasn't the end…merely the end of the beginning.

A whole new world awaited him. And if he was very lucky, which he suspected he may indeed be, it was a world where his mom and dad waited for *him* too.

He wrapped the book carefully in the oilskin and left it in the centre of the floor where anyone who entered would immediately see it. Then he went to join the others.

THE END OF THE BEGINNING.

If you have enjoyed reading Volumes I and II of this series, look out for Volume III which will be coming soon.

The Owners Volume II:

Storm Clouds

– CARMEN CAPUANO –

An environmentally friendly book printed and bound in England by
www.printondemand-worldwide.com

This book is made entirely of chain-of-custody materials